HEARTACHE ON WEST INDIA DOCK ROAD

RENITA D'SILVA

Boldwood

First published in Great Britain in 2025 by Boldwood Books Ltd.

Cover Design by JD Smith Design Ltd.

Cover Images: Shutterstock

A CIP catalogue record for this book is available from the British Library.

Paperback ISBN 978-1-83617-286-4

Large Print ISBN 978-1-83617-285-7

Hardback ISBN 978-1-83617-284-0

Trade Paperback ISBN 978-1-80656-099-8

Ebook ISBN 978-1-83617-287-1

Kindle ISBN 978-1-83617-288-8

Audio CD ISBN 978-1-83617-279-6

MP3 CD ISBN 978-1-83617-280-2

Digital audio download ISBN 978-1-83617-282-6

This book is printed on certified sustainable paper. Boldwood Books is dedicated to putting sustainability at the heart of our business. For more information please visit https://www.boldwoodbooks.com/about-us/sustainability/

Boldwood Books Ltd, 23 Bowerdean Street, London, SW6 3TN

www.boldwoodbooks.com

For Prof Bhaskar Rao
So very inspirational and amazing, so incredibly accomplished,
a brilliant writer and orator.
Whom I look up to and admire and try to emulate.
Thank you SO much for your advice, your support and your
encouragement – I am truly blessed.

"War is an instrument entirely inefficient toward redressing wrong; and multiplies, instead of indemnifying losses."

— THOMAS JEFFERSON (THIRD PRESIDENT OF THE UNITED STATES)

PROLOGUE
1941

Two years into the war, West India Dock Road is tired and looks it, regardless of how much its residents try to spruce it up. The ladies of the street scrub the half-circles in front of their stoops to a shine each morning, no matter that they have been up half the night with the bombing, the East End harangued daily by enemy planes raining their deadly cargo.

This is not the first time the street has seen war, of course. During the Great War too, it suffered. But now, this nightly barrage of enemy ire is knocking away at the residents' morale so that their smiles are brittle, their backs although straight, ready to droop.

Everywhere, there are signs of war. Barrage balloons float tiredly over the Thames. The river is ablaze each night, clouds of navy smoke arcing towards the English sky riddled with German destroyers, orange flames dancing in macabre celebration upon navy, shadow-infested water glowing with an oily sheen.

Double summertime has been introduced with the objective of giving people more daylight hours for work and activities, yet in the East End, with its pall of greasy smog, it appears dark all the time, actual dusk arriving without fanfare and not making much of a difference either way.

There are no wrought-iron railings or gates anywhere in sight; they have been removed to be melted down and used for the war effort.

The factories by the dockside drone and grumble, whether bombed or not, stubbornly continuing to run. The acrid scent of fire and destruction mingles with industry, sugar and jam and custard, leather and melting pitch, a cornucopia of clashing scents.

The haunting strains of a Yiddish song drift on the dust-speckled air: a mother singing to her child.

Over at the bombed-out church, the Catholic contingent of West India Dock Road attend mass religiously, relying upon God's intervention even more so during these uncertain times. They usher along Mrs Murphy, the oldest Irishwoman on the street (much to Mrs Neville's chagrin, for she covets the title), who is getting more confused with each passing day and is often to be found wandering the pavements calling for her long-dead husband, sister and parents. The women kneel on the scarred pews and pray for their beloved lost and missing, fighting and departed, while outside in the churchyard, the gravediggers are busy at work, trying to eke out space in the overcrowded cemetery, sombre notes of funeral hymns wafting on the gritty breeze.

Well before the service is due to begin, Father O'Donnell climbs to the top of a ladder, Paddy and Connor O'Kelly holding it in place as he checks to see what damage last night's air raid has wrought on the already wrecked roof, making sure that it is not in danger of collapsing on the congregation.

'There are at least four birds' nests here with eggs in them,'

Father O'Donnell calls to the boys, who marvel, wide grins gracing their faces.

'A miracle, Father,' Paddy says, 'especially given the bombing.'

'A miracle indeed,' Father O'Donnell agrees, making the sign of the cross. He looks to the heavens and just then, a shaft of sunlight pierces the grey gloom: divine benediction. 'Look at the birds of the air; they neither sow nor reap nor gather into barns, and yet your heavenly Father feeds them,' he is moved into saying.

'Father?' The boys look up at him, their faces rapt, gazes trusting.

It is another miracle, he thinks, that their innocence has lasted as long as it has during these unprecedented times. He makes another sign of the cross, sending up a little prayer. *Please, Lord, long may it continue. Keep them and all of my parishioners safe. Protect them from harm like you have these birds and their eggs who have made their home in the rafters of your house.*

Out loud, he says, in response to the boys' unvoiced question, 'I was quoting from the Bible, Matthew 6:26.'

West India Dock Road is pockmarked with relics of the battering it receives each night. Houses missing, rubble in their stead. Looking for all the world like an aged, cavity-shot mouth with teeth absent, gums sore and bloodied. A haze of smoke and plaster dust staining the ever-present smog.

When the air raid siren sounds, as it does without fail each night, the denizens of the street make their way to the Underground station, stopping whatever they were doing, whether it was bathing in the tin tub (for those who can afford the luxury of one), or watering their aspidistra and watercress and various other flora, all the more precious during these times (Mr Lee, a keen gardener, who can coax even the most reluctant of plants into glorious bloom), or washing the net curtains (Mrs Rosen-baum), or grumbling about the leaking drains and the vermin they attract, not to mention the bedbugs plaguing the tene-ments, all of which the landlord will do nothing about and yet the rent collector will come round steady as clockwork on the day the rent is due (Mrs Boon), or breaking the ice in the water bowl she has set out on the windowsill so the cat that comes to give her company can have something to drink (Mrs Ross), or coaxing her husband to have his bread crusts with dripping, in between worrying about his hacking cough, his chest, already weakened by war, wracked further with infection caused by the damp infesting their tenement block (Mrs Nolan).

They collect in the Underground station, even as some among them help Mrs Nolan cajole her husband, who has a horror of cramped spaces, down the stairs. Others soothe Mrs Murphy, who appears lost, repeatedly asking what's going on, why are they all being herded like cattle into the mouth of the Devil himself, in a plaintive voice that trembles like a sapling during a raging storm.

Once everyone is seated next to the train tracks, some intrepid souls bedding upon the tracks themselves, they wait out the raid, broken nights now part of their routine, as commonplace as the astringent smell of carbolic mingling with the sour undertone of unwashed armpits, the crying of babies, the soothing murmur of weary mothers, the snoring, the laugh-ter, the chatter and the banter, the games of cards and chess.

Mr Ramsey entertains the ladies with his fiddle; Mrs Neville breaking into tuneless song. Mr Barney, turning his face away to hide his grimace at the woman's attempts at singing, passes a flask around with something warming. Mrs Boon shares her fish-paste sandwiches, and Mrs Rosenbaum passes round hard-boiled eggs and *matzo* crackers, all washed down with seed cake, apple turnovers and shortbread, courtesy of Miss Ram. Just the ticket.

Their private sorrows, the burdens and losses they secretly carry, haunt the eyes of every single person in the shelter, and radiate from the new lines etched upon their tired faces, even as they smile and laugh. But their smiles are fragile and their laughter brittle, exploding into a million shards when they are alone, like the buildings crumpling each night under enemy fire as easily as sandcastles too near the sea at high tide subject to the whim of a frisky wave.

Mrs Kerridge keeps on keeping on despite the fact that two of her sons are missing in action and she hasn't heard from her oldest boy since Christmas.

Mrs Ross expends all the love for which she has no outlet, now that her daughter is dead (one of the first casualties of this blasted war), while her son, like Mrs Kerridge's younger boys, is missing in action, and her husband a casualty of the first war, on the cat that started visiting her when she was at her lowest, contemplating taking her own life, going to join her family in heaven. But now she has this feline who appears to need her, and so she showers on the creature all the affection that swells and overflows from her broken heart. The cat purrs and snuggles up to Mrs Ross, looking at her with wide, green eyes the exact shape and colour of her dead daughter's.

Mrs Devlin, who lost her sons and husband to the Great War, was rendered homeless in this one, her house bombed at the very start of the air raids. Now there is just a pile of forlorn bricks where Number 57, West India Dock Road, used to be. Mrs Neville (acknowledged by the children of the street as *the witch*, a notion her toothless gums and wicked cackle and unruly, grey hair do nothing to disabuse), kindly took Mrs Devlin in.

The arrangement suits the two of them very well, for

although the ladies would die rather than admit it, they were lonely before and now they have company, they look very much happier. They grumble and spar and snap at each other, but they also finish each other's sentences like an old married couple. Every once in a while, Mrs Devlin makes noises about moving out but everyone can see that she doesn't really mean it and Mrs Neville has stopped appearing alarmed when Mrs Devlin brings it up.

Paddy O'Kelly swears that Mrs Neville's witchiness has rubbed off on Mrs Devlin and that while Mrs Devlin was harmless before, now *both* women are scary. Paddy is convinced that this is the first step in Mrs Neville's 'grand plan to create a coven of witches and take over the world like Hitler is doing!' The sweet child is tireless in his efforts to make sure that he, his family and his loved ones keep Mrs Neville at a safe distance.

Mrs Porter does not join the rest of the street in taking refuge at the Tube station. She is part of the mobile canteen service, driving her van between shelters and to bombed-out areas, providing much-needed sustenance to whoever needs it, whether that's people being pulled out of the smoking shambles of their homes or those good Samaritans doing the rescuing.

Charity O'Kelly is not at the Tube station either, although her brothers, Fergus, Connor and Paddy are here, playing cards with Mr Lee. Mr Rosenbaum sits beside them, watching Mr Brown and Mr Stone play chess, tutting whenever he thinks one of them has made a silly move, which is nearly all the time.

Charity is in the basement of Mrs Kerridge's house, where she, her brothers and her mother have been staying since the lodging house set up by Charity's parents, which she used to run, was bombed, her father a casualty of it. Charity is keeping vigil beside her mother, both of them praying as above them the phut phut phut of dropping bombs heralds destruction.

Divya Ram, who runs the curry house on West India Dock Road, is at the Underground station passing round the goodies (today, it's apple drops and potato fritters, carrot cake and even fudge made with mock-ingredients, nowhere as sweet as the real thing but nobody seems to mind), which she brings every night without fail, and which are gone in seconds. She and Mrs Rosenbaum are great favourites with Mrs Smith's children. Mrs Smith lives on East India Dock Road and caused a scandal when she became pregnant while her husband was away fighting and hadn't been home on shore leave for months.

'Divine conception it is definitely not,' the ladies of West India Dock Road harrumphed.

Nevertheless, when she went into labour in the Underground station, they all came together and helped deliver her baby, her bonny wee one being born just as the all-clear sounded. But her little boy caused an even greater scandal for he was a beautiful shade of caramel, quite unlike Mrs Smith and her husband, both pale as milk.

Mrs Rosenbaum and Miss Ram take turns holding the baby while Mrs Smith's girls chatter away, telling stories, asking questions, singing songs, while also munching on the snacks both Miss Ram and Mrs Rosenbaum ply them with. Mrs Smith, with a grateful smile of thanks directed at Miss Ram and Mrs Rosenbaum, indulges in a few minutes of well-deserved rest, albeit sitting up, hemmed in by people on all sides; space in the Tube station is at a premium.

Mr Crosby regales the children with tales ('...that get taller by the minute,' Mrs Neville snorts, unimpressed) of his exploits during the Great War.

'I nearly lost me eye, y'know,' he says, as the children hang on to his every word, ignoring Mrs Neville's loud exclamation of, 'Oh for goodness' sake, it was your leg last time.'

'That too,' Mr Crosby says, undeterred by Mrs Neville's interruption, 'but that's a story for another day.' He grins, winking at the children, who are agog. 'Lookit this scar right 'ere; that's where the bullet clipped me eye. One inch lower and I'd be blind, sure as the nose on my face.'

'I have it on good authority you got that scar in a brawl,' Mrs Neville interjects. Again.

'Oh for God's sake, mind yer own, woman,' Mr Crosby says genially.

Mrs Neville harrumphs in response. 'I don't believe in filling those poor bubs' heads with lies, is all.' She sniffs sanctimoniously.

Mr Crosby laughs as if she has cracked the world's funniest joke. 'Well now, woman, I'd be careful making statements such as those, I would. I'm not the one 'appy to allow 'em to believe I'm a witch wot can cast a spell at any minute.'

Over by where Mr Venables is snoozing with his mouth open and loud snores reverberating from it, causing the children no small amount of mirth, Mrs O'Riley and Mrs Boon engage in a heated discussion about rationing: which methods are best for preserving food and whose recipes are better for making use of the meagre ingredients they are provided with and will stretch the furthest.

When the all-clear sounds, they all stand and stretch and sigh and yawn and make their way out, blinking in the fiery, dust- and debris-spattered, smoke-weighted air, wondering if this is the day they will be rendered homeless, even as they keep their fingers crossed and send a prayer heavenward.

When she sees that her home is still standing, Mrs Rosenbaum experiences the usual complex swamp of emotions that have ambushed her since Hitler started singling out, discriminating against and terrorising the Jews. Relief mingling with guilt. *Why me? Why am I spared when so many of my people are suffering? And other innocents too, those fighting the war and those targeted on the home front.*

Although she hasn't discussed it openly with her husband, she knows that he too feels the same way. It is evident in the slight hunch of his shoulders, the small grunt he emits as he settles down in the armchair with his glasses halfway down his nose and the newspaper spread out on his lap.

This is his routine of a morning when he's not busy with his duties as a civil defence worker. And Mrs Rosenbaum, once she's caught up on her knitting for the Women's Voluntary Service, and her daily chores, the dusting and the washing and the ironing, sweeps her stoop to a shine, no matter the weather, even if the frisky breeze, grainy with plaster dust, wilfully chucks the dirt she's just swept clean straight back onto it.

She does this, her eyes stinging with tears, whether from the grit the wind flings at her face or for all those she has lost, she herself does not know. And although she knows her husband inside out, can read his every expression, divine what he's going to say even before he utters a word, she does not understand how he can bear the paper each morning, read about the atrocities being carried out against their people.

Mrs Rosenbaum cleans her house and scrubs the stoop spotless because at least this much is within her control. She does not know the fate of her beloved only sister, bright, fierce Eva, or her children. Eva had insisted on staying in Germany when Hitler began his vendetta against Jews, even when everyone else started to leave, even after Kristallnacht in 1938, the night of broken glass, an organised, nationwide attack against her people. Her sister with whom she was so close growing up in Munich, playing in the woods all day and coming home starving, to Mama's freshly baked *berches challah* with *kugel* and *krautsalat*, followed by Eva's favourite, *kaisertorte*...

Oh, how the memories hurt and stab; how Mrs Rosenbaum wishes she could shout at her sister, cry, *Why didn't you listen to me, silly girl? But you were always the headstrong one, the stubborn and feisty one. It is your strength and also your weakness.*

'You'll be the death of me, Eva,' their mama would cry, frustration and love warring in her voice. 'That sassy attitude will land you in no end of trouble.'

'She was right, wasn't she?' Mrs Rosenbaum rails at her sister in her head. 'Oh, Eva, I don't know where you are, how you are, whether you even *are*. I cannot begin to imagine what they are doing to you and your beautiful children and it is killing me.'

Mr and Mrs Rosenbaum have not been blessed with children. For Mrs Rosenbaum, her sister's children are like her own. Those babes, so very beloved, whom she last saw several months before the war started, she knows they must most likely be in those dreaded camps. She doesn't want to dwell on their fate.

Her heart aches.

And so she sweeps the stoop as if her life depends on it, sniffing as she does so, until her husband comes out of the house and puts his arms around her. Tenderly, he tucks an errant lock of hair behind her ear and whispers, 'That's enough now.'

She rests her head against his heart, its gentle beat steadying her.

And then he leads her into their quiet house, rife with a pondering, weighted silence, where there is too much time to dwell on what is happening to their people around the world.

When the air raid siren sounds again, Mrs Rosenbaum picks

up the bag she has prepared, which is waiting by the door, and makes her way to the Underground station along with her husband and the rest of the street.

The other ladies tease her gently, fondly, that she brings her whole house with her. 'What do you need bedsheets and blankets and towels and food and drink enough to feed an army for, Esther? We're only going to be here a few hours.'

But regardless of the affectionate ribbing, Mrs Rosenbaum is always prepared.

And it has helped. Mrs Rosenbaum's towels and blankets came in use when Mrs Smith went into labour in the Tube station.

Sometimes – often – she feels like a spare part. Her people are dying and what is she doing? Cleaning her stoop, only for a gust of wind to sully it again. A thankless activity, and for what? What purpose does it serve except for getting her out of the house and out of her head, the thoughts going around and around in there?

She has cried in her husband's arms, unable to articulate into words what she is feeling: *What is the use of me? Why am I here, still living, when people are dying in their droves? Children, innocents...*

'Shh...' Her husband pats her back, helpless. Isaac might come across as strong but he cannot cope, she knows, if she falls to pieces. And so, for his sake, she pulls herself together.

But that day in the Underground shelter, when Mrs Smith went into labour and had made use of the towels and blankets Mrs Rosenbaum had packed, she had felt, briefly, purposeful.

Mrs Smith's adorable little girls remind her of her sister's children whom she last saw oh, it feels like a lifetime ago.

It was before the war, around the time when it became dangerous to travel to Germany for worry they would not be able to return again. She has lost count of the number of times she invited her sister and her children here. Begging, pleading, reasoning with Eva in her letters, to please come to England, to safety, and when all else failed, emotionally blackmailing her even, all to no avail.

Eva had countered in her letters:

Don't they discriminate against Jews there too? I read about the riots in the East End where you live: the Battle of Cable Street.

Mrs Rosenbaum had to admit that the uprising had been terrifying but... it was also hopeful and heartwarming. The British Union of Fascists, led by Nazi sympathiser Oswald Mosley, had planned a series of marches through the heart of the East End on Sunday, 4 October 1936 condemning Jews and Jewish businesses. But they were held back by East Enders: Protestants, Catholics and Jews putting on a united front, standing up to them. Many ordinary people had been injured in the ensuing clashes.

Mrs Rosenbaum had written in her reply to her sister:

The East Enders came together to defend us Jews and to stand up to the Fascists on our behalf. You and the children will be safe here.

But Eva was adamant. Her letter was uncompromising:

No place is safe from discrimination and prejudice, Esther. We are staying in Germany. This is our home.

Of course, Mr and Mrs Rosenbaum had oftentimes been at

the receiving end of the hatred and division fostered by the fascists but *nothing* could compare to being made to feel alien and unwanted in your own country. Which is what Mrs Rosenbaum tried to tell Eva. But she had never been as good with words as her sister. She could never win with Eva; her sister was too stubborn, and quick with a retort.

And yet still, Mrs Rosenbaum tried. She wrote:

Here, there are people on our side, Eva.

Eva's reply:

I was born in Germany and I will die here.

Mrs Rosenbaum begged, so emphatic that her pencil tore the paper:

Think of your children.

Eva's response was gentler:

I am thinking of them. I don't want them to see their mother as someone who gives up when the going gets tough. I don't want to uproot them only for them to experience the same hatred there too.

Mrs Rosenbaum wrote back, her tears, her upset spilling onto the letter again, marking the paper, salt and scribble:

They won't. I'll protect them with my life.

Eva wrote:

I know you would.

And this time, Eva's letter too was dotted with wet patches that smelled of the sea; she had also been crying.

But I can't bear to live without them. And I can't bear to leave here, this country where I was born, where the love of my life, the father of my children, is buried.

She refused to come, and then, of course, she couldn't...

Will Mrs Rosenbaum ever see her sister and children again?

No, she can't think this way. This is why she does practical things. But what about the fusty ache of longing and missing, the fug of it settling over everything, tinting it poignant blue? That, she cannot get rid of, no matter how hard she cleans.

Mr and Mrs Rosenbaum, two middle-aged relics about the house, which they bought with such hope, imagining it ringing with the laughter of their children, their cries, their demanding voices, calling for them, imperiously, *Mama, Papa.*

Mr and Mrs Rosenbaum, silent ghosts haunting this abode now heavy with their worries and worst imaginings about the fate of their loved ones, their people in Germany and the countries it has annexed so ruthlessly. Their angst is palpable, threatening to overwhelm them, seething with everything they cannot say, the fears and anxieties that they do not voice to each other, each thinking they will spare the other. And so they brood in isolation, hefting their individual burdens stoically, even though, if they shared them, they would find that they could carry them a little more easily. But who's to tell them?

All is not quite lost, however...

Mr Rosenbaum knows his wife enough to determine when it

all gets just a little too much for her. For that is when he says, gently, 'Shall we go to the curry house?'

And she nods, gifting him a small smile, which makes his heart glow, for he sees in her beloved face, etched with lines of experience and sorrow, the young girl in that crowded dance hall who had smiled shyly at him just so, eyes big and unsure even as she nodded, said yes, she would dance with him, tucking her small hand in his trustingly, so when he closed his palm, hers was completely ensconced.

Thank goodness for the curry house, Mrs Rosenbaum thinks. It is barely two years old, having opened just before the war started. Even so, it is, alongside the public house, the hub of the community, a meeting place for people of the street and beyond, where everyone collects when the reality of war gets too overwhelming. It is warm and noisy, filled with chatter and laughter and companionship, swirling with spicy, sweet scents. It chases away, for a brief while, the anxiety and guilt and upset swarming Mrs Rosenbaum, weighing down her heart.

Thank goodness for gentle Miss Ram, with her smiles and her magic hands with which she concocts such wonderful delicacies even during this time of dearth.

Miss Ram, who makes kosher food – *challah* and *latkes* and *kugel* and *lekach* – for the Jewish residents of the street, and who brings the dishes of Mrs Rosenbaum's childhood, her youth, her mama's beloved memory enshrined in the food she cooked for her family, alive once more.

Miss Ram, loving, kind, warm, wise. Mrs Rosenbaum sometimes likes to imagine, in a secret part of her yearning heart, that, if she had been blessed with a daughter, she would have been exactly like Miss Ram.

Miss Ram who has, despite her tender age, sampled grief,

experienced loss. It is mapped upon her face, in the solemn gravity gilding her voice, the darkness crowding her smile.

Miss Ram who, although she cooks just as wonderfully as ever, no longer takes pleasure in her food, Mrs Rosenbaum has noticed.

Of course, a huge part of it is down to sorrow; Miss Ram lost her lascar friend recently, another casualty of the war. But Mrs Rosenbaum is pretty sure there's something else. That Miss Ram is keeping a secret that is eating away at her. It is evident in the shadows haunting her eyes. In the way she sighs, long and deep and heartfelt, when she thinks nobody is looking.

But, if Mrs Rosenbaum has noticed, then she is sure the others have too. Nothing can be kept from the ladies of West India Dock Road for long. They have a way of divining even the most clandestine of intrigues and they will sniff out whatever it is that Miss Ram is concealing; of this, Mrs Rosenbaum has little doubt.

* * *

'The powers that be missed a trick there, not forming an army of the women of the East End,' Mr Barney the publican grumbles when his missus has given him an earful for having had one too many. 'They would show Hitler what's what and us blokes would have some peace and quiet: a respite from the nagging.'

Mr Barney can't sign up because the smoke inhalation from the fire at the public house just before the war, for which everyone blamed Miss Ram's lascar friend (but just as Miss Ram insisted, he was proven innocent), did for Mr Barney's chest.

'Thank goodness for that!' his patrons exult when they're sure Mrs Barney is not around, nevertheless furtively checking over their shoulders just to make absolutely sure she hasn't materialised suddenly and is within earshot. 'Can you imagine if it was Mrs Barney running the pub? We would have no fun. As it is, we don't when she's around – no offence, Mr Barney.'

'None taken, lads, for don't I know it,' Mr Barney sighs, taking a great big gulp of his ale.

'You might be a publican and all, but that's no excuse for drinking fit to wake the dead.' Mrs Barney sighs grimly, shaking her head at her husband when she's caught him being free and easy with the ale.

'I'm just drowning my woes.'

'What woes?' Mrs Barney queries sternly, hands on hips.

Mr Barney turns away, scowling, murmuring under his breath, 'Well, being married to you, for one.'

'I heard that,' Mrs Barney cries. 'Off to the curry house for you. Go drown your sorrows there with Miss Ram's spiced tea.'

'The pub...'

'...will run better without your intoxicated, too-merry self.'

'Merry?' Mr Barney snorts. 'All the merriness is quite gone.'

'I'm here, aren't I?' Mrs Barney continues, heedless of her husband's grumbling. 'Now scat.'

Mr Barney eschews the cup of spiced tea that Miss Ram brings him, asking for a tall tumbler of water instead and says, miserably to Mr Stone and Mr Brown, Mr Lee and Mr Rosenbaum, 'Mr Churchill should have taken advantage of the women of the East End...'

'How so?' Mr Rosenbaum asks.

'He should have employed them, specifically the ladies of West India Dock Road, foremost my good wife, in intelligence gathering,' Mr Barney says with feeling. 'Set them on the Jerries and they will happily give away their secrets. Master interrogators, that's what they are.'

Before Mr Rosenbaum can reply, Mrs Neville calls, from

where she is sitting with the other ladies across the room, 'Eh, what's that, Mr Barney? Why are you mumbling under your breath? You have something to say, say it to our face.'

'What did I tell you?' Mr Barney sighs. 'Beware if you think you can keep anything from them. And if one of them knows, that means they all do. Oh how they gang up on us poor souls. Nothing can beat the solidarity they employ, especially if it is at the cost of a hapless bloke...'

'Speak up, Mr Barney. You're still mumbling, you know,' Mrs Kerridge cries.

'Singing your praises is all,' Mr Barney mutters, taking a sip of his water and wishing with all his might that it was something stronger.

Where was the good lord Jesus with his changing water into wine miracle when you needed him?

PART I

1

CHARITY

1941

Charity walks down West India Dock Road, this beloved street where she grew up, where she played hide-and-seek as a child among the sheets flapping on the washing lines, where, when she was a little older, she jived to music wafting from the dance hall down the road.

This street whose matrons looked out for her after her da returned from the Great War a ruined man and Mammy took to her bed, worn out from giving birth to Fergus, Connor and Paddy, one after the other, her body giving up on her.

This street where, like elsewhere in the East End, they all scraped and saved to make do, the men queuing for hours to get half a day's casual work at the docks, if that, children wearing clothes too small for them and having toes torn out of shoes as there was no money to buy new ones.

This street where women stretched their meagre budgets to feed their husbands and children, going without themselves.

Some toiled in the rag trade or clocked up ten hours a day behind a sewing machine, backs permanently stooped, eyes squint and eyesight shot from working in the half-light of lamps. Children with scabbed knees and torn clothes played marbles in the gutter, hopscotch on the narrow pavement. Girls skipped to rhymes they'd made up, and ran hoops up and down the road, their voices ringing joyously, plaited with laughter. Boys engaged in a game of street football with a ball they had fashioned from paper and twine, their excited shrieks bouncing off the tenement blocks. When a carriage came down the road, they hopped out of the way, rescuing their ball just in time, pigeons swooping to peck at the steamy pile of horse dung left in the vehicle's wake.

Now the street is melancholy, the high-pitched excitement of children at play just a ghostly impression echoing with phantom wisps of happier times, for most of the children have been evacuated to the country in the hope of safety from the nightly air raids.

Now the loudest sounds reverberating through the street are the bombs dropping and the accompanying groan and shudder and thud of buildings falling, the roaring, raging whoosh of fire. Everyone taking shelter, smiling bravely while being very aware that they are only ever a heartbeat away from destitution, destruction, death.

This street where at the age of fourteen, Charity gave up her secret dream of working at the sugar factory and took over the running of her parents' boarding and lodging house.

Now, Charity's da, Paddy O'Kelly Senior, is no more and neither is the boarding house for which he had such fond hopes.

Charity, her mammy and da and Charity's beau Veer, a

demobbed Indian soldier who had come looking for a place to stay and had stolen Charity's heart, were sheltering in the basement of the lodging house when it was bombed. The terrible memory of it is still fresh in Charity's mind, the acrid scent of fire, the smoke ambushing them, stealing their breath, the heat branding them with scorch marks, the raining plaster dust enveloping them in a foggy miasma of debris.

She thought they would all die in there. But it was only Da who did, his heart – never the same since he came back from the Great War broken by guilt and regret after his comrades died but he was spared – giving up on him.

Charity looks at the gaping hole where the boarding house had stood, a West India Dock Road institution until Hitler's ruthless rampage felled it. A sorry pile of rubble is all that is left. Some ash-stained bricks and a section of wall. Paddy, Charity's youngest brother and her father's namesake, has stuck a flag upon the ruins, which flutters hopefully in the smoggy breeze.

Her brothers are so upbeat and positive, always looking on the bright side, full of life despite being surrounded by death and devastation, doom and gloom. They give her the strength to go on, even after the war has claimed their livelihood.

And Veer does too, of course.

Veer. Charity's heart swells, it glows when she thinks of him.

Her da liked him too, she thinks, experiencing a pang of missing.

It is strange, she muses, but after her da's death, she has felt closer to him. He talks to her like he never did while alive, torn and broken as he was by his experiences in the Great War. She hears his voice all the time.

He had whispered in her ear, 'Go find Veer, make up with him.'

For she had rejected Veer's declaration of love, even though it made her miserable to do so, after they survived the bombing of the lodging house, heeding the warning of Mrs Kerridge and the other ladies of the street: 'He is different. His culture is different. You will not get on, mark our words. And what will you do when your children, God forbid, are mocked, mistreated, shunned because of their father and their colouring?'

Charity had worried, she had agonised. And she had turned her back on her love.

Three things made her change her mind:

It was her brothers, crying, 'But, Charity, he makes you happy.'

It was her mother: 'Charity, my heart, people will talk, whatever you do. They will always have something to say. I was a novice nun, promised to God, but I fell in love with your father, a mere man. That caused a tremendous amount of gossip. But I have never regretted it.' Her mother, who couldn't speak for long without tiring, had smiled gently at Charity and reiterated, 'You must live your life for you, not to try and please people, for there is no pleasing all of them. Veer is a good man. You love each other. You must follow your heart.'

And the third thing: Charity heard Da, his voice clear as hope and bright as sunshine, gilded with a smile. He was the Paddy who had once been the life and soul of West India Dock Road, according to Mrs Kerridge and others who had known him before the Great War.

'A right ladies' man was our Paddy. He'd charm the socks off even wizened old matrons like my ma, so he would,' Mrs Boon had said, her cheeks rosy with reminiscence.

Charity did not recognise this version of her father. She only knew the broken man, quick to upset, to cry, to rage.

But in her dreams, now, when he visited, when he spoke in

her ear, he was that mythical Paddy, the one she had only heard of. Handsome, happy-go-lucky, the man who had, with his wife, opened and run the lodging house on West India Dock Road and was so affable and gregarious that it was always full to bursting.

That man had told her, 'Charity, my heart, love does not come knocking often. With the war, men are scarce on the ground. You have found a good one, who cares for you. Keep a hold of him.'

And so she had gone in search of Veer.

Charity had asked after Veer at the boarding house in Bermondsey where he had been staying.

But... 'He's moved on, love. Dunno where to.' The same response from everyone she asked.

Some of them looking her up and down with hostile gazes. 'And why do *you* want to know a coloured man's whereabouts?'

This was why, she understood, the matrons of West India Dock Road had warned her against Veer.

Finally, one of the lodgers took pity on her. ''E's off doing his duties for the Home Guard during the day, love. You'll find 'im there.'

The Home Guard. Of course. Why hadn't she thought of it? Why hadn't she asked Fergus, who also volunteered for the Home Guard after apprenticing at the shipbuilders' down at the docks?

Because she didn't want to get the boys' hopes up. They loved Veer and had been upset when Charity let him go.

What if, when she went to Veer, he turned her away like she had done him?

'It's because of my colour, isn't it?' he had said when she spurned him, his voice bleeding hurt. 'I thought you were different, Charity.'

The despair in his voice had nearly undone her, but she had stood strong, thinking she was doing the right thing by herself and her family.

Charity had made her way to the Home Guard office when she knew Fergus was at the shipbuilders'. It was entirely possible that Veer would not be there, but instead off doing training exercises, or having language lessons.

'We're being taught German phrases, in the event of an invasion,' Fergus had told her self-importantly.

But she had to try to see Veer. And so she walked to the office of the Home Guard, keeping her fingers crossed.

Everywhere she looked, there were smoking carcasses of houses, soot-stained bricks. Craters on the road, rubble piled high beside it. People queueing at the butchers and greengrocers for the meagre produce clutching their ration books. Faces worn, and yet smiling valiantly. The scent of fire and devastation. London weary, broken, rent apart.

All the while, *Please,* she prayed. *Please don't turn me away.* Alternating between hope and despair.

Then, a miracle. The grit-laden sky parted to let a sliver of sunshine through, making dust motes swirl, haloing the children playing among the debris left over from the previous night's air raid, caressing her face in golden blessing. And Charity heard her da's voice in her head clear as anything: 'He won't turn you away, gel. Believe me, he will not.'

Her da's conviction was reassuring and she quickened her step, but her heart fell when she arrived at the office of the Home Guard to find it empty except for an old man, well past his prime, who peered at her over the top of his thick glasses. 'Miss, 'ow can I 'elp you?'

'I... um... I was looking for...' she began, garnering courage in her suddenly dry throat. 'Mr Veer Singh.'

The old man looked her up and down, his gaze asking, *Why do you want to know*, even as he said, "E's at training. But 'aving said that,' he peered at the clock on the wall opposite, "e should be along right about now.'

And that is when she felt eyes on her.

She turned.

Veer was standing across the road, balancing his crutch with his right hand, the sleeve of his shirt on the other side flapping limply; the loss of his left arm along with the injury to his leg had got him demobbed from the army.

Charity's heart jumped at seeing his beloved face.

How she had missed him. All this time without him, she had been going through the motions but nothing had felt *right*. This, her heart swelling, her entire body glowing, was what he incited in her. Now she felt truly alive.

He was some distance away, but nevertheless, she felt seen, warmed by his gaze, never leaving hers, his face alight.

And all her doubts and torment, her tortured worries about whether he would want to see her after how she had treated him, fell away.

You were right, Da.

'What did I tell you?' She heard her father laugh merrily in her ear.

Veer crossed the road, his gaze full of wonder and love.

Charity was aware that the old man at the office was avidly watching. People going about their business on both sides of the road had also stopped to observe. But she didn't care. She was consumed by happiness.

'You came in search of me,' Veer mouthed when he reached her, stopping an arm's length away.

She wanted to bridge the gap until there was no distance between them, either physical or emotional.

Instead, she wrapped her arms around herself. 'Yes.' She smiled, suddenly shy.

'What can I do for you?' he asked, his face aglow with that smile she would never again take for granted, that lit him up from the inside.

'I have been a fool,' she said. 'I have missed you.' And now she was suddenly struck by doubt, even though he was still smiling. She swallowed. 'Will you...?'

He did not let her finish, drawing her to him with his hand.

And in his embrace, which smelled of him, of warmth and love, she felt complete, even as people in the road tutted, shook their heads and turned away, their expressions variously shocked and horrified, some calling out to her:

'Can't you find someone your own kind?'

'Stop making a spectacle of yourself. This is a respectable street.'

And an old woman carrying a covered basket, a scarf around her head, face scrunched up in a frown, even hissed.

The old man at the office of the Home Guard looked scandalised, his eyes on stalks, but Charity didn't care, either about him, or about the people leering and hurling insults.

She only cared that the man she had turned away had forgiven her immediately.

She had eyes only for him, for the love she saw shining in his eyes.

She only knew one truth: the lodging house that she had run, home to her and her family, had been bombed and they were currently destitute, seeking refuge with Mrs Kerridge; she had had no home to speak of until she was gathered in this man's hug. *He* was her home.

'I love you,' he whispered in her ear, mindless of the spectators they appeared to have attracted, judgemental and angry and mocking.

She opened her mouth, tasted blazing joy, bright orange, burning through her soul, ripping out of her mouth, ecstatic and absolute, as she sang her reply into the dancing, happiness-suffused breeze, gentle as a lover's caress on her flushed cheeks: 'I love you too, with my everything.'

2

CHARITY

'German Q ship sinks in Indian Ocean!' calls the newspaper boy right in Charity's ear, as he walks down West India Dock Road pushing his barrow, which appears to have a loose wheel, for it rattles something terrible, his cap set at a jaunty angle, his voice high and clear, yet to break with that jarring croak of impending adolescence.

Charity is just past the gaping hole where Mrs Devlin's house had once stood.

Every single business and residence on the street is touched by war. Every face is etched with its legacy.

'You all right, luvvie?' Mrs Boon calls to Charity. 'Off to the curry house, are you? Wait a minute, will you, for my creaking joints to co-operate, and I'll join you.'

They are all in the curry house, the residents of the road, those who have survived the continued air raids which began last September and are still ongoing, those who are not evacuated, or at the frontline, or missing in action, or in a German prison, or dead.

Divya, who is flitting between tables balancing platters of

what appear to be her famous potato drops and carrot fritters, smiles when she sees Charity.

Lines of grief tug at the corners of Divya's smile and her sorrow is evident in the shadows populating her eyes. Her beau, Raghu, a lascar by trade who had signed up for war, died at the battlefront earlier this year.

Divya sets the platters down, comes up to Charity and envelops her in a hug. She smells as always of spices and love. She is bony and yet somehow not. Charity can't quite pinpoint how her friend is different, only that she is.

She appears tired, worn. And yet... she seems content too, in a curious way.

Charity can't quite make sense of it. She only knows that something has changed, that something is going on with her friend.

Charity resolves to have a heart-to-heart with her soonest. Somehow, with one thing and another, they've not had the chance to properly catch up and now, with Charity starting work – Charity hugs herself at the prospect, experiencing a complex amalgam of emotions: excitement, anticipation and trepidation – she will have even less time. But she *must* make the time, Charity decides. For Divya is her best friend in all the world.

The matrons of West India Dock Road, while not happy with Charity's liaison with Veer, have nevertheless accepted it.

'If that's what you want,' Mrs Kerridge had said sternly. 'But don't say we didn't warn you.'

Now they sit, knitting for the war effort even as they eat and gossip and complain about the rationing, mouths and hands working busily.

'Do you know what's the answer to all this pain and sadness? Love,' Mrs Porter, who has just come into the curry house after her mobile canteen duties, right on Charity's heels, says. 'I have this woman come in today, battered and bruised she was, caught in the raid last night, see. She showed me the book in her hand, which was the worse for wear, like the rest of her. "I am in a right mess because I wanted to finish the chapter. They were just about to confess their feelings for each other, so I dallied going to the shelter when the siren sounded, wanting to know whether they would kiss." She laughed and winced as the cuts on her face stung, I imagine,' Mrs Porter says, shaking her head. '"And did they?" I asked. She laughed and winced again. "I didn't get that far. I'm glad the book and I both survived, let me tell you. I'll find out now." And even as I was getting her tea ready, she was lost in her book. She told me that the book printing company, Something and Boon –, I remembered the last because of you,' Mrs Porter nods at Mrs Boon, who grins widely, 'were given special dispensation to keep printing – despite paper rationing – as their books were understood to be good for morale. "Bet they didn't take into account that some people might be almost killed trying to find out if the hero and heroine would kiss," I said dryly. But she was not listening. Busy reading, she was, her bruised eyes avid upon the page.' Mrs Porter shakes her head again, but she is smiling. When Divya goes to the kitchen to fetch tea and snacks, Charity lowers herself onto the chair Mrs Kerridge has pulled out for her. She looks around, at Mr Stone and Mr Brown playing chess at their table in the corner, watched avidly by her brothers, Mr Lee, and Mr Rosenbaum, while Mr Barney nurses his glass of water with an unhappy frown.

Mrs Kerridge catches Charity's eye and mouths, 'Your mammy all right?'

'Yes,' Charity says. She had sent the boys ahead while she made sure Mammy was comfortable in Mrs Kerridge's basement before she nipped to the curry house for a bite to eat. Divya would send Charity back with food for her mammy.

The curry house is bustling, warmth and cosiness, scented with cinnamon.

They might be at war, they might be dealing with challenges unique to them, but nevertheless, they have each other, Charity thinks, even as she wonders what's next in store for them.

3

CHARITY

Mrs Neville turns her beady-eyed attention upon Charity. 'How do you feel then? Your first day tomorrow, eh?'

Charity hugs herself and beams.

Divya grins fondly at her friend as she places a heaped plate in front of Charity, accompanied by a steaming cup of spiced tea.

For as long as she can remember, Charity has wanted to be part of the workforce at the sugar factory, seduced by the honey-nectar aroma wafting from it.

When she was younger, she hadn't had the courage to talk to the girls who worked there. They seemed so tight-knit, their easy confidence and their effortless glamour appearing unattainable to Charity's untrained eye.

Now that she's older and, she hopes, wiser, she's had several conversations with the 'sugar girls', as they call themselves, for the factory is operated by women for the most part, since all the able-bodied men are away at war. The sugar girls maintain that working at the factory isn't as glamorous as all that, but nevertheless, Charity's ardour hasn't dulled one bit.

When her father collapsed the week she was leaving school at fourteen, and was advised complete bed rest by the doctor, Charity had no choice but to give up her dream of working at the sugar factory.

'You were but a child but you took over the running of the O'Kelly boarding and lodging house very competently indeed, managing to keep it going even during the war,' Mrs Kerridge says, smiling warmly at Charity. 'And now you are starting a brand-new chapter.'

'I'll drink to that,' says Mr Barney, who is in the curry house, because, in his own words, 'My good wife is terrorising the patrons of the pub and I couldn't bear to see their sorry faces. Don't you go telling her that, mind.'

'She's just doing what she should,' Mrs Neville says sternly, wagging a bony (witchy, Paddy would say) finger at Mr Barney. 'And no matter how you spin it, we know you aren't here of your own accord. She's dispatched you here to sober up, hasn't she? Had one too many with the regulars again, did you?' Mrs Neville cackles.

Over by the men's table, Paddy winces, his expression mirroring that of Mr Barney.

'You say you'll drink to that. Did you forget that all you've got in your hands is water?' Mrs Neville continues, emitting another snort that causes both Paddy and Mr Barney to grimace again.

Mr Barney looks positively miserable and Mr Lee is moved to pat his back and wink at him, whispering softly, so Mrs Neville doesn't hear. But Charity, who is sitting at the edge of the table nearest the men, catches his words: 'I bring *baijiu* later when Mrs Neville gone.'

Baijiu is a potent Chinese liquor – one of Mr Lee's specialities – and Mr Barney perks up considerably, happily gulping his glass of water as if it was a tumbler of ale.

And now, once again, Mrs Neville swivels the spotlight of her attention upon Charity. 'Never mind all that, tell us, Charity, love, how do you feel about starting your new job tomorrow?'

'Excited.' Charity grins.

'So you should be. Working with all that sugar,' Mrs O'Riley sounds wistful. 'I must say, I've quite forgotten how it tastes. Not that you don't try your best with your wonderful desserts,' she says to Divya.

Divya smiles. 'I quite understand what you mean; all the substitutes and mock-ingredients that we have to make do with are not the same as the real thing.'

'Exactly,' Mrs O'Riley sighs. She turns to Charity. 'See if you can bring us back some sugar and jam won't you, love?' Her face glows hopefully at the thought, as does Paddy's over at the men's table for he has asked Charity – several times – for the very same.

Mrs Kerridge glares at Mrs O'Riley. 'Let the poor dear find her feet without you inundating her with demands,' she snaps.

Mrs O'Riley irritates Mrs Kerridge, always has done, for, 'she can eat for England and yet is thin as a rake. Don't know where she puts it all. Hollow legs, that one.' This said with an indignant snort.

Having shut up Mrs O'Riley, who is looking quite crushed, Mrs Kerridge turns back to Charity. 'You have a wonderful first day, love. Don't worry about your mammy or your brothers. We have it all in hand.'

'Thank you.' Charity beams at Mrs Kerridge and the others. 'I can always rely on you all. You helped me when I took over the lodging house, and you have been there for me ever since.'

'Ach, gel, go on with you,' they say, waving her words away, but they sit up straighter in their chairs and preen a little all the same. 'It's nothing.'

'It's everything,' Charity insists. 'Back when I was but a young girl finding my feet, you made sure nobody took advantage of me. You looked out for me.'

The women sniff, their eyes shiny and the tips of their ears red with emotion.

'And now,' Charity says, 'you are helping look after Mammy too. If not for that, I wouldn't be able to work.'

'Ah, it will be a pleasure to rest our feet for a wee bit and natter with our Moira,' Mrs Porter says.

The ladies of the street have drawn up a rota and will take turns to look in on her mother while Charity is at work. Divya will be providing all of her meals.

Knowing that Mammy will have company and be looked after is a load off Charity's mind. She tries to put that into words, feeling choked with emotion: 'Your kindness means that I can work at the sugar factory, follow my dream.'

'I've heard that it's not all it's cracked up to be, mind,' Mrs Kerridge says.

'It doesn't matter. At least now I have the chance to find out for myself if it really is as great as I've built it up to be in my head. I am only going to go and do what I've fantasised about for so long.'

'So you are,' they say, beaming widely, fondly at her.

Charity places a hand upon her heart, which is beating with excitement, feeling ensconced in the warmth and love of all here at West India Dock Road. Once again, as she has been doing since she got the job, she sends a prayer of thanks heavenward.

4

CHARITY

'Have you heard from our Jack Devine then, lass?' Mr Stone asks Divya.

'No,' Divya says, in reply to Mr Stone's question, sounding worried, the shadows crowding her eyes darkening.

'It would be wonderful if Mr Devine married Miss Ram, when he is released from the German prison,' Paddy had remarked the other day, his eyes glowing. 'He likes her, I can tell from his letters.'

Divya writes to Jack on behalf of the street, for he is beloved by everyone, and when his replies arrive, she reads them out aloud for he makes sure to include a message for everyone on West India Dock Road.

'But Miss Ram doesn't like him in that way,' Connor, who rarely spoke if he could help it, had said. 'She loves Mr Kumar, doesn't she, Charity?'

Charity nodded, wowed as always by her younger brother's perception.

'But Mr Kumar died in the battlefield,' Paddy said. 'And Miss Ram is sad. Mr Devine will cheer her up.'

Once again, Charity could only nod, overcome by admiration and love for her younger brothers, who were so discerning and yet so innocent with it. For Paddy had echoed Charity's hopes, that Jack Devine, her childhood friend, would be freed soon and that Divya would turn to him for comfort and perhaps, eventually, love, getting her happy ever after like Charity herself has with Veer.

'I haven't heard from Jack for a while,' Divya is saying. 'I do hope he is all right.'

'Of course he is,' Mrs Kerridge tuts.

Charity's heart goes out to Mrs Kerridge. Her two younger sons are missing in action and she hasn't heard from her eldest lately and yet she smiles and keeps on going, chivvying the street and boosting morale, refusing to let her worries get her down.

Mrs Kerridge has been so good to Charity, always there with advice and kindness and, after Charity, her siblings and Mammy were rendered homeless when the boarding house was bombed, insisting that they stay with her.

In the weeks since, in between organising the funeral for her da and making sure her brothers and mother were all right, Charity had done her bit for the war effort through the Women's Voluntary Service, alongside the other women of the street. But she felt it wasn't enough. She wanted to do more as well as pay Mrs Kerridge back.

She is glad she is clocking in at the sugar factory tomorrow, just the thought affording her a jolt of joy.

This way, she will be able to pay rent to Mrs Kerridge, although the older woman has stated firmly that she will not hear of it.

But Charity wants to do so anyway. It is the only way she can square with her conscience, even though Mrs Kerridge says, often enough, smiling fondly at her, 'I am glad of the company, my dear. You are the daughter I never had.'

'But it's not only me; it's Mammy and my brothers too,' Charity had agonised.

'The more, the merrier. I miss having my boys around.' And at this, Mrs Kerridge's eyes clouded briefly. But then she took a deep breath and smiled brightly at Charity. 'You, your mammy and brothers can stay for as long as you need. I love having you all here.'

But even though they were pooling rations, it was still a big commitment and Charity was very aware of it, however much Mrs Kerridge protested that it was a pleasure having them.

Moreover, although Mrs Kerridge has grudgingly accepted Charity's relationship with Veer, she is not one to mince words. 'I worry about you, you know. We've watched you grow from a tiny sproglet into such an amazing woman, Charity, love. You deserve happiness, not the pain that will surely follow if you continue your dalliance with Mr Singh.' A raised eyebrow, then, 'For while we understand and accept you and the person you choose to love, not everyone will. Look at Mrs Smith and what she has to deal with...'

Charity had been at the greengrocer's the day before yesterday, trying to get some fruit for her mammy.

Divya provided wonderful, wholesome meals for Mammy despite the scarcity of ingredients, but Charity was nevertheless worried about her mother. Since the bombing of the lodging house, when they had all suffered from smoke inhalation, her mammy was even weaker than before, and going steadily downhill. Never a good eater, she was now eating even less, saying her throat hurt to swallow. Which was why Charity had been at the greengrocer's, clutching her ration card, hoping she'd find fruit which she could boil and mash for Mammy, so it was easy on her bruised throat.

And that was when she'd heard the commotion.

A harsh voice had yelled, 'The likes of ye are not welcome 'ere among us respectable folk!'

Charity had turned to look, just like everyone else had been doing.

The abuse had been directed at Mrs Smith, who had been in the queue behind her, holding her bubba, her girls playing on the street with the other children.

Most people had taken one look at the infant, huffed and moved away.

But others had been openly rude. 'Some nerve you 'ave, go on off with ye and your 'arf-caste.'

Mrs Smith had understandably been upset, her mouth set in a tight line, expression brittle, eyes shiny, even as she had held her babe to her chest as if her life had depended on it.

Her girls had stopped playing and had come running up to their mother, breathless, identical worried expressions gracing their small, upturned faces as they'd looked to her for explanation and direction.

Charity had been about to say something but Mrs Neville, who had been behind Mrs Smith, had turned to the woman who had been rude. 'Our Gladys, there's no need for that. She has just as much right to be here as anyone else.'

The woman, 'Our Gladys', had given Mrs Smith a dirty look before muttering under her breath and walking away; clearly, she hadn't wanted to be anywhere near Mrs Smith.

Mrs Smith had thanked Mrs Neville with tears in her eyes.

'Ach, it's nothing,' Mrs Neville had said.

'It means a lot,' Mrs Smith had said. 'You are so nice to me. I wish everyone was the same.'

Mrs Neville's cheeks had been pink with embarrassment. Charity had had no doubt she was thinking of how she herself had talked about Mrs Smith behind her back. For the gossip mills had been working overtime among the matrons of West India Dock Road since Mrs Smith had given birth to a child of a different skin colour.

'We knew the babe wasn't her husband's. Didn't I tell you, he hasn't been home on shore leave since the start of the war?' Mrs Neville had sniffed.

'He will get a surprise when he comes home, so he will, the poor sod,' Mrs O'Riley had sighed.

They might have passed judgement on Mrs Smith but the ladies of West India Dock Road were essentially kind, and good to her and her children.

But the same could not be said of everyone else...

'You can't change people, luvvie,' Mrs Neville had said to Mrs Smith gently.

Mrs Smith's girls had tugged at their mother's skirt. 'Why are people so mean to Jimmy?'

Mrs Smith had smiled brightly at her daughters. 'It's all right, girls.'

'It's not nice, Ma. They cross the road when they see him. They call him names and you too. And they shake their heads when they see us.'

Charity had felt tears prick her eyes.

'He's only a baby. He hasn't done anything wrong,' the girls had said indignantly, hands on hips, with the innocence and flawless logic of children.

If only adults would think this way, Charity had thought.

She had seen the sadness in Mrs Smith's gaze as she'd gently stroked her baby's cheeks.

'He's beautiful,' Charity had said and she'd smiled gratefully at Charity but her eyes had been stark, her expression resigned.

Charity had looked at the sleeping babe, his beautiful golden hue. Mrs Smith's girls had hit the nail on the head. How could anyone condemn this babe, his glorious innocence, treat him as less, shun him?

Charity knows that this is exactly what she can expect if she continues her relationship with Veer, marries him and has his children like she very much wants to.

This is what Mrs Kerridge and the other ladies on West India Dock Road worry about on her behalf. This is why they warned her against Veer, for, 'We care for you, gel. We want the best for you.'

But Charity wants Veer. He is the best for her.

'You have had a hard life. Why are you hellbent upon choosing the hard path again?' Mrs Kerridge has tutted.

But how can you choose who you fall in love with? Charity loves Veer, and that's that. She understands where Mrs Kerridge and the other well-meaning ladies are coming from. But, like her mother did when she left the convent to marry Paddy, causing quite the stir, Charity too will deal with whatever the future has in store for them.

Nevertheless, it is hard to be stoic, and for her resolve not to waver when she and Veer are subject to prejudice.

When she is out with Veer, people give them a wide berth.

Now that Charity and her family are lodging with Mrs Kerridge, and Veer is at a boarding house in Stepney, they don't get much time together, having to make do with snatched moments here and there. Veer is busy with his duties with the Home Guard during the day and the only time Charity sees him is when he drops by the curry house of an evening. Afterwards, she walks with him a bit of the way to his boarding house and that's the only time alone they get. But even that is soured by people's reactions to the two of them together.

The other day, an elderly man queuing at the pie and mash shop had cried, eyes flashing with venom, 'Shame on you, lass, stepping out with a coloured man.'

Fed up, she had retorted, angrily, 'Shame on you, sir, for seeing colour instead of a courageous soldier, who has fought for our country.'

Afterwards, Veer had said, eyes soft with emotion, 'That was brave, my love, but you can't fight everyone.'

'I will if I have to,' she declared.

'I wish it was different. But this is what is bound to happen if we stay together. I should stop seeing you for your own sake.'

'Don't you say that,' she said fiercely. 'I want you and only you.'

He smiled and gently cupped her face and she angled it towards him.

A man coming out of the pub down the road did a double take, crying, 'For shame.'

Charity felt tears of anger bud, as much from the man's comment as from the despair writ large upon Veer's face.

She was composing a retort when Veer touched her arm gently, saying, 'Charity, love, it's not worth it.'

The man had stood in their way, shooting daggers at Veer's hand upon Charity's arm until Veer dropped it and stepped away from Charity.

'Not only is he black but he is missing a limb. You can do better than that, surely?' he had sneered.

'I don't want to do better. For me, this brave man who gave up his arm for this country is the best,' she said, holding the man's gaze until he turned away, but not before spitting vehemently in the street right next to their feet.

It took all of Charity's willpower neither to flinch nor to jump away from the dregs of the spittle, drops of which had splashed her.

The vitriol and abuse they endure daily upsets Charity, makes her so very angry. But Veer is inured to it.

'It is what it is,' he says, sounding defeated. Resigned.

Charity realises now how Divya must have felt when she first arrived in this country, and what she must have experienced when she stood by Raghu when the entire street was against him, convinced he had started the fire at the public house just before the war. She fancies that she understands Divya better now she is facing a little of what Divya and Veer and other people of colour must experience as a matter of course.

But although the hatred and the anger directed at her and Veer hurts very much, she will take it.

For the alternative is losing Veer, and *that,* she will not countenance.

5

CHARITY

Speaking of Veer, here he is now, with Fergus, glimpsed as they come past the window of the curry house and walk through the door.

Veer's face lights up when he sees Charity, and her heart, as always, blooms at the sight of him.

She glows and the ladies gathered in the curry house shake their heads, muttering, 'Young love, eh?' But they are smiling.

Paddy and Connor rush up to Veer and Fergus, Paddy doing the talking while Connor is content to grin and hang back. 'Mr Brown beat Mr Stone in one game of chess and then in the next one, Mr Stone beat Mr Brown, so they are even,' Paddy recounts breathlessly.

Veer sets his crutch down as he lowers himself into the chair beside Charity.

'Hello, ladies,' he says to the matrons and they smile at him.

'If only I was younger, you'd have serious competition, Charity, my girl,' Mrs Neville sighs.

Paddy looks horrified.

'Does she mean she would have liked to be with Mr Singh,

marry him even, if she was younger?' he whispers furiously to Charity, his eyes on stalks.

'It's just an expression, Paddy,' Charity smiles, ruffling his hair.

'But Mr Singh would never be with her, for she's a witch,' Paddy says. And then, clapping a hand over his mouth, 'Oh, do you think she might brew a spell to make herself younger?'

'Paddy...' Charity begins.

'Beware, Charity, she might cast a spell on you as you are her enemy since she likes Mr Singh. I better warn Mr Singh too,' Paddy says, watching in barely controlled upset as Veer grins at Mrs Neville.

'You are looking especially well today, Mrs Neville,' he says.

She turns quite pink. 'Aw, you charmer,' she says, waving a hand coquettishly at him.

Paddy looks even more distressed, shaking his head at Veer and frantically gesticulating a warning to him behind Mrs Neville's back.

'What's the matter, Paddy, love, do you need the toilet?' Mrs Boon asks kindly and Paddy blushes and runs back to sit with the men, shaking his head vigorously while his brothers burst out laughing.

Divya comes from the kitchen with a heaping plate of potato pakoras and another of freshly baked oat biscuits along with a cup of cinnamon spiced tea, which she sets in front of Veer.

'Just the ticket, Miss Ram,' Veer says and she beams, the shadows dispersing from her eyes, briefly.

'So how do you feel? Are you all ready to start work tomorrow?' Veer asks Charity, smiling warmly at her.

'Yes, I am,' she whispers, with wonder and thrill.

It was Veer who had given her the idea.

'I volunteer with the WVS but it's not enough. I want to do more for the war effort,' she had said to him.

Veer had smiled gently at her. 'You also look after your brothers and your mammy too, not to mention anybody else who needs help on the street and beyond. In addition to that, you have been looking in on Mrs Murphy.'

'It's not only myself; it's all of us on the street who do it,' she had said to Veer.

'I know. But I don't think anyone else does quite as much; you fill every minute and then some. Now I see why Fergus ran away to sign up even though he's only fifteen. He takes after you, Charity. Wanting to help, to go above and beyond. I love that about you and your brothers.'

'I feel bad, staying with Mrs Kerridge. I want to pay her rent but can't as we lost everything when the boarding house was bombed.'

'Charity, you would do the same if it was the other way round.'

'I would but even so, it doesn't sit right with me.' She had taken a breath, then tried to put into words what she had been feeling ever since the lodging house was bombed. 'Us O'Kellys have always been independent, not relying on anyone, making our own way, you know? I want a source of income and also to recompense Mrs Kerridge for her kindness whether she wants it or not,' she said fiercely.

Veer had smiled tenderly at her. 'You are quite something, my love. If Mrs Kerridge is determined, you are even more so.' And then, after a bit, he had said, 'You told me your dream was to be a sugar girl. So why don't you see if they need people over at the factory?'

His words had made her heart bloom. She herself had briefly considered it but had thought it too precious a fantasy to tarnish with the brush of reality. But when Veer, her beloved, thoughtful beau, had mentioned it, she thought, *why not?*

And so she went to the factory, this place that she had built up in her mind as something unattainable, and asked if they were looking for people to work there.

'We always need people,' they said. 'When can you start?'

She had come away with her heart aglow. Unable to quite believe it.

She still cannot, even as Veer says, now, beaming at her, that smile he reserves just for her, 'You are going to be a sugar girl.'

'Yes,' she whispers. 'I am.'

And she tastes her dream, soon to be reality, molasses sweet in her mouth.

6

DIVYA

25 April 1941

My dearest Raghu,

This morning, I had come back from the Tube station, up the stairs and into a decrepit world, smoke and rubble, sundered by war. I had washed and was changing in preparation for starting the day when I experienced this flutter, soft as an angel's kiss, in my stomach.

Overcome by awe and wonder, I caressed my stomach, cooing to our child.

And our babe responded with another flutter!

A hello from inside the womb!

Oh the wonderful miracle of it!

Tears started in my eyes. Tears of joy and gratitude. Of wistfulness and ache.

I wish you were here, to experience it too, our baby talking to us.

I will protect you with my everything, I promised, and our babe responded with what felt like tiny bubbles being blown beneath my hand.

I want to keep this secret to myself for a little longer but I know I don't have much time.

Truth be told, I am nervous about telling everyone. I worry that they will judge, that they will malign this baby who is so precious, so wanted. I don't want their reaction to leach away the joy, the wonder I feel.

I haven't even been able to talk to Charity but I know she suspects something. I fret that the matrons of the street, with their unerring nose for divining secrets, will find out before I share my news with Charity. I really don't want that to happen. I want to be the one to tell her but I am apprehensive of the reception to my news – yes, even from Charity.

I am convinced that Charity will be happy for me but even so I... I worry that she may worry for me, and that that might chip away at the happiness I am feeling.

I know that sooner rather than later, someone will clock that I am growing big with child, no matter that I wear clothes with the specific purpose of disguising it, which I am managing to, just about. But... the way I am walking is changing too and I cannot rush down the steps of the Tube station any more. I worry about slipping, hurting our child.

I hate to think of anyone not being receptive to this child I long for. And I know this is silly but I worry that our babe, even though it's in my womb, will pick up on it.

But the world is going to find out, soon, whether I share my news with them or not, and I am afraid. Anxious.

This is why I go to church whenever I have a minute. I feel at peace there. I pray to all the gods and goddesses, Hindu and Christian, and fancy the prayers making their way heavenward through the bombed-out roof.

I place my anxieties into the hands of the deities and hope and believe that they and you, alongside my parents and your ma, are looking out for me and our babe.

And I come back strengthened.

I have been writing this after everyone has left the curry house after supper, blackout blinds drawn, lamp light flickering, the faint tang of spice in the air, our babe snug in my womb, one ear peeled for the air raid siren.

Ah, now here it is. I better go. More soon, my beloved.

Love always,

Divya and babe

7

CHARITY

Everyone has been fed and Divya has come to sit down at the table beside Charity and Veer.

Close up, Divya looks even more tired and the unease Charity has been harbouring with regard to her friend intensifies.

'Are you not sleeping, Divya?' The question she really wants to ask is what's eating away at her friend, why she doesn't seem herself – worried, but also, strangely, content too – but for that, she must catch Divya alone, which has proven difficult.

They are both busy all day.

And in the evenings, Charity has Mammy to look after and stay with. While everyone else, including Charity's brothers, goes to the Tube station when the air raid siren sounds, Charity and her mammy bed down in Mrs Kerridge's basement.

Charity has come to treasure that time with her mammy. She climbs into bed beside her mother and they pray together.

Mammy is getting more fragile by the day. She has gone rapidly downhill since Da's death. She is finding eating, talking and even breathing more difficult now. The doctor says there isn't anything he can do.

'I don't have much time left, my love,' she tells Charity often.

'Don't say that, Mammy!' Charity cries each time.

'I want to prepare you, my love,' Mammy had said, the other night, smiling softly at Charity. 'I am ready to go, meet the Lord, join your da, look out for you all from there.'

And Charity could see that Mammy really was ready, although selfishly, Charity was not prepared to let her go. It seemed like she had only just got close to Mammy and she wanted more time with her...

Mammy had taken to her bed after Paddy was born, her health, never the best, wrecked, her back giving way after having three boys in quick succession.

Even though she knew Mammy couldn't help it, Charity had nevertheless resented the fact that she had to do everything on her own. She had done her duty by her parents, looking after them, feeding them, but she never had time to sit and chat with them, for there was the boarding house to run and the boys to see to.

But when the boarding house was bombed, Charity was suddenly at a loose end and she took to sitting with Mammy.

And they talked.

Like hearing her da's voice in her head only after he was gone, Charity has gotten close to her mammy, finally, only to have precious little time with her.

Even the Ursuline nuns, whose order Mammy had joined, leaving when she fell in love with Charity's da, have said that Mammy doesn't have long.

'Charity, love, you and your brothers must be prepared to let her go,' they've warned.

Charity hasn't told the boys yet; she cannot find the words.

But... they have taken the loss of their father in their stride and she hopes they will cope when Mammy goes too. This is at least one thing that the war has prepared them all for: loss. It is as commonplace as breathing. The gravediggers over at the church have never been busier. The cemetery is full to the brim and the problem, Father O'Donnell says, is finding space to bury yet another of his flock.

In Mammy's case, Charity understands that death will be a release after being bedridden for so many years. And Mammy has her faith so she is not worried or afraid; in fact, she welcomes it.

Charity is hopeful that she will hear her mother's voice too, after she is gone, like she does her da's.

But for now Mammy is here and Charity treasures the nights she spends with her in the basement.

Mammy cups her face and says, in her soft whisper of a voice, halting after each word, to take a breath, 'It is good to see you happy, my heart.'

And yes, all things considered, despite her angst about losing Mammy soon, Charity is happy.

Her brothers are doing all right.

She has found love in Veer.

And her dream is being realised. She is going to work in the sugar factory.

Charity had been worried about how Mammy would take to the idea.

It has always been Charity looking after Mammy: bringing her meals, helping her to and from the privy. Mammy might be bedridden but she is also fiercely proud and very private, which is why she had refused the help of the ladies of West India Dock Road when she fell ill after Paddy was born.

But when Charity started work at the sugar factory, unlike

when she used to run the lodging house, she would be away all day and Mammy would have no choice but to rely on the ladies of West India Dock Road to look in on her and give her a hand.

So, the evening after she went to the sugar factory and they said that they did have vacancies, she had climbed into bed with her mother, held her fragile body and said, hesitantly, 'Mammy, Mrs Kerridge is very kind having all of us stay with her, and she says we are welcome to stay for as long as we want and I know she means it, but it's never sat right with me. I would like to pay her back and the only way to do so is to start working. I've inquired at the sugar factory and they said they need people urgently.' Just saying the words made her heart jump. 'But if I do join, it means the ladies of the street must look in on you during the day.'

She watched her mother, waiting for a look of horror or upset. It never came. Instead, her mother smiled and said, 'Of course you must work. We cannot be dependent on Mrs Kerridge's charity forever. I will be all right, my heart.'

'Are you sure, Mammy? You don't mind the ladies coming in to see you, helping you to the privy?' she asked anxiously. 'It will be Divya for the most part but there will be times when the curry house is busy and she won't be able to get away, so the others will pitch in.'

'I will be fine. It will all work out for the best. Don't you worry about me,' Mammy said.

And Charity hugged her mammy, her heart aglow, for finally, her long put to bed fantasy of being part of the workforce at the sugar factory was coming true!

As if she had divined her thoughts, her mammy said, 'You are finally achieving your dream.'

Charity was surprised. She had not shared her secret desire

with Mammy, or even Divya. Only Veer had known, or so she thought.

'How did you know?' she asked.

'Ah, love, I know you.' Mammy cupped her face gently, her touch feather light. 'It was never your wish to run the lodging house. That was your father's dream for you.'

'Yes,' Charity said.

Mammy smiled at her daughter gently. 'Now go and realise your dream, my heart. I will be fine.'

Charity, her heart full, could only nod.

Mammy said, softly, her gaze full of love, 'Shall we recite the rosary, then?'

Charity nodded.

And together, they said the rosary and afterwards read the Bible while overhead, enemy machines wreaked havoc upon their beloved East End.

'Charity, where have you disappeared to?' Veer's voice, threaded with laughter, brings her back into the present.

She is in the curry house, on the eve of starting her new job at the sugar factory, sitting beside the two people she loves most in the world apart from her family.

But now Charity looks at her friend and feels that she has failed her.

Divya has dark circles under her eyes.

None of them are sleeping at night due to the incessant bombing.

But in Divya's case, it is more than that. It is grief. And something else too. What?

How do you go on after the love of your life is gone? Charity has wondered since Divya received the dreaded telegram informing her of Raghu's death.

Charity cannot begin to imagine. Those few days when she had turned Veer away, she had felt undone. The world rendered colourless.

For Divya, that must be the case every day without any hope of relief. For her love is never coming back.

'You know you can talk to me, at any time,' Charity has said often to Divya.

'I know,' Divya has assured her.

And yet, Charity gets the feeling there's something Divya is not sharing. What is it that is so difficult that she cannot tell her best friend?

Guilt pricks at Charity. She has felt out of her depth, not knowing how to help Divya navigate her grief. But that's no excuse. She can't shake the feeling that she should have done more.

She takes Divya's hand. 'Are you all right?' she asks, thinking of that tower of letters by Divya's pillow.

Raghu, Divya's beau, a lascar, had thought himself not good enough for her, and so he had signed up for war without leaving a forwarding address.

Divya loved him and wanted only him. But she didn't know where he was, if he was alive. Even so, Divya had written to him religiously, and as she had nowhere to send the letters, they remained upon her bed, the pile growing every day.

And then when Veer came in search of Charity's lodging house, located opposite the best curry house ever, according to a certain lascar in his barracks, Divya had an address to post the letters to.

Raghu had replied, telling her that he had been wounded and recovering in a convalescent home in Guildford.

An ecstatic Divya had gone to see him last Christmas,

although nobody but Veer and Charity knew about this. The others thought Divya was visiting a fellow *ayah* whom she had met during her journey to England.

It proved fortunate, for Raghu was killed in action not long after. He had died with Divya's letters nestling next to his heart.

That was how the powers that be knew where to send the telegram informing next of kin of his death.

Divya has gone on, grieving for her love, but still cooking, still smiling.

And still writing letters to her love that multiply upon her bed. Charity has seen them there, an ever-growing pile going nowhere, and it is the saddest sight.

'Yes, I'm fine, my friend,' Divya says, in answer to Charity's question.

But Charity is not convinced.

For she glimpsed something in Divya's eyes, a shadow, a secret, just for a brief moment before she smiled widely, saying – too brightly – to Charity, 'Don't you worry about me.'

Charity looks at Veer and he raises an eyebrow at her.

He too has noticed, she is sure.

She had confided to Veer the previous evening, 'I am worried about Divya.'

To which he replied, 'You care about everyone; that is one of the things I love the most about you. You are fiercely loyal, a wonderful friend.'

'But that is exactly it, Veer. I haven't been a good friend to her. I've been caught up in my own affairs, far too much,' she'd fretted.

He put his arm around her, gathered her close. 'I promise you that she knows you are there for her,' he whispered against her hair and she heard his words reverberate in his ribcage against which she was nestled. 'And for now, that seems to be enough for her. When she needs you, she will ask, I am sure.'

Charity had nodded, hearing his heart beat steadily beneath her cheek, feeling comforted.

She had said, breathing him in, 'I am so glad I have you.'

'And I still can't believe my luck to have the love of the most beautiful, kindest woman in the world.'

She had, like he expected, laughed, delight and embarrassment at his over the top compliment, and she had heard his rumble of laughter start deep in his chest and explode out of his mouth, an avalanche of chuckles, festive, wonderful.

Beloved.

'Shame on you,' a gravelly voice thick with disdain boomed out of the darkness.

They had stopped at the corner of the street, thick with shadows, where they would part ways, Charity to Mrs Kerridge's, and Veer to his boarding house.

It was the opaque darkness of blackout and nobody was about which was why they had been brave enough to hug.

Upon hearing the angry shout, Veer immediately released Charity from his embrace and she felt bereft, cold without the warm enveloping of his love.

The man who had been walking past, eyes shooting amber sparks at Veer, growled, 'Find someone your own kind.'

Veer's shoulders slumped in defeat while Charity bristled.

'He's a celebrated soldier...'

'Shame on you,' the man spat again and then he was gone, leaving Charity shaking with upset, calling after him, even though he was out of earshot, 'He fought for our country. He's worth a thousand of you!'

And Veer, as always, said softly, 'You can't change them, my love. Leave it be.'

Now, in the curry house, the discussion is about Charity's friend Jack Devine.

Paddy is saying, 'Mr Devine is amazing. Do you know, he is teaching the prison guards English. That's what he wrote in his last letter.'

'That lad is quite something,' Mrs Kerridge says fondly.

'We all miss him sorely, we do,' Mrs Neville sighs.

'It's been a while since his last letter,' Mrs Boon remarks. 'Hope he's all right.'

'He is an' all,' Mrs Neville says stoutly. 'His letter is on its way even now, you mark my words.'

Divya walks past Charity and looking at her, Charity is troubled once again by growing unease.

'Divya...' Charity begins.

But Divya stops her, holding Charity's hands in hers and looking into Charity's eyes. 'Missy, you worry too much.'

'But you—'

'I am *fine*. I am concerned for Jack.'

'I am too,' Charity says. 'He is in my prayers, always.'

'I do hope his letter is on its way, just as Mrs Neville says,' Divya says. Then, firmly, 'Now I want you to concentrate on starting work tomorrow. Your dream job. A sugar girl.'

And Charity beams, a thrill rocking through her. It feels so good no matter how many times she hears it.

She, Charity O'Kelly, a sugar girl.

But then she turns again to Divya, refusing to be diverted. 'You're sure there's nothing you aren't telling me?'

'Charity, if I need anything, I will come to you first,' Divya says affectionately, holding Charity's gaze.

Charity nods, then realises that Divya has not really answered her question. The skein of worry with regard to her friend nags at her again. Why is Divya avoiding the issue?

She opens her mouth to ask Divya this when the door to the curry house opens, letting in a gust of evening air, flavoured with earth and grit.

'Who is it, I wonder? I thought we were all here,' Divya says even as they all turn to look at the stranger, standing shyly, hesitantly at the door to the curry house.

PART II

8

RUTH

Ruth clutches the letter to her chest and peers at the street.

It is, like all the others she has passed on the way here, cobbled and very slightly crooked, busy with houses and businesses on either side, but also riddled here and there with gaping holes where buildings had once stood, she imagines. Now there are only piles of sorry bricks, under the smoggy glower of sky.

Relics of war.

The street appears deserted. The setting sun gilds it in a golden glow, making even the rubble appear romantic, the houses still standing haloed a dreamy, reddish gold.

Is this where she will finally find who she is looking for, what she has come here for?

And again, she thinks, *Why me? Why not you, Eva? By rights, it should be you.*

Her heart ululating in pain and loss. So much loss.

This street, basking in the loving crimson-rose kiss of fast-disappearing sun, appears peaceful, for the moment at least.

A world away from Germany and Hitler's ruthless pogrom against their kind.

Why didn't you come here, to safety, Eva, when you could? Why did you stay there? Why?

But Ruth, more than anyone, knows why. The same reason her father stayed in Germany instead of travelling to India, to relative safety, with his German Jewish wife and their children. Even though he was ostracised from his family, he could still have gone elsewhere in the country of his birth and started anew. Or like he did, too late for him to take advantage of it, he could have built bridges with his family and moved back into their fold.

But no. Germany was the country he had adopted and he hadn't wanted to leave, fighting against Hitler's increasingly determined and despicable campaign to rid 'his' land of Jews to the bitter end.

Eva was the same. 'This is my country just as much as Hitler's. This is where I was born, where my love was born and is buried, where my children were born. And this is where I will stay.'

But if you stay here, you will most likely die, as will all of us foolish enough to do so, Ruth had thought but did not say. For it was a truth understood by all of them, those foolhardy souls of Jewish blood stubbornly staying on in Germany until it was too late to leave.

Ruth too had been convinced she would not leave, meaning to continue in her father's footsteps, like him, 'until the bitter end.' After all, she had nothing to live for.

But Eva had had other plans for her protégée, the girl she had taken under her wing...

And so here Ruth is, on West India Dock Road, which looks

calm, shimmering in the cerise-saffron twilight glow. But Ruth knows, better than most, that appearances can be deceptive. That nowhere is safe, not now.

There are signs of war everywhere. Hillocks of dirt and debris swept by the side of the road, broken bricks stained with soot and stamped by fire, all that is left of people's residences.

As she was walking here, she'd watched a boy of around her brother's age – the thought of her brother causing her heart to bleed afresh – juggling pieces of wood from a splintered door, it appeared, judging from the hinges still attached to some of the pieces. How did he keep them from stabbing his hand?

'Be careful with that. It might take out your eye,' she had warned.

'Hold your horses, miss.' He had grinned cheekily at her, handling the wood with the breezy confidence of childhood, the conviction that he would be fine.

It was a blessing that the war hadn't bled it out of him.

Now, she stands in the middle of West India Dock Road and, as she looks at the gaps where houses should be, she is struck by a sudden thought. Something she hadn't considered before but really should have.

Why hadn't she?

Because the whole journey had been surreal, everything from the time they had come for Eva and her children, and Eva, in an act of immense love and sacrifice, had pushed Ruth out of the back door, pressing a letter into her hands and asking her to please deliver it to her sister in England.

'But how?' Ruth had asked, her heart jumping with fear as the pounding on the front door increased in volume and strength.

'Go to your grandfather's friend, Karl Hoffman,' Eva had

whispered, her breath hot and urgent in Ruth's ear. 'He has your passport and the relevant documentation for travelling to England. Your opa entrusted him with it, and a packet of money for safekeeping, for an eventuality such as this.' Then, 'Please find my sister. Give her this letter. Tell her I'm all right and so are the children.'

Her eyes wild as they'd met Ruth's for they both knew that by the time Ruth arrived in England, this would most likely not be true.

But because Eva wanted her to find her sister and give her a missive from her, Ruth has come all this way only to stop short now.

What if the house she is looking for has been bombed? What if the woman she wants is no longer here? What if she has been a casualty of war? What will she do then?

Ruth thinks of the officers in the train on the way here, how they had checked everyone's passports and when they had come to the German Jew sitting opposite her, they had appeared grim, lips disappearing as they conferred among themselves.

The man opposite Ruth must have endured God knows what horrors, overcoming countless obstacles to arrive at this moment in time, in this country which was supposedly on his side.

He had sat on the train appearing to shrink into himself, taking up as little space as possible, his face lined and drawn with everything he had experienced, his eyes bleeding wounds.

The officers had shaken their heads, said to him, sombrely, 'You will be sent to an internment camp.'

He had looked bewildered, thinking, no doubt, *I escaped one camp only to be sent to another?* Out loud, he had said, his voice an apology, 'But I thought you were... you...'

He couldn't finish the sentence.

But Ruth had known what he had been about to say: *I thought you were on our side, the side of the Jews.*

And Ruth had sent a little prayer of thanks to her father for her Indian name and complexion, and to her beloved opa for her passport, which he had somehow used his influence to get out of being stamped with J for Jew, and entrusted to Karl Hoffman for safekeeping so his grandchildren could escape to safety if it came to that.

Her heart keening as she'd thought of the other passports, her brother's, her father's, her mother's, Opa's and Oma's, which would never be used again...

When they'd disembarked the train and the man opposite was led away by the officers, Ruth had thought, *I'm glad I look Indian and have an Indian surname. Being brown and looked down upon for it is far preferable, it appears, to being a German Jew.*

She'd felt ashamed at the thought but couldn't help it all the same.

As she'd prepared to exit the railway station, she'd heard shouts, cries of, 'Hey, can't you read?'

She'd stopped, shocked, when a man's foot appeared in front of her, blocking her way.

She had been even more stunned at the anger, the vitriol aimed at her. 'Yes, I was speaking to you.' The man's face was red and snarling as he pointed at the sign above her, which read: *No Blacks or Coloureds.*

'Use the other exit,' he'd barked.

Clutching her case, determinedly not thinking of another railway station where she had waited with her mother and brother for Opa to collect them, engulfed by fog, ambushed by the painful cries of men being beaten and kicked and abused, refusing to dwell on omens and signs, Ruth had walked through the exit reserved for non-whites, alongside a surge of dark-skinned people, into a different country and a different life, stripped of family, and deliberately hiding the Jewish part of her identity.

9

RUTH

Now, steps faltering, Ruth walks down the street, peering at the house numbers as the sun sets and gloom sets in.

She is clutching her case with one hand and the letter to her chest with the other, praying, *Please.*

She hadn't realised that she was so invested in Eva's wish for her, until there was a possibility that it might not happen.

44, 46... ah here it is. Number 48.

She lets out a breath.

It is still standing.

A narrow house. Neat and staid. The half-crescent circling the stoop and the cobbles around it shined to perfection.

The street is quiet. Empty.

Is it always like this? Ruth wonders. *Where* is *everyone?*

It is like a ghost road, the eerie, unnatural silence thick with wisps of impressions, reverberating with haunting memories of happier times when it was busy and bustling...

Stop it. You're letting your imagination run away with you.

On the other streets she passed to get here, there were

people milling. Sitting outside their front doors on chairs and nattering while getting on with their chores.

But here, there's nobody about.

She looks up at the house. Blackout curtains neatly drawn across the windows. A shuttered residence, giving nothing away.

She takes a breath. Walks to the front door.

Knocks.

Waits.

It appears deserted. Like the rest of the street.

She waits a beat. Two. Three.

Knocks again.

Nothing.

She steps back.

Looks up at the house.

It is as mysteriously enigmatic as before. Hugging its secrets tightly to itself.

Weariness engulfs her. She has been journeying with single-minded purpose since they came for Eva and her children and Eva handed Ruth the letter and whispered, 'Please. Leave Germany. Go to England. Karl will arrange it. Find my sister and give her my letter. Please do this for me.'

Eva has done so much for Ruth.

Ruth wants to give back. Honour the request of the woman who has been like a mother to her in these past few horrific months of her life. And she wants to realise the hopes of her grandfather who had thought far ahead, making sure his grand-children could escape even if he wasn't there to help, arranging for Karl to come to their aid and for Eva to facilitate it.

And so, she had kept her head down and emptied her mind of all thought except doing what Eva and her opa wanted. Throughout the fraught journey here, Ruth had worried that someone would stop her, that they would send her back.

But she never envisioned that she would arrive here, at the house and yet not find the person to whom she had to deliver Eva's message.

She looks up and down the street again.

Nothing has changed in the last few minutes except for dusk settling lazily: a dark, shadow-infested mantle.

The street is still completely, uncomprehendingly empty. *Where is everyone?* she wonders, again.

She stands still. Listens.

The whirr and drone and grumble of factories from further down by the docks. The cawing of crows and the screech of seagulls from somewhere hidden in the smoggy screen above.

The swell and splish of the Thames in the distance.

And wait, is that...? Yes, the muted hum of human laughter and conversation, wafting on the earthy, smoke- and dust-flavoured breeze, which strokes her cheeks with a nippy bite.

She walks towards the sound.

Ah, a public house. The laughter, the noise louder as she approaches, and she is ambushed by the darkly bitter, vinegary fug of ale.

Here too blackout curtains grace the windows but this place is definitely occupied.

Even so, she hesitates at the entrance. Should she?

The voices that she has heard are masculine, throaty and full-bodied, their good humour no doubt helped along by the brew they are consuming. The woman she wants is most likely not within.

Once again, she looks up and down the street, hoping she missed something. Someone. But no, she is the only person out and about.

She looks towards the docks. The sun has set, and all she can see are silhouettes of buildings, grey and imposing, factories churning columns of smoke. Barrage balloons floating tiredly. The sky is clammy grey, heavy with grit. In the distance, the twinkle and shine of water, dark and swelling, lit here and there with silvery ripples.

Stop hesitating, her conscience chastises. *You've come this far. You must do this for Eva's sake. Even if her sister isn't inside, someone in there will surely know where she is.*

She takes a breath and walks up the steps of the pub.

The laughter and noise louder now, raucous and merry, accompanied by the tangy pungency of brewing hops.

She lifts her hand and, taking another bolstering breath, pushes the door open.

Ah, here's her answer to where everyone is. Some of the street is here, the male contingent at least, she thinks.

Men huddle over their pints of ale, some jolly, others looking gloomy and miserable. They are either very old or very young, but every one of them appears weary and run down.

There's a woman behind the bar, the only female here by the looks of it.

But she appears competent and well able to handle the mob, her smile, that she beams upon Ruth, resolute and steely, even as she wipes her hands on her apron and says, warmly, 'What can I do for you, gel?'

Ruth clears her throat, finds her voice and asks after Eva's sister.

'Ah, she'll be at the curry house.' The woman smiles. 'Everyone who is anyone on this street, apart from those who like their brew, are all in there. My husband too.' At this, a frown graces her kind features. 'I'm hoping he's sobered up summat.' And then, once again smiling at Ruth, 'Cross the road, gel and you will see the curry house. You can't miss it. There's a great big sign outside in case you were in any doubt.'

As soon as Ruth leaves the pub, shivering after the cosy warmth inside – it is quite decidedly nippy now the sun has set – she sees it.

Divya's Curry House, the faded sign reads. The Indian connection incites a jolt of warmth, mingled with pain as memories of Papa, as well as their brief sojourn in India after Papa's death, assault her, bittersweet and poignant.

She crosses the road, her case juddering over the cobbles.

Ah, now she's standing in front of the curry house. How did she miss it before? How did she not see the sign? If she peers through the narrow sliver of gap between the blackout curtains and the window frame, she can just make out faint impressions of golden light dancing inside.

And she can hear the murmur of conversation permeating from it, on a delicious, spice-scented breeze.

The lady at the pub said the woman Ruth is looking for would be here. It appeared as if she knew her. That means Ruth will be able to realise Eva's wish, hand her sister her letter.

Taking a deep breath, she walks up to the front door.

And with another breath, she pushes it open.

10

CHARITY

The stranger who has just entered the curry house is a girl around Charity's age.

She has caramel skin, a pert nose and wide, brown eyes. Her golden-brown curls, loosely held together by a clip, cascade down her back, several of them escaping to frame her heart-shaped face. Lines of weariness and suffering tug at her features but it is her eyes that Charity recognises and responds to, her heart swelling with empathy. For they bear the stark, hollow pain of having seen and endured too much, that all of them wear. A legacy of the war they are all living through. Their lips might lift in smiles but it is the eyes that give everyone away.

The girl stands timidly at the door, shifting her weight from one leg to another, blinking in the spotlight of the collective gaze. She is carrying a battered case in one hand and clutching what appears to be a letter in the other.

'Come in, child, out of the cold and sit down. Spring might be tipping into summer but there is, as ever, a nip to the air of an evening.' It is, as always, Mrs Kerridge who takes the lead and smiles warmly at the newcomer.

And now, the girl speaks, her words tentative, her gaze flitting between all of them, 'Um... I... I went to the pub...'

She speaks English with an accent. Hard to place. A bit like Divya's but softer, with an European lilt. German, at a guess.

'The landlady at the pub—'

'My good wife,' Mr Barney says.

'Let the gel speak,' Mrs Neville cries and Mr Barney gulps down the dregs of water from his glass, looking suitably chastised.

'The lady at the pub,' the girl says again hesitantly in her soft, lovely voice. 'She said to come here.'

'That's right, my dear. We all collect here of an evening,' Mrs Kerridge says kindly. 'Were you looking for anyone in particular or just fancied a bite to eat and to rest your feet a tad?'

'Um...' The girl swallows, her gaze once again sweeping over all of them. 'I'm looking for Mrs Esther Rosenbaum?' The last raised in question. Adding, 'I knocked on her door, but there was no answer. Is she here?'

Mrs Rosenbaum stands, one hand upon her heart.

Over by where the men are playing chess, Mr Rosenbaum stands too and approaches his wife.

Mrs Rosenbaum is the quietest of the ladies of West India Dock Road. She blends into the background, usually. But she is always there if you are in trouble, or in need of something. She's the first to offer practical help. She is always unfailingly kind.

Now she is looking at the girl with curiosity, worry and hope warring on her face.

'Mrs Rosenbaum?' the girl says.

'Yes?' Mrs Rosenbaum's voice is soft, a fluttering whisper dancing on the wings of vibrant hope.

'I... I have a letter for you. From your sister.'

Mrs Rosenbaum startles, falling backward, and even as everyone rushes to her aid, her husband gets there first.

When she comes to from her fainting spell, Mrs Rosenbaum, who is a petite, lighter-haired, lighter-skinned version of Eva, takes Ruth's hand, her grip fragile yet hopeful, her sister's letter clasped to her chest, and she says, eyes bright with all the burning questions she wants to ask but is dreading the answers to, 'Come with me. Please. Let's go to my house.'

And, flanked by Mrs Rosenbaum and her tall, quiet husband, Ruth walks across the street, to the staid house which had appeared so shuttered and still when Ruth had knocked and not received an answer.

Ruth marvels at the neatness, the paving stones around the stoop scrubbed to a shine, and the house itself, so immaculately tidy, not a thing out of place, the photographs on the walls, on the dresser, a shrine to all the Rosenbaums' loved ones.

Eva is in so many of them. As a child, her sister beside her, both girls grinning widely. With her husband and children. Smiling. Happy. Younger. Carefree. Before Hitler started his campaign of rage and hate and division and destruction.

Ruth has no photos. She has nothing. Only the faces of her family stamped behind her eyelids, calling to her, their eyes bright with pain. And love.

All her worldly possessions are in her case: a change of clothes and other basic necessities. She has them thanks to the kindness and generosity of Opa's friend Karl, who had helped her get away even though it put him at risk. She does not have anything personal at all. The Nazis had appropriated their house and everything in it, as well as Opa's garment shops.

Opa, Elijah didn't make it but I did.

And on the heels of that, another thought, one that's always hovering: *Why me? Why was I spared? Why not my innocent brother? Why not Opa or Oma or Papa or Mama or Eva or her beautiful children?*

'My sister, she's alive?' Mrs Rosenbaum asks, her eyes bright, tears shining upon her lashes, one hand upon her heart.

What will Ruth tell her?

The horror of the Gestapo at the door, breaking it down, yelling, 'We know you are in there!'

Eva slipping Ruth the letter for Esther. Pushing Ruth out the back door just as the Gestapo broke the front door down.

And when Ruth hesitated, 'Please.' Eva sounding desperate like she had never been before, her voice cracking, affording Ruth a glimpse into the vulnerable woman beneath. 'I have to go to my children.'

Ruth had done as she said, even as her heart shrivelled from the shame of it. The cowardliness of leaving Eva and her children to their desperate fate while she escaped. She had run to Karl Hoffman, a German who vehemently disagreed with the atrocities wrought by his country on his fellow Jews and took a stance against it. He was active in the resistance. Sometime during the terrible build up to Kristallnacht, Opa must have entrusted the contents of his hiding place under the loose floorboard in the bedroom he shared with Oma, which he had shown Ruth once, to Karl, making sure Eva knew about this. Karl had equipped Ruth with a travelling case with essentials and managed to smuggle her out of Germany and into England. Ruth does not know what strings he pulled to get her the right papers, what he did to secure for her a visa for entry into Britain, and how much trouble he himself was in because of it.

All through the terrifying journey, as official after official checked her passport, at each hurdle, she thought, *This is it, I will be caught and sent back*, a small voice at the back of her head whispering, *It will only be right if you do,* all the while being bombarded by horrific imaginings of what had happened in that house after she left. Eva and her children being led away by the Gestapo, almost certainly to the concentration camps...

Ruth had grabbed the letter like it was a lifeline. And she had tried to push everything away, concentrating on doing what Eva had asked of her: getting her letter to her sister. But she heard their cries anyway. They reverberated in her ears; they were there when she closed her eyes, all her lost loved ones. And even as her passport and entry papers survived the hard-faced scrutiny of the officials, she wondered why she was spared, the purple wash of guilt threatening to swamp her...

'Ruth?' Mrs Rosenbaum prompts gently, looking at her with such stark hope in her eyes.

Ruth blinks, coming back into the here and now. Mrs Rosenbaum. The intensity of her gaze that Ruth wants to shy away from.

But the very least she can do, *must* do, is to meet Esther Rosenbaum's gaze, and not look away.

What should she say?

She swallows.

And speaks the truth. 'I... I don't know. Eva sent me away to safety, just as they... we were ousted from our hiding place by the Gestapo.' Her voice wavers. But she continues. She must. This woman deserves to know the likely fate of her sister and niece and nephew. 'Your sister... Eva saved my life. She told me to find my grandfather's friend, who had my passport. My grandfather never got it stamped...'

Mrs Rosenbaum nods. She no doubt knows about the directive Hitler brought into force in 1938, requiring all Jews to have their passports stamped with the letter J.

'They...' Ruth forces the words out of her dry, hoarse throat. 'Eva and her children were most likely taken to the camps.'

In that sterile, ordinary room, the words are as potent as bombs.

Mrs Rosenbaum nods. Swallows. Closes her eyes.

Her husband, who has paled, his mouth set in a grim line, puts his arm around her.

Ruth reaches across, takes her hand in her own.

'My mother, Naomi, she was Eva's childhood friend.'

Now Mrs Rosenbaum opens her eyes and looks up at Ruth, teardrops dancing silver-bright upon her wet lashes.

'And mine,' she says. 'Naomi Goldberg.'

Ruth's mama's name on Mrs Rosenbaum's lips is like a prayer.

'Ah, the three of us were thick as thieves. We would play together all summer in the woods behind our houses until our mothers called us for dinner. Oh, those were the days!' Mrs Rosenbaum sniffs. Her voice is wistful and faraway. She is gazing into the distance, somewhere beyond Ruth's shoulder, peering into the past, happy and unsullied by war and pain, all that was to come.

And then, eyes alight, as if she's only just realising it: 'You're Naomi's *daughter*.'

'Yes,' Ruth says, thinking of Mama. Oh, how she misses her! Her hugs, being wrapped in her scent of roses and love. Her habit of feeding everyone, as if food was the answer to everything: heartache and illness and prejudice and war. *Pflaumenkuchen* when there was something to celebrate, moist and jammy, the *streusel* crumbling in her mouth, sugary cinnamon. Happiness, for Ruth, tastes of her mother's *Pflaumenkuchen*, although she cannot recall the last time she was happy...

Chicken soup with *matzo* balls when they were ill. 'Eat up. It will make you better in a tick,' Mama would beam. 'That's a promise.'

'She was so bright,' Mrs Rosenbaum is saying. 'She came to England to study.'

'Yes, Cambridge. That's where she met my father. He was Indian.'

Mrs Rosenbaum smiles through her tears. 'You have Naomi's features; I don't know why I didn't notice it before.' Then, softly, 'Your beautiful complexion must be your father's gift to you.'

It hasn't felt beautiful. Or like a gift. It has felt cursed. Jews are being prosecuted. So she is better off hiding her Jewish identity. But she cannot hide her Indianness which is stamped upon her skin, marking her as different. Other. Unbelonging, twice over. She belongs nowhere.

'I hope you don't mind me asking, Ruth, but why did you all stay in Germany?' Mrs Rosenbaum says.

Ruth takes a breath. Another.

Why? Why had they? It is a question she has tortured herself with over and over.

Germany. Her country. Theirs. Which turned against them. Taking so much from her. Everything.

She feels a touch. Opens her eyes. She hadn't realised she'd shut them. Mrs Rosenbaum, looking at her with such empathy. Mr Rosenbaum beside her, quietly offering support and strength with his gentle gaze.

'My papa, he was ostracised by his family when he married Mama,' Ruth says, when she can speak. 'Opa and Oma, Mama's parents...'

'Yes, I knew them well. I spent many glorious afternoons at their home. We were neighbours growing up.'

'They weren't happy either, about Mama marrying an Indian man. But Papa, he was very charming.' Ruth wills her voice to stay steady as she talks about her beloved father. 'He won them round. We lived with Opa and Oma.'

'They were so respected. Your opa's garment shop was the place to go to in Munich,' Mrs Rosenbaum says, eyes sparkling with reminiscence.

And now Ruth sees how much she resembles her sister. It is a gift. Eva returned briefly to her.

'Yes. Papa joined him in running the shop. It expanded. They even opened branches in Frankfurt, Hamburg and Cologne.' She takes a breath. 'They did well for a time until Hitler started his discrimination against Jews.'

'Why didn't you leave?' Mrs Rosenbaum asks again softly.

'Papa was with the resistance. Opa's shop was not only the most respected garment shop in Munich, but also the headquarters for the resistance. Papa, he couldn't, wouldn't leave. He wanted to stay and fight for the country he had adopted as his own after his parents shunned him for marrying a white woman.'

Mrs Rosenbaum nods, eyes haunted. 'My sister refused to leave too.'

'Papa was arrested. His friend tried to get him out but... We don't know what happened, but the night before he was to be free, he died.' Ruth's voice wavers once more. *He was murdered by the Nazis*, she thinks, but can't say the words out loud.

Mrs Rosenbaum understands, for she squeezes Ruth's hand gently.

Ruth nods her gratitude, swallows. 'Afterwards, we did leave. We went to India.' She takes a breath.

India. The land of her father, which he never got to return to. Heat and spices and rituals. Disorientating. Stunning. She tastes the humid, burning tang of it in her mouth. 'Before he was arrested, Papa... Perhaps he had an inkling that the Gestapo were onto him, for he... he had tried to make amends with his family. After his death, we found a letter pleading with us to go to India if anything happened to him. He had written to his parents and we were now very welcome there. We went, and it was quite an adjustment, especially for Mama.'

She thinks of Mama, a pale facsimile of her former vibrant self after she lost Papa, the love of her life. Mama had travelled to India for it was Papa's wish for them, but she had struggled to adjust there, out of place in a foreign country, with its alien language and customs, missing her parents, her husband and all that was familiar. 'Papa's parents were very good to us and my brother, Elijah, he loved it there.'

Elijah had been spoilt rotten by Papa's parents, who were old and ground down by life. Grieving for their son, they had poured all their love on Elijah, who they said, reminded them of Papa as a child.

'But then, Papa's parents died within six months of each

other and his brother wanted nothing to do with us. So we returned to Germany...'

Ruth is once again ambushed by memories. The train station. The fog blinding them to the sadistic violence. But they had heard it all the same. Anguished cries, agonised screams, bitter wails, pain-soaked pleas amplified in the torturous mist, wet and moist and rife and seething. The savage grind, the vicious thud of boots. The zinging thwack of whips, the muffled cries as they connected with vulnerable human flesh...

12

RUTH

October 1938
Munich, Germany

Ruth waits at the train station, shivering, pulling her brother, whose teeth chatter audibly, closer to her. After the orange heat of India, the cold is a shock, and their thin coats are no protection. They are all too flimsy. They should have expected it and been better prepared. But, when leaving India, the weather was the last thing on their minds, for they had been kicked out of the house with not much more than the clothes on their backs, no sooner had Papa's parents been cremated...

Pain ambushes her, along with the scorching burn of anger and upset.

Mama had been stoic but Ruth had raged against Papa's brother – her uncle – had yelled, 'Your parents would have wanted us here!'

'But they are not here. And it is I and my wife and children who looked after them, took care of them while my upstart brother was living it up abroad. You don't belong here; you never have.'

Ruth was about to retort but Elijah had started to cry and Mama had gathered both of her children to her and stood up to her brother-in-law, saying in her quiet, dignified voice, 'We are leaving. We will not bother you again.'

Now, Ruth and her brother cuddle for warmth, hunched against the biting wind. Their mother – always straight-backed and well turned out and elegant – droops, lines of grief dragging down her lips. Mama used to be ever the optimist, before Papa's death. But since she lost the love of her life, followed by the events in India, she is beaten by life, diminished.

Ruth tries to ignore the pain that lances her with frost-edged knives and stands up straighter, pushing her shoulders back, her brother clinging to her. Elijah is eight years old and has already experienced such upheaval in his life: the imprisonment and subsequent death of his father, the move to India, losing the paternal grandparents whom he knew briefly but loved absolutely, in that unquestioning way of children, and now, their return back to Germany, away from his cousins, Papa's brother's children, whom he had also loved.

'Our little miracle,' Mama and Papa had called Elijah fondly.

They had tried for more children after Ruth – 'Both of us wanted a big family' – but Mama suffered miscarriage after miscarriage. Then, when Ruth was twelve and they had all but given up, Elijah had come along. An unexpected but very welcome addition to their family.

A happy, easy-going, delightful child usually, but now, he appears on the verge of tears, his little face blue and nose red from the cold, eyes ringed with exhaustion. Ruth smiles determinedly at Elijah, trying to buck him up. But he is looking at Mama, who is staring straight ahead, at nothing at all, for gloomy fog has enveloped them, shrouding them in its icy coffin, stroking their cheeks with deathly tentacles.

'Opa will be here soon,' Ruth reassures her brother.

Her brother's teeth click and clash as he asks, looking worriedly up at her, 'Will he find us in this?'

The hand with which he is gesturing at the mist encasing them is shaking as much as his teeth, Ruth notes, her heart going out to her brother even as she gathers him closer to her.

The ghostly screen of fog, cloistering the station like a particularly frosty witch's breath, stings and chastises, slimy breath depositing frozen kisses upon Ruth's cheeks.

'Of course he will; he knows we are coming and he will not rest until he finds us,' she says brightly, keeping her fingers crossed, hoping that the letters Mama wrote Oma and Opa informing them of their arrival had reached her grandparents.

Oma's letters to them in India had been desperately bright and yet failed to mask the undercurrent of unease that pulsed through them.

Mama, instead of being cheered, which was clearly Oma's intention, was troubled. She would hand each letter to Ruth. 'Tell me if I am wrong, but from what Oma is not saying, it appears things are getting worse at home. Hitler is more openly anti-Semitic by the day, passing all these laws designed to exclude, tax, fine and punish Jews. I think this was what your papa was anticipating, which is why he swallowed his pride, mended the rift with his parents and made arrangements for us to travel to India. I only wish...' And here, Mama's gaze became faraway, wistful, desperately sad, '...that he could have come too.'

Ruth had taken Mama's hand in hers. It had felt so fragile. Her mother had lost weight since losing her husband; she was paper-thin skin over a collection of bones. 'Me too,' she had said, thinking of her father's parents' looks of longing and nostalgia when with Elijah, the pain and sorrow shadowing their smiles as they had discovered their son in their grandson and longed for him and mourned the precious time they had lost because of their estrangement.

'I worry for Opa and Oma,' Mama was saying.

'Mama,' Ruth said, trying to inject confidence that she did not feel into her voice. 'Opa and Oma will be fine. They own the biggest garment store in Munich, perhaps all of Germany, in addition to their other stores all over the country...' But inside, she was thinking, and she was sure Mama was too, that none of that had helped Papa. The Nazis had got to him regardless, killed him the day before he was to be released from prison. Ruth was sure that was what had happened and she knew Mama and Opa and Oma knew it too. Only Elijah was spared the knowledge.

'But—' Mama appeared troubled, her brow furrowed, knotting her hands compulsively in that way she did when she was anxious.

'And not only that,' Ruth said brightly, 'Opa, as you said, has connections among the most influential—'

'That will no longer offer protection for Jews. Here, read your oma's latest letter; she's tried to be jocular about it, but I think it is absolutely shocking that they've to add Israel and Sara to their names as their given names don't sound Jewish enough. And that is not all: they need to carry an identity card at all times and there's talk all Jewish passports will need to be stamped with an identifying J...'

'But surely that's...' Ruth was so upset that she couldn't get the words out, even as she marvelled at her father's foresight. Somehow, he had seen this coming and tried to make sure his family was far away, even if that meant trying to get back in touch with the family who had so unceremoniously cut ties with him when he married outside his community, married for love.

Now, here they are, back in Germany despite Papa's best-laid plans, in Munich railway station, waiting for Opa to collect them. Opa, who is usually very punctual; one of the maxims he lives his life by is: 'Better early than late.'

Why then is he not here?

She squashes her worry down, says, for her brother's benefit, 'Opa will slash this fog bubble with his sword, for he is a daring knight and you his brave accomplice.'

Her brother's violet-tinged lips lift upwards in a tentative smile.

Encouraged, Ruth nudges her brother. 'Opa will part the door of this fog igloo and scoop us up like ice cream. We're definitely the right temperature for it.'

And now Elijah manages a proper, teeth-clinking smile.

It breaks her heart, the sight of her brother so small and vulnerable and blue with cold and she urges Opa here faster. *What is keeping him?* she wonders again, a skein of worry wrapping itself around her heart.

It will be okay, she tells herself, pushing her anxiety resolutely away. *We are here now. Opa and Oma will have received at least one of our letters. Mama made sure to post them at each stage of our journey.*

Opa will come. But even if he doesn't, we can take a carriage. She mentally calculates if the meagre cache of money left after booking their passage back here will be enough. *I don't think we have enough but surely the carriage groom will know Opa. Who doesn't? He'll take credit. When we arrive at Opa and Oma's, Opa will make sure to compensate him with a hefty tip.*

And once we get to Opa and Oma's, all will be well.

13

RUTH

Crash.

Marching boots.

Breaking glass.

Cries. Shouts. Screams of pain.

Swearing: 'Bloody Jews.'

Elijah looks up at Ruth and their mama, his lower lip trembling preparatory to tears, even as Mama and Ruth exchange shocked glances while trying to keep calm for Elijah's sake. Ruth's heart is pounding with panic and she is quite sure Mama's is too. What is going on?

The fog obliterates, disorientates.

They cannot see anything.

But noises pierce through. Sounds of bullying, blustering, grunting.

Anguished cries. Painful gasps. Lobbed insults. Potent, soul-destroying word grenades: *'Juden Raus! Auf Nach Palästina!' Jews out, out to Palestine!*

Glass clinking as if in celebration before it shatters.

A jarring note of festive cheer with violent undertones.

Not being able to see what is going on only makes it scarier.

Ruth's brother's mouth is an O of terror, his eyes brimming with anxiety too mature for his tender years.

Ruth meets her mother's eyes and they are clear for perhaps the first time since Papa died.

The fog of pain and sorrow has lifted from her eyes but Ruth flinches from the clarity. For there is fear there and a desperate worry that Ruth would rather not see. She would have preferred the opaque mist obscuring her mother's emotions.

'Jewish pigs, off with you. Your kind do not belong in our country.'

Her mother recoils as if slapped while Elijah huddles closer into Ruth.

'Mama,' Ruth says, deciding that it is foolish to wait for Opa here, 'we need to get a carriage.'

'We'll wait until this, whatever it is, calms...'

But the sound of more trucks pulling up, involuntary moans of pain, swearing and hurled insults – *what* is *going on?* – gives no indication of calming soon.

'I didn't realise it was *this* bad,' Mama whispers, her brown eyes glinting like melting chocolate. Her gaze is stark, her too-pale cheeks tinted purple with cold as, from near enough to touch, they hear the painful slam of a rod making violent contact with skin, the sickening crack of breaking bones, the plaintive whimper of a grown man in pain. The thunk and shudder of boots ripping flesh. The accompanying insults.

Ruth tries to cover her brother's ears but it is too late.

He whispers, tears trembling on his lashes, his lower lip jutting out with the effort of holding his upset in. 'Why are they saying that, doing that? Why do they hate Jews? Will they do it to us too?'

And again, Ruth's eyes meet Mama's.

'No, they won't,' she manages to say decisively, although she doesn't believe it for a minute. 'Opa is so well respected, they just wouldn't dare.'

'Yes.' Her brother nods, his worried expression easing slightly, only for his face to scrunch up again as there are more yells, further shouting, hitting, swearing, crying.

A train hisses into the station, steam briefly displacing the mask of fog, and they see rows and rows of men being herded, none too gently, into it.

'This country is my home,' one of the men protests.

'You don't belong here, Jew.' The Nazi storm trooper nearest him aims a kick at the man, who falls backward and would have slipped onto the tracks if one of those already on board hadn't pulled him onto the train.

Ruth gathers her brother's face into the folds of her thin coat, trying vainly to protect him from this ruthless violence. A cold that has nothing to do with fog is creeping through her, chilling her very bones.

She cannot believe what she is seeing. This is *Germany*. Their *home*. They are Jewish. But they *belong*. Don't they? This is their country just as much as the Nazis'. So why are they treating Jews in this way? And even though she told Elijah the stormtroopers wouldn't turn on them because of who Opa is, she does not quite believe it and the precariousness of their situation terrifies her. *Stop being scared,* she tells herself. *Be brave like Papa was and fight the regime. Be the resistance. Show them what they're doing is wrong.*

But there is a small voice at the back of her head saying, *But Papa lost the fight. They killed him.*

Holding her shivering, tearful brother, seeing the fear Mama is trying to but can't quite hide, despite the bravado of her conscience, Ruth shivers and it is nothing to do with the cold and all to do with the panicked terror that is gripping her heart in a vice.

What have they come back to?

Should they have stayed in India despite Papa's brother kicking them out?

But they knew nobody there other than their uncle and his family – and he didn't want them. They had no money and no means of livelihood in a country that was foreign to them.

And so they had booked a passage with what little money they had and returned to the only country they knew, the place they had called home, where they were born, but which has changed irrevocably, become even more alien and forbidding to their kind in the time they have been away.

The agonised screams of grown men at a freezing train station a world away from sun-scorched India vocalise the yawning cries inside of Ruth. *What have we done? Were we wrong to come back?*

A man sobs, heartrendingly. 'Please, my child is sick. I—'

A resounding thump and he falls silent.

Ruth shudders, along with her mother. Her brother, his face hiding in her coat, is sobbing silently.

Ruth's heart stutters as she is struck by a sudden, terrifying premise. Has Opa been arrested? Is that why he isn't here? Or... is he one of the men being packed into the trains like animals?

Bitter bile ambushes her mouth. She feels sick.

But... her brother is clinging to her. Fear and upset have rendered her mother immobile. Ruth has to be strong.

And so, she pushes away the nausea, swallows down the bile, tries to focus her thoughts...

Opa is not one of the men being abused here. He is on their way to pick them up.

He will...

But her determinedly positive inner spiel is interrupted by a storm trooper barking, right next to them, so they all, Mama, Elijah and Ruth, flinch as one, 'Off with you lot. Jews not welcome or wanted here. You do not belong.'

How did he guess they are Jews? Ruth wonders, heart scrambling within the confines of her chest.

Thwack.

The soldier whips the man in front of him ruthlessly.

Elijah jerks, letting out an involuntary whimper.

The soldier was addressing the man he just hit, not them, Ruth understands.

Nevertheless, as she hugs her brother's shaking body, trying to offer solace she doesn't have, the storm trooper's terrible actions ringing in her ears, she turns to her mother.

Her mother reads the words she is not saying and together, they slip unobtrusively towards the exit, Ruth gently nudging her terrified brother along.

They are almost there when...

'Wait.'

14

RUTH

It is the soldier who hit his hapless victim senseless.

Wielding the whip and a smirk that highlights the cruel glints in his icicle-blue eyes.

'Who are you? Where have you come from?' He clicks his fingers as he holds his palm out. 'Documents?'

Ruth's fingers are trembling as she digs in her bag for their passports and tickets; she volunteered to be in charge of the paperwork to save her mother the trouble.

She can't find the folder with their documents even though she has kept them safe, she is sure – they had to show them when they exited their train, and she is certain she had tucked them back in her bag; she is usually very careful and meticulous.

But these are not usual circumstances.

Panic mounting up her throat, choking her, tasting of the sea in her mouth, juddering with each terrified heartbeat against her chest even as the soldier sighs with impatience.

'Well?' His blue eyes flashing black sparks.

Where is the folder? Her fingers fumble, grasping air.

Her mother's troubled eyes upon her.

She is reduced by fear to a child again. She wants to sob like her brother is doing, silently, his shoulders shuddering against her.

She is tired: of putting on a brave face, of hiding her missing for her father, pretending she is all right, that she has taken his loss in her stride, for Mama's sake. For she can see that Mama, while undone by her own grief, also worries about her children too, and she has Elijah's sorrow and incomprehension, his plaintive queries of, 'But *why* is he never coming back? He promised he would,' to deal with.

But the truth is that for Ruth, the ache of missing Papa, instead of diminishing, is growing by the day. His loss is always there, glaring and irreplaceable. After Mama and Elijah were asleep – they had all shared a room in India – she would cry silently into her pillow each night, when she had tried and failed to manifest him back into existence. Papa, the sheer comfort of him, the strength he imparted, his confidence, his humour, the way just by being there, beaming his kind smile, he made everything all right.

Now, more than anything, as her shaking fingers root around desperately in her bag, she wants her father, yearns for his quiet reassurance. He would have stood up to this man who just whipped another into submission.

'Papers,' the man barks, a fleck of sour spittle landing on Ruth's cheek.

She flinches and her brother cannot help an involuntary moan from escaping, his little body trembling even more, if possible.

'Please, my child is upset.' Her mother's voice is unrecognisable, a cowed wisp of a plea. 'We are German, we were born and have lived here for most of our lives. We have been away but we're back now.'

'Child or not, upset or not, nobody is allowed into this country without the relevant paperwork. I will not take your word for it unless accompanied by proof,' the man grinds out even as he stamps his boot-clad feet, the whip hissing impatiently, ominously, in the hand not held out for their passports.

Thankfully, just then, Ruth's shivering palm folds around the familiar packet containing their passports.

'Here.' She wants to shove the wallet at the monstrous man, a righteous flame of fiery ire briefly pushing away the panic. But sense – and fear making a speedy comeback – wins out and she hands it over docilely.

'These better not be Polish passports or you'll be marched right back, into the trains with those Jews.'

He flings the word 'Jews' at them like an obscenity.

What's wrong with being a Jew? Ruth wants to yell. But her angry bluster is just that...

Against Ruth, her brother is trembling violently. Her mother is trying to stand tall but her shoulders stoop all the same, her eyes, which had flickered with relief when Ruth found the passports, now anxiously studying the man as he leafs through them. Ruth can see from the way she bites her lower lip the fear she is failing to conceal. The panic Ruth herself feels.

Finally, the man looks up at Ruth's mother with a leer.

'You are Finkelstein's daughter?' he sneers.

Ruth seethes at the disrespectful way he says her grandfather's name, her opa, who is invited to the tables and intimate parlours of Germany's elite. How dare he, this mere speck of a man, young enough to be—

Her mother, as if divining the direction of Ruth's thoughts, reaches for Ruth's palm, squeezes it. Her way of saying, *Calm, Ruth.*

This is the way it has always been between them: Mama intuiting Ruth's thoughts before she speaks them.

Ruth is her father's pet – was (even now, even here, in the midst of peril, she experiences a sharply intense stab of grief). But her mother is the one who gets her.

'Well?' the soldier spits.

'Yes,' her mother says, her voice gentle in the face of the soldier's fury: soft, but not meek like previously, and unwavering. Ruth knows she is scared but she seems to have garnered courage from deep within her, having realised that her daughter is flagging.

'You need to get your passports stamped with a J for Jew.' He spits the word 'Jew' at Mama, pronouncing it like a slur. 'And your children need to have Jewish names added on.'

Ruth feels fury rise up her throat, bitter red, even as entreaties and groans and the strident bellows of bullies heckling orders resonate from around the station. This unasked for, unjust oppression rankling, anathema to the socialist ideals she absorbed on her father's knee.

And again, her mother quietly presses her palm. *Not now.*

As if reminding her just of what is at stake, her brother presses closer to her. He hasn't stopped shuddering.

Not now, Ruth tells herself. *We'll get to Opa and Oma's first. But where is Opa? Please let my grandparents be okay.*

'Being a Jew is bad enough, but you sullied your bloodline even further by tainting it black. I'll never understand you people,' the soldier barks, shaking his head, disdain and disgust dripping from his voice.

Ruth folds her hands into fists to contain her fiery anger.

The man's slimy gaze travels over Ruth, leering and lecherous. Ruth wants to stare defiantly at him but she looks down at her brother's tousled head instead and that centres her, even as her wounded heart bleeds over its boiling, raging core.

She hates this injustice, this discrimination, this man who thinks he is better than them just because of his race. She will do something about it. She will fight. She will not take this lying down. She understands now, finally, why her father was so active in the resistance.

Truth be told, secretly, Ruth has been angry with her father while also mourning him. He must have known what he was doing was dangerous.

Ruth had often raged against her father, even as she grieved for him. *If you knew they might come for you, hurt you, and you must have done, for you went to great lengths to make sure your family was spared, then why did you do it at all? Why didn't you give it up, stay safe? Then we could all have gone to India together.*

But now, tasting fury and helplessness, bilious bitter in her mouth, she understands. She is fired up by the passion to retaliate, to do *something*, anything, to not feel so completely powerless, at the mercy of this sneering bully.

She promises herself that if they escape this interrogation unscathed, she will continue what her father started, become active in the resistance. She and Opa will plan it together. Fresh terror stamps her heart. *Why is Opa not here? Has something...?*

No. He is fine. He has to be.

'You tired of him, your black beau, did you? Was he not able to give you what you wanted?' The storm trooper laughs.

Her mother says nothing, but Ruth can feel her blanch. Her body contracts with pain as her hand in Ruth's goes slack.

Ruth digs her nails into the flesh of her palm hard enough to draw blood and yet it doesn't ease her rage.

She hates this man with a roiling, incandescent fury. She

wants to lash out, hurt him, scratch at his face until the smirk is quite wiped out. But...

Not now.

Right now, getting her brother to warmth and safety is the priority.

She chants, *I hate you, you beast,* in her head over and over, so it takes a beat to make sense of the man's words: 'You can go.'

She snatches their passports from him without looking at him.

Her whole body is shaking, whether from rage or relief, she is unable to determine.

Of course he had to let them go. He wouldn't risk going against her grandfather, who has the ear of the people who run this country, perhaps not Hitler himself, but definitely his aides.

But given what is going on, is that even true any more?

Opa... where are you?

And they did get Opa's son-in-law, didn't they? Have they got to him too? And, she wonders again, is he one of the people they are pushing onto the trains so unceremoniously, so violently?

But... this soldier said something about these men having Polish passports, didn't he? So maybe that means Opa is spared, for Opa has a German passport.

Then why is her grandfather not here? Opa, who is *never* late for anything.

Ruth, standing shivering in a country she does not recognise nor understand any more, her brother's blue-lipped shudders running through her, angry though she is, hatred for this man coursing through her, is also immensely grateful that he is letting them go, family connections or not.

'Be sure to get the passports stamped.' With another lascivious glance that rapes Ruth and her mother, the soldier walks away.

'Pig,' Ruth mutters.

The Nazi stops, turns.

Her mother glares at Ruth, terror and rage.

The man winks at them and turns back.

Her mother's lengthy exhale mirrors Ruth's own as they lug their trunks down the station steps, the cold air sharp as a slap, her sobbing brother clinging to Ruth.

'No credit for Jews,' the taxi driver sneers.

Ruth is furious, and hurting on behalf of her traumatised brother. Elijah is trying to be quiet, to be strong, but his little body has not stopped shaking, his sorrow and incomprehension manifesting in hiccupping sobs he can't contain.

And to top it all, it is absolutely freezing, their breath manifesting as icy puffs, her brother's upset visible on his face as his tears solidify in salty trails, shimmering icicles on his eyelashes.

And now this.

Ruth is absolutely fed up.

The fog is still as dense as ever, a screen obscuring everything, rendering solid structures as shimmering mirages, murky silhouettes. In some ways, perhaps, that is a blessing as this city she loves, her home, has transformed, in the time they have been away, into a hostile stranger. The violence of boots and truncheons ripping flesh, moans of pain, yells of, 'Jews out to Palestine', haven't ceased, mingling with the whistles and creaks, hiss and grind of trains, the shuffles and shoves as men – Jews – are marched onto them. The scent of ice and hate, incomprehension and panic, blood and frost, iron-blue.

Trucks pulling up, the screech of brakes, men whipped, pulled, pushed, abused. 'Get out. You have no place here, filthy Jews.'

Elijah is shivering more from fear than with cold and if Ruth is honest, she is just as terrified. She never thought this country would change so much in the short time they have been away, becoming unrecognisable. While Opa – never a devoted correspondent – didn't hint at this, Oma had. But her letters, even though they'd revealed her rising anxiety (although that had never been her intention, her obfuscation inadvertently giving away more than she wanted to), did not betray the extent to which it has changed for the worse. Making them, Jews born and brought up in Germany, feel unwelcome, unwanted, alien in their own country.

How dare they?

The anger is welcome. It masks the fear, scorches it in a flaming-orange wave.

Her brother's skin is bloodless, tinted an alarming shade of violet. He is shuddering even more now, his teeth chattering. Ruth is worried that he will collapse if he is not out of the cold and soon.

All the anger and frustration she is feeling erupts and no amount of her mother's increasingly urgent non-verbal cues for calm can cool her down.

'What do you mean, no credit? Do you know who my grandfather is?'

She squashes the voice in her head saying, *Your grandfather's status might no longer be of use in this new, malevolent Munich.*

And there is another voice, her father's back in happier times, when they would discuss politics, heated debates about their socialist ideals: 'Claiming your grandfather's pedigree and contacts goes against all the values you have so feistily embraced and so loudly and vehemently advocated, Ruth, my love.'

'Yes,' the taxi driver replies coolly. 'I know who your grandfather is. A bloody Jew.'

'How dare—'

He does not let her finish. 'And you are even worse,' the taxi driver leers. 'Watch your mouth, you dirty, black, Jewish half-caste.'

And now Ruth charges even as her brother cries, 'No!' and her mother holds her back, just about, Ruth thrashing against the confines of her mother's arms.

The taxi driver grins, unperturbed, inviting her ire, revelling in her loss of control, commenting, 'You are a slur on Aryan soil.'

Ruth none too gently throws off the shackles of her mother's embrace.

It is another voice that stops her committing a foolish act in her rash fury that she might sorely regret.

A familiar, beloved voice raised in angst: 'My *bubbale*...' Her grandfather, jumping out of his car which is parked haphazardly behind the taxi. 'So sorry I'm late.'

Her brother flings himself at his grandfather. Her mother cannot stop the relief moistening her eyes as she clasps her hands together at the welcome sight of her father.

Ruth stands with her fists bunched by her sides, heaving, gasping with rage and relief. He's fine. Opa is fine. The fear she'd not wanted to articulate taking leave of her in a lengthy exhale, weary exhaustion left in its wake, alongside the remnants of the bright, blazing fury.

The taxi driver smirks. 'Saved in the nick of time, eh, from prison, or worse. But you'll end up there anyway, with that temper and that skin, mark my words, black Jew.'

And before she can respond, he drives off, spewing a spurt of exhaust in her face, petrol fumes and bitter heat, anger frozen into a hard ball in her chest.

And then she is enveloped in the familiar tobacco and bergamot scent of her grandfather, his warm coat around her, sinking into his chest: security, shelter, safety.

'Sorry I'm late, my *bubbale*, my beloved. Was stuck behind those blasted trucks all the way to the station and not one of them gave way.' Her grandfather's voice tight with the fury that is an echo of the one seething within Ruth. Then, in a gentler tone, 'Let's get you home.'

Hidden within the folds of her grandfather's coat, safe against his beating heart, she allows herself finally to shed fierce, hot tears, her pain muffled by his clothes, anger and frustration and weariness, before she sniffs, composes herself, pulls away and smiles brightly up at her grandfather.

'Yes, Opa, let's go home.'

16

RUTH

Ruth watches from the window of Opa's car as the city flashes past, different to the one she, Mama and Elijah had left to go to India after Papa died.

Soldiers barging into houses, returning with defeated men, hunched shoulders, wives' and children's shocked faces pressed to the windows as their loved ones are pushed violently into waiting trucks.

Ruth turns away and shuts her eyes, holding her brother, whose sobs have gradually quietened.

A small blessing.

She doesn't know if she is offering comfort or deriving it.

What does it matter?

Everything has changed.

Their father is no more.

They are unwelcome in his country.

And the country of their birth, the one that had provided solace and succour to her papa when his family had shunned him for marrying Mama, the beloved city they and their opa and oma call home, has transformed beyond recognition and what's more, does not want them either.

Thankfully, Elijah, with the hearty resilience of children, reverts to almost his normal self, his hiccupping sobs dying down and disappearing altogether when they arrive at Opa and Oma's home, Oma making an absolute fuss of him.

He has two helpings of Oma's famous chicken soup with *matzo* balls, and a huge slice of *strudel*.

In contrast, Ruth cannot eat much of Oma's food, although she is hungry and it is as delicious as she remembers. She is still shaking inside from their encounter with the soldier and the taxi driver.

After his meal, Elijah wilts, his eyelids drooping.

But every time Mama says, 'Bedtime,' he jerks awake, sitting upright, smiling at all of them in turn in his sweet, irresistible way. 'I want to stay with you all, please?'

None of them has the heart to refuse.

In the end, it is Ruth who carries her brother to bed, his sleeping body heavy and warm against hers. This boy she loves with her everything and had vowed to protect when their father went to prison and never returned and she witnessed his bewildered, uncomprehending hurt.

When Ruth comes back down after tucking her brother in, Mama is talking about what they witnessed at the station. 'The soldiers... they were being inhumane.' Mama shudders.

The memory of it makes Ruth nauseous. She cannot push the soldier's cruel, cold, blue gaze as he checked their passports from her mind.

'Talks between Germany and Poland failed and so Polish Jews are being deported,' Oma says. 'Some of them grew up here. This country is their home. I heard they had little or no notice. It happened literally overnight.' Oma's eyes are moist with pain, her voice resonating with it.

'That is bad enough. But do they have to be so violent?' Mama cries.

'The atrocities against us Jews are getting worse. Since Hitler came to power and passed the Enabling Act, it has been bad, as you know. But not as obvious as it has been recently.' Oma sighs deeply. 'It is as if they don't care about hiding their prejudice any longer. It is out in the open. We are aliens in our own country, the Reich Citizenship Law that Hitler passed in '35 making us ineligible for citizenship. Yellow benches for Jews only. Special number plates on Jewish-owned cars...'

Had Opa's car sported a special number plate? Ruth cannot recall. She usually notices everything but she had been flustered as she climbed into the car, and more than a little upset. And when they reached here, she just wanted to run indoors, into Oma's welcoming arms, her vanilla-scented embrace, the house blessedly warm and gloriously unchanged, just as in her memories, smelling of chicken soup and baked *strudel*, buttery dough, boozy raisins, apples and caramelised sugar.

'Graffiti on Jewish businesses...' Oma sighs, sharing a look with Opa.

'Not yours surely, Opa?' Ruth is shocked.

'Once or twice, my *bubbale*,' Opa says tiredly, looking down at his hands, which he is knitting together.

'What! They can't do this. You should complain. You know the mayor...' she protests, ire rising fiery in her chest.

Opa's words are soft, resigned. 'My *bubbale*, it was just a couple of times. Petty people led by—'

'But you can't just take it,' she interjects, tasting raging heat on her tongue, the anger welcome after the nauseating upset since her confrontation with the soldier and the taxi driver, the knowledge that she was scared and wanted her father causing her to feel out of her depth, helpless.

'No, and we won't. Which is why I'm a member of the resistance.' Opa smiles gently at her.

Oma tuts, shaking her head at Opa.

Ruth's mother: 'Tate, must you persist in doing so? We worry for you...'

'If nobody does anything, how will there be change?' Ruth says hotly.

She is rewarded by a wink from Opa, while her mother, ignoring her interruption, appeals directly to her father. 'If you will do it, please be careful, promise me. The more obvious they become, the less you must be,' Ruth's mother cries. 'I can't bear to lose you too...' Her eyes shining with the memory of her husband.

Ruth's heart heavy, sorrow displacing anger.

'I know, *meine leibe*, my love,' Opa says softly. 'I'm always careful.'

'What will happen to those poor men who were being packed so ruthlessly into the trains?' Mama asks, her mind, like Ruth's, still struggling to make sense of what they saw.

'That's the tragedy. Poland is refusing to take them.' Opa sighs deeply.

Mama shivers. 'But what will they do? Where will they go? What is happening to the world?'

'Well, whatever it is it cannot be fixed tonight. You're home now. Have a good night's rest. Things always look better in the morning.'

In a voice barely above a whisper, Mama says, 'Not for those men or their families.'

From her faraway look, Ruth knows what she's thinking: that her husband, the love of her life, will still be gone in the morning.

17

RUTH

1941
England

Mrs Rosenbaum places *matzo* crackers in front of Ruth.

'Call me Esther,' she had said, gently, when she'd led Ruth into her house. 'And he,' nodding fondly at Mr Rosenbaum, 'is Isaac.'

She hands Ruth a mug of tea. 'Chicory,' she says apologetically. 'Because of the rationing. Now, drink up,' she says, smiling warmly at her.

Ruth takes a sip of her tea. It is bitter and earthy, masking the taste of salt and sorrow in her mouth.

Mr Rosenbaum – Isaac – she must remember to call these kind people by their given names – who is also drinking the tea, smiles gently at her.

'Stay with us, please,' Mrs Rosenbaum, Esther, says. 'It is dusk already and the air raid will commence soon, if the last few months are anything to go by.' She sighs. 'We all go to the Underground station and take shelter there.'

'Thank you, that is very kind of you,' Ruth says.

Esther beams while her husband smiles, looking from his wife to Ruth.

After a bit: 'What happened then, after you returned to Munich?' Esther asks softly.

Ruth takes a deep breath and looks over Esther's shoulder, into the past.

After they came back to Germany, it seemed that every hour brought more bad news and yet...

And yet, if she had to go back, she would live those days again, savour every moment, however fraught, for then, they were all together apart from Papa; she had Mama, Opa, Oma and beloved Elijah with her.

18

RUTH

October 1938
Munich, Germany

A new day in this new, hostile Germany.

Mama and Ruth are on their way to register Elijah at his new school a few blocks away. They had both been agonising about how Elijah might be feeling, whether he might be apprehensive about starting school in Germany again after his sojourn away. But they needn't have worried. Elijah woke this morning happy and excited, eager to start school.

Ruth is altogether more subdued. She was on track for Cambridge, her parents' alma mater, until her father's death and their subsequent move to India. She had briefly considered applying while in India but hadn't the heart to leave Mama, who was grieving for Papa and out of her depth, and Elijah, and moving to the other side of the world from them. They had already lost Papa and she worried that they would find it very hard to adjust to her being gone too...

And so, she had put her dream on hold. And now, with all

that is going on, the fear and worry they are experiencing, she feels she cannot leave Mama and Elijah and go to England. These are strange, uncertain times, and she knows that Mama and Elijah, Opa and Oma would want her with them. So she will not go to Cambridge as she had once hoped.

She has considered applying to university here but...

'They've banned Jewish students from taking exams in pharmacy, medicine and the law,' Oma had said the previous night, wringing her hands, looking distressed. 'They might soon ban other subjects too, you never know.'

'How can they do that?' Mama stole the words right out of Ruth's mouth. 'How has it come to this?' She had lowered herself onto a chair, looking winded, and Ruth could see that she was revisiting the scene at the station when they arrived, her face deathly pale.

So, Ruth had dumbed down her own rage, and said lightly, 'I will do my own independent study at home for now, Mama. I think that's for the best.'

Mama's shining, relieved gaze had mirrored Oma's, and Ruth was glad that she had held back her impulse, reined in her anger.

Now, Ruth wonders, is it just her imagination, a reflection of her glum and sombre mood following their experience at the train station, causing her to detect a troubled atmosphere in the city, a seething undertone threaded with menace?

But as they walk through the park opposite the school, they come across one of the benches Oma had been talking about the previous evening, painted yellow, inscribed, *Fur Juden*.

Everywhere in the world – India, her father's country of birth, Germany, her mother's – is rife with injustice, inequality, division.

A woman, laden with shopping, perches on the bench, emitting a sigh of relief as she sets her bags down on the seat beside her, wiping her face with the ends of the sunshine-coloured scarf covering her head, protection against the nippy, frost-edged wind.

A man walks past, spits, 'Filthy Jew,' at her and crosses the road.

The woman flushes beneath her scarf, collects her shopping and stands wearily.

Ruth turns to the man, eyes blazing, about to follow him and give him a piece of her mind, but her mother clasps her hand, nodding at Elijah, who is skipping ahead. He has already made a friend, and they are chatting away, tousled heads close together, Elijah's dark, his companion's blond, the boy's mother smiling at them.

'Not now,' Mama warns.

Ruth reluctantly decides that Mama is right and addresses the woman who was on the receiving end of that man's prejudice. 'Why didn't you say anything?'

'This isn't the first time it has happened.' The woman sighs. 'This is how it is now. And if we do anything, speak up, we'd be in the wrong. We're always in the wrong.' Bitterness pulsing in the woman's voice.

'But—'

'Ruth!' Elijah calls from up ahead, his voice bright and clear as sunlit hope, gilded with a smile. 'Come and meet my friend.'

Elijah goes into school happily with his new friend, barely pausing to wave goodbye to his mother and sister.

Mama and Ruth walk back home without incident. Each a prisoner to her thoughts. Mama's shoulders slumped with weighted grief, the depression that has plagued her since losing her husband taking hold now she doesn't have to dredge up a smile, the brittle façade of normality such as it is, for Elijah.

The bench is empty on their way back.

When they get home, Ruth's mother asks Oma, who is at the kitchen table, her head in her hands, a cup of coffee going cold beside her. 'Mutter, what's happened?' And, as her gaze takes in her father, who should be at the shop but who is sitting beside Oma, a hand resting on her back, offering succour, 'Tate, why are you home at this time?' Mama's voice is taut with the worry Ruth herself feels.

'Hans is looking after the shop,' Opa says. His voice is calm but his eyes betray the anxiety he is trying hard to conceal.

'What's happened?' Mama asks again. 'Mutter?'

A tiny sniffle escapes Oma and the fear Ruth has been trying to dumb down erupts in a violent explosion of throbbing panic. Her whole body feels wobbly with it.

'I got word at the shop,' Opa is saying. 'Monika...'

'My best friend since we were toddlers.' Oma's voice a lament.

'Her husband Pavel was one of those deported yesterday.' Opa sighs.

'I didn't know he had a Polish passport. He was born here,' Oma whispers, kneading her palms as she finally looks up at her daughter and grandchild. Her face is waxen, streaked with tears.

Ruth feels a reciprocal sob choke her throat, alongside shock at seeing her usually calm and composed Oma like this.

She recalls the soldiers kicking and pushing the men while calling them names.

'Did something happen to him?' Her voice is a tentative whisper.

'I don't know about him, where he is, how he is. It's... it's Monika. She...' Oma cannot continue.

Opa strokes her back gently even as he says, 'The Gestapo

looted their house, the front half of which is their place of business. And Monika...' Opa sighs deeply.

Oma shudders.

Ruth has a frantic urge to shut her ears. Whatever it is, she does not want to know.

'She committed suicide,' Opa says shortly.

'She could have called me,' Oma keens. 'No, *I* should have called her. But I didn't think she... they had anything to worry about since they grew up here... I didn't *think*...'

'*Mutter*...' Mama kneels beside her mother, gently gathering her in her arms. There are tears in Mama's eyes.

'Monika... she's always been fragile, more so since their only son died in the war. Fighting for this country.' Oma's voice fierce with bitterness, an echo of that of the woman from the bench earlier. 'And now... they grab Pavel, shove him into their truck like he is an animal, loot their house and business and she couldn't take it. She couldn't take it.'

Even as Oma sobs, Opa is whispering something, seemingly to himself. Ruth only manages to catch the words because she is standing next to him.

'Poland doesn't want them. So what will become of those men?'

19

RUTH

That evening, after their dinner of potato and meat *kugel*, Elijah, who is tired out from his first day at school, puts up only a token protest when Mama declares it is time for bed.

'But—'

'No buts, you have to be up early for school tomorrow,' Mama says.

Ruth, noticing how worn out Mama is from the emotion of the day, holds her hand out to her brother. 'Come on, sport, I'll tell you a story.'

He beams up at her. 'Will I be in it?'

'You and the friends you made today too.'

He grins widely, jumping off his chair, slipping his small hand trustingly in hers.

As she leads him up the stairs, her mother smiles gratefully at her.

Elijah's head starts drooping five minutes into the story.

She drops a kiss on his velvet cheek, breathing in his small boy smell: innocence, purity, faith.

As she walks downstairs to join the others, Oma, steadier

now, although the lines around her eyes give away her grief for her friend, is saying, 'We need to leave before we're next. The smart ones have already left.'

'I agree,' Ruth's mother says with a sigh.

Ruth waits for Opa to counter with, *Why should we run away? This is our home. We have as much right to be here as anyone.*

But instead: 'Yes, I agree that we must leave,' he mumbles, sounding distressed. 'But I worry that it is already too late.'

Opa, what about your principles? Ruth thinks, feeling very sad.

But she knows what Opa's reply would be: *Ah, my* bubbale. *What are principles in the face of life and death?*

He has been a different man since his son-in-law died. Beaten. Resigned.

Ruth has refused to see it, countenance it, but now she does.

She thinks of Elijah, tired out from his first day at school, sleeping peacefully upstairs, his dream-warm cheek, the smile fluttering on his lips.

He is only just getting settled after the trauma he's endured: losing his father, the sojourn in India, his paternal grandparents dying and immediately after, being kicked out of their house by Papa's brother, their anguished escape here, the horrible scene at the train station.

'We cannot displace Elijah, not again,' she says, skipping down the last of the stairs and coming to sit beside Opa, Oma and Mama at the kitchen table, which smells of caramelised apples, fried onions and angst.

She is speared by three pairs of eyes, identical worried expressions gracing Opa, Oma and Mama's drawn faces.

'I understand what you're saying about us leaving,' Ruth says. 'But we've only just come back. And Elijah... he has had so much change already.'

'Yes,' Mama agrees.

'But things here are only going to get worse, I fear.' Oma
sounds oh-so very weary. 'We have stayed on, hoping that our
fellow countrymen will see sense, stand up to Hitler, do the
right thing. But perhaps now it is time to accept that nothing is
going to change and make plans to leave.'

Opa sighs. '*Mein liebling*, I don't know if it is any better elsewhere. From what I've heard from those who've tried to leave,
we are not welcome anywhere. South Africa and Palestine have
limited the number of Jews that are admitted. Great Britain
admits only a small number of refugees, as does Canada.' He
takes a breath, then, 'And like Ruth rightly pointed out, we must
think of Elijah. It would be very traumatic for him if we were to
unsettle him again, leave the country only to be denied entry
elsewhere.'

Tears shine in Mama's eyes as she nods, compulsively knitting her palms together.

Ruth too feels tears of frustration, anxiety and helplessness
stab at her eyes.

Oma drops her head into her hands: a gesture of despair.

Opa lays a loving hand on her back, strokes it.

He is looking pale, washed out. Old. He's never looked this
burdened before, anxiety carving lines onto his handsome face.
It momentarily blindsides Ruth, and makes her very afraid, even
more so than she already is.

She takes a breath and another, reining in her fear. She
looks at Oma, Opa, Mama in turn and says, 'So, the worst that
can happen is that we cannot leave and things get very difficult
for us here. Then we will fight it.'

It is Oma who speaks. '*Liebling*, people are dying. Hitler and
his men, they don't see sense.'

Even though her words cause a fresh stab of fear, Ruth says,
'By staying and putting up resistance, we'll make them.'

Oma tuts.

Mama shakes her head. 'Ruth, your papa tried...'

She cannot finish the sentence, her face bright with sorrow.

'Mama, Papa tried and he would expect the same from us.'

'No, he would rather we were safe, which was why he arranged for us to go to India.'

'But if we cannot leave, then we must take a stand against what is happening. For if we don't, then who will?'

Oma sighs while Mama sucks her teeth.

'Oh, to have the conviction and passion of the young.' Opa's smile is immensely sad. It appears to Ruth as if he has already given up.

The fear threatens to engulf her and so she cries, 'Opa, we can't just give in! Give up.'

'My *bubbale*, we have to be very careful,' Opa says, at the same time as Mama cries, 'This is not a game, Ruth!'

Opa continues gently. 'You and Elijah have your whole lives ahead of you. The Gestapo are already watching the shop since your father was arrested. We cannot put a foot out of line.'

Ruth is terrified at the thought of the Gestapo watching Opa's every move. Those same soldiers who had been so ruthless at the railway station, who had treated their fellow human beings so inhumanely. The danger they are in strikes her all at once and she is breathless with panic.

Opa picks up on her fear, says firmly, 'Now, Ruth, all is not lost yet. I have friends in high places who hate what Hitler is doing and are willing to help even if it means they are in danger. They will try and get us out. I'm holding out for certainty in these uncertain times, not vague promises, which is why it will take longer. I've heard stories of Jews fleeing Germany and arriving at the borders of other countries seeking refuge, only to be denied entry. I don't want that happening to us, especially given what you and Elijah have been through already. I want to know that wherever we end up, we will be welcome. It will happen, my *bubbale*, so please don't worry. All is not lost, not yet, all right?' He smiles gently at her.

She can only nod, her entire body weary, mouth bitter with fear and anxiety.

When she finally falls asleep, she dreams of her father.

He is crying. 'We must fight, till the bitter end, for our principles. They have no right to treat us like second-class citizens, to discriminate against us. This is our country and we deserve to be here just as much as anyone else.'

Papa was distributing anti-Nazi pamphlets, tucked within the garments he sold, when he was caught. But even as he was led away, she was told he'd said, 'We must not back down. Long live freedom!'

In Ruth's dream, it is what he is shouting as he is shot, his lifeblood flowing as a river, seeping into the pile of leaflets scattered around his spreadeagled, too still, finally quiet body, obliterating the legend, *Down With Hitler!*

20

RUTH

A knock on her door jolts Ruth from her nightmare.

Opa's voice, creeping in alongside the dewy, honey-butter light of a new dawn.

'There is always light even after the darkest night,' Oma had told a young Ruth, snuggled in her lap, nearly falling asleep. 'It finds a way to illuminate even the most neglected or skilfully hidden corners, to expose the dark parts of a soul secret from the most discerning of gazes.' The moral to a fairy tale which Ruth doesn't recall now suddenly rings clear, several years later.

Her head is full of her father. His last moments as imagined by her...

She shakes her head to chase the dark, horrifying images away.

'My *bubbale*,' her grandfather's voice floating through the door, wrapping itself around her like a warm, soothing hug. 'I don't think I was clear last night. You must have got the wrong impression. These might be dangerous times but that doesn't mean I'm doing nothing, *meine liebe*.'

Her heart warms even as fresh tears seep into the pillow

drenched with a night's worth of dream-thrashed, memory-soaked sorrow.

'Don't think for a moment that I've given in. Now that would be cowardice. I have served this country, fought for it, been part of it. Myself and generations before me. There is no way that I am backing down now, especially given what happened to your papa.'

At Opa's words, vivid images from Ruth's nightmare ricochet before her eyes.

'Until we leave, I will be part of the resistance. It is what your papa would have wanted,' Opa says.

Ruth opens the door. Opa is standing there in his pyjamas. His face is busy with lines and very wan, dark shadows crowding his eyes. It appears that he has not slept well either.

'But, Opa, you said that the Gestapo are watching the shop,' Ruth says.

'Ah, but there are ways and means to get around them.' Opa smiles, tapping his nose. 'As I said, I'm arranging for us to leave but until that comes through, we are continuing what your father started, printing and distributing anti-Nazi leaflets like your papa was doing, educating those blinkered enough to believe the despotic regime's propaganda about what's really going on.' He takes a breath. 'And we will keep on doing so, wherever we end up next.'

Ruth nods, thinking of her dream, her father's blood staining the pamphlets that he had distributed along with the garments he sold.

'I'd like to help,' she says.

Opa smiles warmly at her, eyes crinkling. He cups her face with his gnarled hand. 'I am so proud of the woman you're growing into, my *bubbale*. So strong and principled and wonderful.'

I'm far from wonderful, Opa, she thinks. *I'm terrified, worried out of my mind.*

Nevertheless, the ice that has taken her heart hostage since they arrived back in Germany thaws a little.

'Now come and join us for breakfast,' Opa says. 'Your oma has made your favourite: *matzo brai*.'

21

RUTH

Over the coming weeks, Ruth helps Opa with creating, assembling and printing anti-Nazi leaflets to distribute. Since the shop is watched, Ruth designs the pamphlets at home and then Opa clandestinely hands the designs over to Papa's friend Johannes, who runs a printing press and is active in the resistance, printing them in such a way so as to not arouse suspicion. Once that is done, they go about distributing them, a tricky operation as they have to do so without drawing suspicion upon themselves.

But they do manage it as Opa knows all the people active in the resistance in Munich and beyond, Mama's friend and one-time neighbour Eva among them.

When Johannes's printing press comes under scrutiny, Ruth writes out the leaflets by hand, Eva and her fellow members helping to distribute them.

Doing this focuses Ruth's mind, stops her feeling helpless as each day brings more horrible news, new ways in which Jews are targeted and oppressed.

Oma returns home from the market one day trembling from head to toe.

Ruth and Mama – Elijah is at school and Opa at the shop – cluster around Oma. 'What happened?'

'I...' Oma's eyes shine with incomprehension and hurt. 'I saw Birgitta in the market. I've known her for years. She's come to my home.' Oma's eyes glittering, ornamented with tears that dangle from her lashes, dot her cheeks. 'We've sat right here and shared recipes and meals. But just now she... she ignored me when I said hello to her. When the Nazi she was with asked, "Do you know this woman?", she laughed, said, "I don't liaise with filthy Jews." She did not look at me. But... the look he gave me...' Oma starts shaking again, even her teeth chattering as she continues. 'He yelled at me then. "Stop accosting respectable Aryans, Jew." He said "Jew" like it was a swear word. Like I was beneath contempt. Then...' Oma shuts her eyes tight, tears squeezing from beneath swollen lids, 'he spat at the ground right next to me, missing me by inches. And through it all, Birgitta stood straight-backed, smiling, as if I was a nobody. No, worse than a nobody. I... I'm ashamed to say I ran, came home. I...'

Mama holds Oma as she sobs, her face contorted with the same pain and sadness that Ruth is feeling.

Once Oma's sobs have quietened down somewhat, Mama turns to Ruth, wringing her hands. 'Ruth, have you heard from Opa about what is happening with our plans to leave?'

'He said his friend Karl is in the process of arranging the requisite documentation for us,' Ruth says.

Mama kneads her hands. 'I hope it comes through soon. We can't stay where we are not wanted. They've already sent away those with Polish passports. This is only going to get worse. Principles are no use against fists. We must leave when we can.'

Ruth is overcome suddenly. It is all too much. She runs to her room, her grandmother's sobs echoing in her ears.

She is still in there, trying to exhaust all her hurt – at her grandmother's tears, Oma who is so dignified, and usually so strong, but just now shown to be an old, very upset woman, bewildered by the hate directed at her – into her much-abused pillow, when she feels small arms around her.

Her brother, having come home from school – *is it that time already?* – has climbed into bed with her, comforting her as best he can.

'Why are you sad? Don't be sad,' he pleads, voice trembling.

Although she feels too overwhelmed and upset to reassure him, she manages a weak smile for his benefit.

They lie there, side by side, she and Elijah, staring at the ceiling, which undulates before her eyes, and her brother says, 'When I am sad, you tell me a story to cheer me up. So now I will tell you one.'

And now she turns to him and her smile, although shaky, is genuine.

'Oh, you will, will you?'

'Yes,' he says, earnestly. 'Listen. Once upon a time, there was a very brave girl called Ruth...'

'This story features a heroine called Ruth, does it?' she asks, and her voice is dancing now, her brother, as always, harbinger of the joy that she thought was lost forever.

'Yes,' her brother says, nodding busily, his voice sincere. 'Your stories always have a hero named Elijah so this one will have a heroine named Ruth.'

'Go on.' She laughs. 'I'm all ears.'

And hearing the chuckle in her voice, her brother beams even as he says, 'Now listen carefully. No more interrupting, all right? There was once a brave girl called Ruth who was not afraid of anything, even horrible, scary monsters...'

And this is how Mama finds them, Ruth smiling as she listens to her brother narrate a story about a heroine who is courageous, feisty and devil-may-care, taking on monsters twice her size without batting an eyelid...

Mama climbs into bed with them, soon followed by Oma, bringing *apfelkuchen*, and they all eat it while squashed onto Ruth's bed, unmindful of the crumbs going everywhere.

And when Opa comes home from the shop, he climbs in too, next to Oma.

And they lie there, nearly on top of each other, taking turns making up stories until the room is rife with shadows and their stomachs growl with new hunger.

It is one of the best afternoons of Ruth's life and she will store it away, the memory of all her beloveds bundled into her bed, the love and togetherness, Papa also very much present if not physically, then in spirit, for they take turns making up stories featuring him, each one more extravagant and heroic than the last, their eyes shining with missing and longing.

It is a gift that Ruth will cherish in years to come, gently unpacking it from memory to treasure when she needs it the most.

22

RUTH

That evening, after supper, Elijah fast asleep and the rest of them winding down, Oma recounts the incident for Opa, tight-lipped now, not emotional like before, in a deadpan voice.

'It is just a phase. We are living in a civilised country. This cannot continue. Most people are decent. They will see sense,' Opa says when Oma has finished speaking.

But his voice lacks conviction. His eyes are troubled, his body defeated as he puts his hand on Oma's and tenderly strokes her palm.

The 'phase' drags on.

Everywhere, they are made to feel unwelcome.

Thankfully, Elijah is unaffected. If he is subjected to any abuse or discrimination, it seems to go right over his head. He is happy at school, secure within his circle of friends who appear to have accepted him unconditionally – a blessing.

Opa's face sports new lines. He is hunched with the weight of worry. He returns from the shop each afternoon with his shoulders just that bit more stooped than before.

'I suspect he is not telling us everything,' Oma frets. 'I think that Karl is finding it even more difficult than they initially suspected to get us out of Germany. We should not have left it so late. And perhaps you and the children should have stayed in India, Naomi, *meine liebe*.' Oma sighs.

'Yes,' Mama agrees, kneading her palms, her eyes bloodshot. Then, softly, her voice yellow with despair, 'You know, I never thought this day would come when in our own country, we would be made to feel like the enemy. They have declared war on us. In our hometown where we were once respected, now we are reviled. They are stripping us of our dignity, by their words, their actions, making us feel other. Less human.'

Mama's voice, crackling with pain, fear, incites reciprocal terror in Ruth's heart.

She says, intending her voice to be bright, full of conviction, but it quivers, 'This is a phase. It will pass.' If she repeats it often enough, these empty words might feel true, become true.

'Why is it taking so long for us to leave, Tate?' Mama asks Opa that evening, after Elijah is asleep, while Oma sits, tight-lipped, face pale, hands clasped on her lap so rigidly that the knuckles stand up pale as ghosts. 'Surely with your connections, we should have been able to get the necessary documents...'

Mama's voice tails off upon seeing the helplessness on her father's face.

Although Opa tries for a reassuring smile, it wobbles, pulling down at the corners even as he says, 'The Polish passport holders evicted from here are in holding camps, refused entry by Poland.' Opa sighs deeply, running a weary hand down his face. 'Jews are not welcome anywhere. The Evian conference achieved nothing. Countries have updated their entry requirements, essentially barring us.'

Mama's face falls. Oma is staring at her bloodless knuckles as if they have the answers to their dilemma.

Ruth wants to shake away the pall that has settled over the room. And so she says, her voice determinedly cheery, trying to comfort herself as much as anyone, 'The documents will come, won't they, Opa? They're just taking longer, that's all. And meanwhile, whatever is happening, we are dealing with it, resisting it. And in any case, it cannot continue. It's just a phase.'

Surely she is right? Although when she hears about yet another injustice against Jews, when she sees Oma and Mama and Opa so disheartened, she is incensed, distressed and fearful in equal measure, a very big part of her wants to stay right here, in Opa and Oma's house where she grew up and which is associated with such happy memories. It is comfort and familiarity. And even though she feels guilty for her selfishness, she can't help hoping that whatever is happening won't affect them, that they will be shielded from it. After all, Opa is so well respected...

Well, he *was*...

The truth is, Ruth is so very tired. She wants to go to sleep and wake up with everything back to how it was when Papa was alive. Then too, Hitler was persecuting Jews but nothing compared to what he is doing now.

She does not want to be displaced again, tossed rudderless into an uncertain world instead of being cushioned within the warmth and shelter of her grandparents' home, protecting them from the horror, the racism, the abuse outside its four walls.

And then...

Monday morning heralds a new week in a new month in this fragmenting world, and dawns with icy showers chilling to the bone. Freezing, yes, but nevertheless with no witching premonition of what is to come...

23

RUTH

1941
England

'I knew it was bad,' Esther says softly. 'But I did not realise the extent of it.'

The shadows in the room have lengthened, playing upon their faces, the light from the lamp casting Esther and Isaac in a mellow, gold glow.

'My sister, in her letters, gave nothing away. I begged her to bring her children and come here. But she would not. And later, I suppose, just like you and your family, she could not.' Esther sighs, her voice sad.

'She was very active in the resistance,' Ruth says, thinking, *Oh, Eva, I hope you and your children are all right.* Although she knows in her heart, that aches and bleeds for them, that they are anything but. 'She distributed the leaflets I made, but that was only part of what she was doing.'

'She was always fiery, that girl.' Esther's voice is a lament of longing.

'We felt so impotent, all of us. Hitler and his Nazis were committing all these horrible injustices and we wanted to do *something*,' Ruth says.

Esther nods. 'I do understand. But Eva... she had her children to think of.'

'Yes.' Ruth sniffs. 'But she would argue that she *was* thinking of them, was doing it for them.' She takes a breath, tries to explain. 'When you are fired up, angry, you just... you want to make a difference. I had lost my father. Eva had lost her husband. We wanted their deaths to not have been in vain...'

'I think I understand now why she absolutely refused to come here, why she always had an excuse,' Esther says, eyes bright with sorrow. 'When she wouldn't heed my pleas to come, I begged her to at least send the children.'

'They are her life. She wouldn't part with them.'

'That's what she said in her letters.' Esther sighs. 'I thought, perhaps if I visited her, persuaded her in person...' Esther's voice trails off, her gaze far away, tinged navy with what might have been.

'I told Esther that was a bad idea. She may not be able to come back, I said.' Mr Rosenbaum, Isaac, speaks for the first time. He is a silent man, content to listen, brow furrowed in intense concentration.

'My sister agreed with Isaac. In every letter I wrote, I put forth the idea of me coming to see her and the kids, and in her replies, Eva resisted it.' A pause, then, her voice wet with tears, Esther continues. 'Anyway, it is what it is. Here we are now.' After a bit, she says, softly, 'And your family, Ruth? They didn't manage to get away either, I take it?'

Ruth takes a breath. Another. Trying to compose herself.

'You don't have to tell us if you don't want to, love,' Esther says gently.

It is painful to talk about all that happened.

But in a strange way, much as it hurts, it is also cathartic. It is bittersweet agony but also painful joy, for it brings Ruth's beloved family back to her in a different, more tangible way than when she is visiting them in her memories.

'I want to,' she says, swallowing past the grief clogging her throat, thinking back to that time, each day feeling endless as she and Opa busied themselves with anti-Nazi leaflets while they waited for their paperwork to come through so they could leave Germany. A part of Ruth never losing hope that things would go back to normal, that they could continue as they had, stay on at Oma and Opa's...

'It was becoming harder to leave Germany,' she says. 'And despite the fact that the atrocities against us Jews were multiplying, we kept thinking, *this is the turning point, surely? It cannot get worse than this.* But it did. It did.' She swallows down brine and bile, trying to put into words how things had been, then. So very fraught, every moment of every day lived on a knife edge. 'I don't know how to explain it,' she says, twisting her hands. 'This trust we harboured despite all evidence to the contrary. This, completely misplaced as it turned out, belief in our country, its people...' She takes a breath. 'Our people had fought for Germany in the first war...' She tastes salt in her mouth. 'Surely that would count for something, we thought.'

'I understand,' Esther says softly. 'My sister was the same.'

Ruth nods. 'My mama met with Eva a couple of times and always returned looking brighter, happier. They were such good friends.'

'Yes,' Esther says, her eyes sparkling. 'We all were but I lost touch with Naomi once I moved here and she moved back to Germany after Cambridge.'

'Germany...' Ruth sighs. 'It changed so much in the time we were in India.'

In the dim light, shadows flicker upon Esther's and her husband's faces, their gazes bright with understanding. It gives Ruth the strength to go on. 'And yet, we harboured hope that the changes could be reversed. After all, we told ourselves, it is the twentieth century, not the dark ages. We kept waiting for our fellow Germans, whom we'd grown up with, our friends, our neighbours, to see sense, stand up to Hitler, do the right thing. We were so naïve, I see now. Opa and Oma, Mama, all of us.' Her mouth thick with sorrow and regret, bilious yellow. 'During that time, the light in our lives, the one who brought comfort, normalcy, was Elijah. My little brother, only eight. Entirely clueless to the undercurrents seething through the house. We were so grateful for him.' She thinks of his wide smile that lit him up from within, his hugs, the way he looked up at her, so trustingly, in the utter belief that she'd make things better for him. *I failed you, Elijah, I'm so sorry.*

Esther squeezes her hand and she is grateful for it.

When she can speak, she says, 'He had had so much upheaval in his young life. He was so perplexed when Papa went to prison and never came back. Then we decamped to India, and although he adjusted to life there better than myself and Mama, he missed his papa and Opa and Oma dreadfully. Germany, too. And then the grandparents he was just getting to know and love died and he was uprooted again, separated from the cousins, Papa's brother's children, whom he had befriended. Then when we returned to Germany, that scene at the train station... And yet, he took it all in his stride. Coming back to a country that was full of violence, starting again at a new school. He was a beacon of joy and innocence. He was blessed with such a sunny personality. So affectionate and capable of such love and happiness. It helped that, for his sake, we had to act as if nothing was wrong. To go on as normal, although nothing was.' She pauses again, overcome.

Esther puts her arm around her.

Ruth rests her head in the crook of her shoulder. She smells of roses and sweat.

Ruth closes her eyes and tries to pretend she is being held by Mama.

Through the lump choking her throat, she manages, her voice a whisper, 'And then November arrived, and everything changed once more. And this time, we couldn't shield Elijah, couldn't pretend all was well any longer...'

24

RUTH

Monday 7 November 1938
Munich, Germany

Elijah is off school for he is not feeling well – just a cold – but he is hot and uncomfortable with it.

'I am ill,' he sniffs, cheeks flushed, when Ruth comes into his room to check on him. He asks if she can stay with him, saying, 'Tell me the special stories you make up, with me fighting dragons and baddies. It will make my sore head better, please?'

Those big eyes pleading, how can she refuse?

They have a great time, she and Elijah. Lounging in bed all day, playing I spy and hide and seek among the sheets after she has regaled him with stories. Planning what they will be in the future. Singing at the top of their voices, pretending the bed is an alien spaceship and when they've exhausted themselves, lying side by side in silent companionship, happy together, safe, loved.

With him, she is a child again, briefly setting aside her burden of worry, her torment about the divisions in this country, her doubts about whether whatever is happening will get worse, and will they be able to escape before then. Her anxiety about whether they should leave at all, and if they do manage to, whether it will be too much for Elijah, who has been remarkably resilient so far, to cope with. Her qualms about whether wanting to leave, run away, is cowardly. Her worry about what she and Opa are doing by handing out the anti-Nazi leaflets will get them all caught and put not only her and Opa, but Mama, Oma and beloved, innocent Elijah in danger. She lies awake deep into the fraught, susurrating hours of night, agonising about this last, picturing Elijah being tortured, hurt, because of her.

Oma and Mama look in on them every so often, plying them with food: *latkes* and *hamantaschen* and *sufganiyot*.

'You know what, I do not think you are ill at all, you cheeky boy,' Ruth says, tickling her brother's neck, his mouth smeared with jelly, face dotted with poppy seeds, smelling of sweetness and pastry.

'I am. Here, feel. My head is hot.'

Ruth places a hand on his forehead and recoils in mock-horror. 'It nearly burned me. You are Superfireman!'

He throws back his head and laughs, infectious, tumbling, rollercoaster giggles that go on and on.

Oma and Mama pop their heads round the door and join in. A festive celebration of glorious, unrestrained mirth. A brief respite from a world that is splintering around them.

Afterwards, Ruth will look back and be grateful that they had it: that one perfect, beautiful day. But it will make what is to come all the more horrific.

25

RUTH

The perfect day continues until Opa comes home.

By this time, Elijah has decided he is better and they are all gathered in the kitchen. Elijah is colouring at the table while Ruth and her mother help Oma bake *challah* buns, Opa's favourite, and *Gewürzplätchen*, Elijah's request; he loves the gingerbread biscuits. 'Especially when you make them, Oma,' he had said, grinning charmingly at his grandmother.

She had beamed at him, ruffled his hair and said that she would make a hundred just for him, which made his eyes pop in awe and wonder.

Oma and Mama are also making *Mandeltorte*, almond cake, having decided to go all out.

'To cheer me up because I have been ill,' Elijah says earnestly and they all nod, hiding their smiles behind their hands.

The kitchen is toasty and scented with sweet dough. Snow falls gently outdoors, swirling lazily outside the window and settling in starry, cotton flakes on the sill, lending it a frosty, opaque sheen, making Ruth glad to be indoors.

Mama and Oma reminisce as they roll out pastry, both in aprons, working in tandem, their velvet voices, the occasional music of their laughter festooning the room in happy swirls.

Elijah hums as he colours, his tongue poking out of his mouth as he concentrates. Ruth looks at her family in the warm, snug kitchen and thinks, with a stab in her heart, *I wish Papa was here.*

That afternoon, after they had exhausted their games and she'd tired of making up stories, lying side by side in Elijah's bed and looking up at the ceiling, her brother's eyes heavy with the languor of imminent slumber, he had said softly, 'I miss Papa so much.'

His words had lanced Ruth's heart. She had held her brother close, breathed in his lemon and mischief scent. Whispered, 'I miss him too.'

Only after her brother fell asleep did she allow the tears stabbing her eyes access, the ceiling undulating above her, creamy white, imagining her father's lifeblood staining the pamphlets he was distributing, that had led to his arrest, fiery crimson.

Would that be her fate, and Opa's too, if they couldn't leave Germany in time, and if they were caught? And if so, what would happen to Oma and Mama and Elijah? Would they be in danger? Was it right what she was doing if it meant putting her most beloved in harm's way?

Ruth is jolted out of her ruminations by a knock on the front door.

The kitchen smells sweet.

Her brother is humming as he colours.

Her mother and grandmother are baking and stirring. Soup and *challah* and *mandeltorte* and *Gewürzplätchen*, the honey and spice scent of gingerbread and cake festooning the air.

She has been lost in musing, cosy in her family's bosom, love and comfort alongside sadness with regard to her absent father and the ever-present worry about what is going on in the world outside their four walls.

'Your opa is here.' Mama holds up floury hands. 'Will you get the door?'

One look at Opa's face, the weary hunch of his shoulders, and Ruth sees that it is not good news.

She doesn't want to ask but... 'What's the matter?'

He shrugs wearily as he follows her into the kitchen.

Outside, the snow falls in slick flurries. Her grandfather's coat and hair dusted with it, silvery white.

The fragrant kitchen is suddenly frosty. Broody with shadows.

Ruth pulls out a chair. Her grandfather slumps into it.

As if understanding Opa is in need of comfort, Elijah stops colouring and climbs into his grandfather's lap.

Opa buries his face in his grandson's hair, breathing in deeply of his scent: innocence and purity unsullied by bigotry.

His womenfolk have gathered around the table, pausing in what they were doing, looking at him with concern writ large upon their faces.

'Here,' Oma says, laying a steaming cup of herb-infused tea in front of her husband.

Mama wipes her floury hands on her apron, a dusting of flour coating the floor mimicking the snow slurry building up on the windowsill.

Opa takes a sip of his tea, sighing deeply.

And above the tousled head of his grandson, he looks at his wife, his daughter, his granddaughter. 'Shall we eat?'

Ruth's grandfather barely picks at his food. He does not

touch the steaming bowl of soup Oma places in front of him and shreds his *challah* bun to crumbs.

'I'm not hungry,' he says apologetically, when his wife raises an enquiring eyebrow.

It scares Ruth seeing her grandfather so dejected and she can see that Oma and Mama are worried too. None of them do justice to the food.

Only Elijah eats enthusiastically, two helpings of soup, two *challah* buns, with a large slice of *Mandeltorte* and three *Gewürzplätchen* for afters. If the boy was ill, he's definitely on the mend now.

Afterwards, when he is in danger of falling asleep at the table, Ruth takes him up to bed.

When she comes downstairs after Elijah is asleep, Mama, Opa and Oma are gathered around the kitchen table looking grim.

'What's wrong, Opa?' she asks.

'Herschel Grynszpan, a German Jew of Polish origin living in Paris, has shot Ernst vom Rath, a German embassy official, in protest against the expulsion of his parents, Polish Jews from Hanover who were hounded out of the country in October,' Opa says.

'We were caught up in that when we returned from India,' Ruth says softly, hearing the agonised screams, the thwack of whips connecting with tender flesh at the train station.

She sees the memory reflected in Mama's eyes. Mama shivers and hugs herself.

'Vom Rath is not dead but is seriously injured and fighting for his life.' Opa sighs when he's finished speaking, the only sound in the warm kitchen now chilled by this news.

'Well at least this Herschel Grynszpan took a stand,' Ruth says but the words tremble as they whisper out of her mouth.

'There will be repercussions for all of us,' Opa mutters. 'Worse if vom Rath dies.'

The stove hisses and in the terrible silence following Opa's pronouncement, it is like the whizz of a bullet. The harsh precursor to violence.

26

RUTH

They are silent for a long time after Opa tells them about the German embassy official, vom Rath being shot at by Grynszpan.

Ruth's gaze travels almost involuntarily to her mother, the horror rendering her a child again, in need of comfort.

But her mother is unravelling herself, her face whiter than the snow outside.

'If this vom Rath dies, there will be retaliation. We need to leave before things get even worse than they already are.' Oma frets, wringing her hands. 'How much longer before our papers are ready?'

Opa runs a weary hand down his face. 'It's taking longer than expected to get clearance. Especially since Dev was imprisoned...'

At the mention of Papa, Ruth looks again at Mama, who is clutching her heart with a pale hand, her eyes haunted.

'Also,' Opa speaks into the stricken silence, 'I don't want the children's passports to be stamped with a J. That big, red J is all the knowledge they need to condemn us, ostracise us, turn us away. Poland is refusing entry to the Jews deported from here.

Other countries talk the talk but when it comes to inviting us...'
Her grandfather sighs, leaving the rest of his sentence hanging.

'You fought in the war alongside your German brothers for
the motherland. You earned your limp and an Iron Cross for it.
We've dutifully paid our taxes year after year, contributed to the
economy, are law-abiding citizens and yet none of it counts,'
Oma says, cradling her head in her hands, her face etched with
despair.

'We are Jews and thus to be abhorred, not welcome
anywhere, our character, our qualities wiped out, made invisi-
ble.' Opa is bitter in a way Ruth hasn't heard before.

It is unusual for Ruth's grandfather to be so down; he is
normally upbeat, trying to boost morale. But this news has
taken it out of him.

Ruth understands suddenly that he must have been enter-
taining these feelings for a while, even, perhaps spoken of them
in private with his friends, but he has kept them from his family.
Now it appears he is too defeated to think optimistically, too
weary to fight.

It ignites terror in Ruth's chest, panic that threatens to engulf
her. Opa is the strong one. If he gives up, what then? She silently
urges him to be the Opa she knows and looks up to and not this
exhausted, fearful old man with the sheen of tears in his eyes.

'The sooner we leave, the better,' Oma says. 'It doesn't matter
if the kids' passports are stamped with a J. We need to get out of
here. It's dangerous to stay.'

Ruth watches her grandfather swallow, then wipe a hand
across his face. He looks up then, right at her. And he must see
something in her expression, the fear that is choking the breath
from her, perhaps, for, finally, he sits up straight, pushing his
shoulders back with visible effort. Then he smiles, the worry

lines easing from his forehead, although his eyes are still cloudy with shadows.

When he speaks next, it is in an altogether different, bright and passionate tone. 'This oppression can't continue, not in the middle of Europe in the twentieth century.'

'But it is,' Oma mutters. 'You always say we are a shrewd race. But the Nazis have stronger fists that they don't hesitate to use to control us.'

Capitalism, Ruth thinks, the root of all evil. The 'I'm better than you' ideology. Socialism is the answer: everyone equal. No one person above another. But that won't suit the Nazis, of course.

'And they will get even more brutal and ruthless now a Jew has dared stand up to one of them.' Oma shudders, wrapping her arms around herself. 'I hope vom Rath recovers. I dread to think what will happen if he dies.'

Tears shiver in Mama's eyes, her hands clasped tightly together.

Ruth waits in vain for Opa's reassurance but the effort of being cheerful seems to have exhausted him, for he is silent, the food that had been so lovingly prepared, uneaten, the warm and toasty kitchen now cold with misgiving.

27

RUTH

Ruth cannot fall asleep. She tosses and turns as she recalls the defeated expression on Opa's face, how he had looked so very old and beaten. She is troubled by premonition, hounded by the sinister, looming spectre of doom.

Finally she gives up trying to sleep, pushing the sheets aside, standing up and stretching. Outside, snow is still falling silently, a whirling constellation of flakes dropping from the sky, obscuring everything in a creamy, white glow. She is heading to the kitchen for a drink of water when she hears sounds from Opa and Oma's room. They are awake, talking in whispers which, although hushed, thrum with a pulsing urgency that gives Ruth pause.

Her feet have stalled outside their room and she eavesdrops almost without meaning to.

'I've known Christoph for years and when he spat at the shop as he walked past, I couldn't take it. "You are my friend, Christoph, what is this you're doing?" I yelled.' Opa's voice haemorrhaging pain. 'Do you know what he said?'

'I can guess.' Oma sounds immensely sad and weary.

'"The only friends your kind make are with other Jews," he said. I grew up with the man, have known him, his family from the time I was a teen. What is Hitler doing to our country and our people? Turning our friends and fellows against each other. People I know and care for transforming into horrible strangers propagating violence. I have to turn away from these men I no longer recognise because I'm ashamed for them, afraid of what they will do in their new, hate-filled guises. They smeared the word "Jew" all over the shop windows and I... no one helped while I washed it off. Instead, they stood there and laughed. My supposed friends.'

Ruth starts walking back to her room, forgetting to get the water, the despair and upset in Opa's voice ringing in her ears, drowning out Oma's agonised, 'Why didn't you tell me?'

'I wanted to spare you. I thought that it would boil over, they'd get it out of their system and that would be that,' Opa says and something in his voice, a deeper hurt, gives Ruth pause once more. He speaks again, his words coming in a gush. 'But... I was still shaking from my encounter with Christoph, when Heinrich Müller, who has had his eye on my business, swaggered – that's the only word for it – into the shop and offered to buy it for a tenth of what it is worth! And do you know what he said? "I'm doing you a favour before the party snatches it for nothing."' Opa pauses. 'But you know what's the worst thing? I believe him. I do.' His voice is breaking. 'I never thought it would come to this but... this government is capable of anything. I... I've heard stories.' His voice a whisper but carrying, as it is throbbing with pain. 'Jews shot down like animals at the border while trying to escape. Jews sent to concentration camps, accused of smuggling for carrying more than ten marks upon their person...'

Oma says, her voice wet, 'We should have left much earlier.

Naomi and the children shouldn't have returned from India. The children... I worry... they've been through so much. We've lived but they...' Oma stops speaking, unable to continue.

Ruth rocks on her feet, her heart seized with terror, even as she tries to process what Opa has said, what he has endured. All these weeks he'd come back home smiling from the shop, bearing treats for them, never giving anything away, making out that whatever was happening was just a phase that would pass.

Now she understands why he was so adamant that she stay at home and create the leaflets the few times she had offered to come into the shop with him and work there. 'Oma and your mama need company here, my *bubbale*,' he'd said gently, smiling tenderly at her. He was protecting her from the abuse and discrimination she too would face if she went with him to the shop.

She'd seen it happening, at the train station when they'd arrived, and to that woman on the bench reserved for Jews, but it hadn't touched her, touched them, or so she'd thought.

'Dev saw it coming. That was why he wanted Naomi and the children out of the way. When we got Naomi's letters telling us that they were returning home because Dev's brother had kicked them out, it was too late to ask them to stay back instead. They had already set out for here.' There is a world of sorrow and regret in Oma's voice. 'We should have got our visas done when Hitler started his hate campaign. We should have left when we had the chance,' Oma repeats, her voice shaking like a building in an earthquake.

'What's done is done,' Opa says and the sigh of defeat that accompanies his words is a lance in Ruth's heart.

She had been hoping, despite everything she'd heard so far, that Opa would reassure Oma, tell her she was wrong, that it wasn't as bad as all that.

But...

It is much worse than she thought.

'In any case,' Opa is saying, 'Karl is trying his hardest, pulling all the strings he can to get our paperwork ready. Should be done by next week, I'm hoping.'

'Let's hope it's not too late,' Oma whispers.

Her grandparents are silent now and Ruth makes her way back to her room, her legs jellied with fear.

Sleep evades her all night, and when she does manage to doze, she is tormented by horrific images: her family bleeding onto the leaflets Ruth has designed, the slogan on them, *Down with Hitler!* shimmering scarlet with the lifeblood of those she loves most in the world.

28

RUTH

Morning dawns bright and cloudless, the sky the white of purity, the garden clothed in a serenely sparkling snow fleece.

But gloom pervades indoors, the cloud of foreboding hovering since Opa told them about the shooting of the German embassy official in Paris.

They are waiting, all of them except Elijah, for the repercussions, even as they hope that the German official recovers and there will be none.

But they know that even if vom Rath does pull through, Herschel Grynszpan's actions will not go unpunished and there will be a backlash for all of them.

What they are unaware of, for now, is that the horrific fallout from an act of violence committed in Paris will bring the savage atrocities against their race that they have so far managed to keep outside the four walls of this, their haven, inside their home, rendering it and their hearts chillier than the wintry snowstorm.

But that is yet to come.

Now, Ruth sits up in bed after a restless, sleep-deprived night when Elijah bounds into her room, and arranges her features into a smile.

As always, her exuberant brother cheers her up, the put-on smile morphing into a genuine one.

Elijah, who has no clue what's going on, is as happily affectionate as ever, throwing his arms around Ruth, declaring, brightly, 'I feel all right today. Look!' He takes her hand and lays it upon his forehead. 'It's not hot any more.'

Our plans to leave Germany being on hold because of not managing to get the requisite paperwork has been good for Elijah, she tells herself, even as she hears Oma's whisper, fear and caution, in her head: 'Let's hope it's not too late.'

It's been good for Elijah.

Reiterating this in her head eases her doubts a smidgen.

The nightmares that have plagued Elijah since their father's death have reduced since their return to Germany. He has made friends here; he loves school and learning. And thankfully, he hasn't experienced or picked up on any anti-Semitism; he's had none directed at him. That doesn't mean that it won't happen. That he will be sheltered always. But for now, he is blessedly unaware of the tension and stress the rest of them are experiencing.

So, worrying though it is, with every day bringing worse news, rendering it more difficult and dangerous for Jews to remain in Germany, at least for now, staying here has been good for her brother; of this much, Ruth is certain.

He somersaults upon her bed, a bundle of lively energy. 'I'm better. I can go to school today.'

'Okay then, sport. See you this evening.'

Elijah gives her a tight, lingering hug. 'I had a great time yesterday. Spending the day with you healed me.'

Her heart overflows with love and warmth. Opa's announcement and the long night after had wiped out the happiness of the day preceding it. She buries her face in her brother's hair to hide her tears.

'Me too,' she says.

But then...

Just as Opa is getting ready to leave for the shop – he's leaving later today and Ruth opted to stay behind at home, helping a wan-looking Oma prepare breakfast and Opa's packed lunch, rather than walking to the school to drop Elijah off with Mama – Mama and Elijah are back.

'They let Hans in, and even Klaus, who's always getting in trouble, but not me,' Elijah says indignantly but there are tears flowering in his eyes.

'Go to your room and change, Elijah. I'll be there in a minute. We'll have another fun day like yesterday, what do you say?'

But her words do not lift her brother's spirits. He appears dejected even as he nods.

Ruth is gentle as she gives her brother a hug, planting kisses on his tousled hair even as her heart breaks, aches for him, her whole body rigid with upset on his behalf.

Once a downhearted Elijah pulls himself up the stairs, clinging to the banister, his school bag thudding on each step, Mama lowers herself gently onto the table and buries her face in her hands.

'They're banning Jewish children from schools.'

'What!' Ruth feels fiery anger explode within her, briefly displacing the sorrow and heartache.

'The world has gone mad. I have given up trying to make sense of it. First, my husband and now this. Is there no peace, unity, a sense of community, togetherness anywhere any more?' Mama's voice despairing.

Opa lays a hand gently on Ruth's mother's shoulder.

'I'm afraid this is just the beginning.' He sighs and there is such pain in his voice, his eyes heavy with it. 'They've been waiting for an excuse to openly castigate and oppress us and this shooting of vom Rath gave them just that.'

'We can't just take it,' Ruth cries.

And now her mother looks at Ruth. Her eyes, like her son's just now, are garlanded with tears, but her voice is steely as she says, 'And what do you suggest we do?'

'We...' Ruth blusters. 'We...' She looks at Opa, who shrugs.

'We wait to hear what's next,' Opa says.

'That's it?' She is incredulous.

'We cannot fight unless we know exactly what we're dealing with.'

'We know what we are dealing with. Prejudice. Racism. Ostracism. Discrimination against a community. Capitalism gone wrong.'

'Don't shout, Ruth. You'll upset your brother more than he is already.' Mama's voice sharp.

Hurt stabbing Ruth even though she understands that Mama is afraid and that it is making her lash out.

This situation is bringing out the worst in all of them.

'There must be something we can do, surely,' she says in a softer tone.

'All this is happening because that boy, a teenager, upset with the way his parents and his fellows were treated, turned on an authority figure who happened to be vom Rath.' Mama sighs. 'We are all suffering the consequences.'

'But we can't just take it,' Ruth persists.

'If we take a stand, we will be punished,' Oma says tightly.

'We're being punished anyway just because we are Jews,' Ruth bursts out. 'Are we meant to hide and cower and act the way they've labelled us as though we've done something wrong, as if we are a sin, a blemish, a mistake, dirty, inferior, for the rest of our lives?'

'Ruth...' her mother chastises, but the heat has gone out of her voice; she is too defeated to continue.

'Ruth, my *bubbale*, I too am tired of being made to feel in the wrong,' Oma sighs. 'I am fed up with being pushed around, shoved, loathed, ignored, shouted at. It has been insidious, the change since Hitler came to power. And now, all of a sudden, it is so obvious. Those who oppose it are sent to concentration camps, prison, worse...' Here, she pauses, eyes shining with sadness, thinking, like they all are, of Ruth's papa, who dared do something about the injustices taking place in his adopted country and lost his life for it.

Oma takes a breath. 'Those canny enough to see ahead, left. Your papa made sure you did too but circumstances dictated otherwise and you ended up back here...' She sighs again deeply. 'Your opa and I stayed, believing in the good of our fellow countrymen. That surely people would protest, wake up, realise how wrong it was, the burning of Jewish texts, the sacking and discrediting of Jewish intellectuals, professors. We took it, hoping that it would surely stop soon. But recently, it's become worse, blatant and now this... this attack on that diplomat is just an excuse for more violence, more exclusion, more sanctions against us. I kept thinking that this country is better than its leadership. I never gave up hoping that the people I grew up with, my friends, would see sense. But they too are drunk on feeling superior to someone else. It's human nature. I cautioned myself against becoming too sensitive, paranoid, seeing meanness everywhere. But...' Oma's voice stripped raw. 'That is the state of this country now. Living an ordinary life, working, sharing a meal with friends is a luxury, an impossibility for us. For those we consider friends think of us as the enemy, other, alien. And now we have to put up with being treated as robbers and murderers as well as for our grandchildren, innocents, to be banned from learning...'

'Enough, *meine liebe*,' Opa says, laying a cautionary palm on Oma's.

Oma nods, leaning into her husband.

To Ruth, Opa says, 'My *bubbale*, come with me.'

Opa leads Ruth up to the bedroom he shares with Oma.

She pauses outside Elijah's room. His door is not completely shut and she peers inside. Her brother is lying face down on his bed, still wearing his school clothes and shoes. He's asleep, tears having dried in salty tracks upon his face.

Sleeping through trauma is Elijah's way of coping. He takes after their father in that respect. He will wake later, sobbing, from the nightmare that has plagued him since his father's death, that had stopped recently. But Ruth knows now that it will start again. Elijah is always besieged by nightmares when he goes to bed in tears. It is the way his mind processes hurt, pain too incomprehensible to fathom.

Her heart goes out to her little brother lying there so vulnerable. She recalls his laughter the previous day as they played and talked, remembers him humming as he coloured in the warm and fragrant kitchen yesterday evening, his joy this morning.

Her brother sniffles in his sleep, restless, a remembered hiccup of a sob escaping his slightly open mouth.

Her chest aches with love and pain.

Opa gently nudges her past her brother's room, whispering, 'You can see to him later, my *bubbale*. He will be okay, I am sure.'

But there is no conviction in her grandfather's voice.

29

RUTH

As they enter her grandparents' bedroom, Ruth is reminded of Opa and Oma's hushed whispers from the night before.

Now Opa moves the bed away from the wall. He counts the tiles on the floor, 'One, two, three, the third floorboard to the left, slightly scuffed, see?'

'Opa...'

'My *bubbale*, this is important.' The plea in Opa's voice shuts her up at the same time as it scares her even more than she already is. 'Now,' he says. 'This floorboard is loose. You prise it up just so.'

He does as he says to reveal a box tucked into the space beneath, which he opens.

'Here, I've been secreting money, valuables, documents.'

She is shocked. One hand on her heart, which is thumping wildly. 'For how long?'

'A while,' Opa says.

It must have been since Papa was imprisoned and later, killed, Ruth guesses.

'Now you know,' he says. 'Just in case.'

Just in case of what? She cannot ask. Instead, 'Opa, there was no need for me to know. You will be here to retrieve them, if it comes to that, which it won't,' she says fiercely.

'Yes, I know, my *bubbale*.' His voice is gentle and so very fond. It makes her ache.

'But it is to set an old man's heart at rest, eh?'

'You have years to go yet.' Her fear makes her voice sound harsh.

'Of course I do.' He smiles affectionately at her and winks, his eyes shimmering.

Her heart is ambushed by fresh sorrow and panic.

For Opa's wink is the saddest thing. An attempt at levity in this horribly tense situation.

'I... I don't know if we did the right thing by returning to Germany, Opa,' she says, her voice shaking.

He pats her head gently. 'Look forward, not back,' he says, but his voice wavers and his hand on her head is heavy, weighted as the sigh of a doomed man.

30

RUTH

1941
England

Ruth blinks, coming back into the present.

The room is dark; the lamps have gone out.

Shadows dance upon Esther and Isaac's faces, their eyes bright with empathy and sadness.

She takes a sip of her chicory tea.

'It's gone cold,' Esther protests. 'I'll make some more.'

'No, this is okay,' Ruth says. The bitter, sluggish dregs of the tea mask the sorrow in her mouth, the briny taste of pain and regret choking her.

'I'm so sorry for what you went through,' Esther says. 'We both are.' She looks at Isaac, who nods. 'We had no idea, not a clue it was so bad. Eva was so determinedly cheery in her letters, the few that managed to arrive, anyway.'

Tears sparkle in Esther's eyes.

'It got worse,' Ruth manages through the lump that has taken her throat captive.

'You don't have to...' Esther begins.

'I want to,' Ruth says. She does. Speaking about it for the first time – she never did so with Eva as they had all lived through it and it was too close then, too much – allows her to make sense of it and also, even though it hurts terribly, it is a gift to remember her beloved in this way. Recounting aloud brings back memories she had forgotten, little things, the way Elijah's face lit up when he looked at her, the feel of her brother, his warm weight in her arms.

'I want to,' she says again.

And, taking a deep breath, she travels back into the past. Those last few days when everything unravelled, when her life changed irrevocably, forever...

31

RUTH

November 1938
Munich, Germany

Just when they thought it couldn't get any worse, it does. They are at the synagogue when it happens.

In retaliation for the shooting of vom Rath, not only have Jewish children been banned from school, but Jewish cultural activities suspended and the circulation of Jewish newspapers and magazines stopped.

Jews Declare War on the German People, the German newspapers propound.

It is a mad world. Everything subverted.

'Lies, all lies. How can they print this, propagate hate? It wasn't war. It was a furiously upset seventeen-year-old Grynszpan lashing out.' In Ruth's frustrated impotence, as she sees her brother's sadness, her mother and grandparents' fear – yes, even her grandfather who, along with Papa, Ruth thought invincible but now realises is just a frail, scared old man trying his hardest to be strong for his family – Ruth is a broken record.

'They *are* doing it,' Mama says and there is immense tiredness in her voice; she sounds much older than her years.

'We must do something.' Ruth has said this a hundred times, wringing her hands, pacing the house.

'What do you suggest?' There is no fire in her mother's voice, just apathy. Defeat.

And again, Ruth comes up blank.

Her brother's nightmares have started again. Ruth holds him, tries in vain to console him: her brother, who should be happy, carefree, going to school; who was doing so, until they decreed he couldn't just because of his race. As always, Ruth is consumed with anger that has no outlet.

Opa hasn't gone to his shop. He was getting ready that morning when Oma said, gently touching his hand, 'Stay home today.'

Before, Opa would have chuckled, made a joke, said, 'I'm not scared. Why should I hide?'

But this morning, he nodded.

Ruth read the resignation in his slumped shoulders and her heart seized with fear.

Now, Mama says, 'Let's go to the synagogue.'

'Prayer, Mama?'

'It is as good a plan as any. We need to be together at a time like this. Band with others going through this. Eva said she would be there.'

Mama had taken Elijah, who was getting restless cooped up at home, to visit Eva the previous day. 'Her children have been banned from school too, so at least Elijah will have company,' Mama had said. She had invited Ruth along too but Ruth had opted to stay with Oma, who was looking very down.

Elijah had returned from visiting with Eva and her children

looking happier, more like his usual self. Mama too looked better, more upbeat than she had in days.

'Eva is good for the soul. She reminds me of you, Ruth. She's feisty, active in the resistance. She's very impressed with you. She asked me to let you know that she loves what you are doing with the leaflets and pamphlets. She has distributed them amongst her network and they are making sure to send them far and wide.'

Ruth had beamed, her heart swelling. She had been so disheartened lately, wondering, what was the point of it all? But now, finally, something positive: her creating the leaflets at home was having *some* effect. It was not all for nothing.

As if Mama had intuited the direction of her thoughts, she said, 'Eva said it all helps, makes a difference. She is so brave, that woman. She is a widow, like me, with children Elijah's age, and yet, she is fighting the regime. "I will go crazy if I don't do something. It makes me so angry, Naomi," she said. I told her I heard the same from you every day. She said that she would love to see you again.' For since they returned to Germany from India, Ruth had not seen Eva and her children.

Now, Mama says, 'Eva will be at the synagogue. You can talk to her about ways in which you can fight whatever is happening.'

And for the first time all week, Ruth feels a flicker of hope-fulness.

The streets leading to the synagogue appear deserted. Eerily still. A menacing calm with troubled undertones. Ruth feels apprehension tickle her spine. She sees the same worry reflected in the set of Opa's mouth, the way the muscle in his jaw is working overtime, in Oma's joined hands, knuckles standing to attention, her rigid stance, in Mama's chewing of her lower lip, in the way her grip around Elijah tightens and the smile she is affecting for her son droops when he is not looking.

The synagogue, in contrast, is an oasis of safety. When they enter, Ruth can breathe again, the tension leaving her, and she sees that it has the same effect on Opa, Oma and Mama.

When Ruth meets Eva, she remembers afresh just how much she has always liked her. Eva is warm, down to earth and passionate about the resistance. She takes Ruth's hands in both of hers while beside them, her children chat to Elijah, Opa, Oma and Mama watching indulgently.

'We are all so very impressed with your leaflets. You have been doing each by hand! I cannot imagine how long it must have taken you.' She smiles at Ruth.

'It allows me to keep the anger and helplessness at bay,' Ruth says.

Eva's eyes light up. 'Yes, that's exactly how I feel too.' Then, eyebrow raised, she says, 'Would you be interested in discussing more ways in which we can fight back?'

Ruth doesn't have to think twice. 'I would like that very much,' she says.

'It is extremely dangerous and risky work.' Eva looks at Ruth, her gaze assessing.

'I know,' Ruth says. 'But I am so angry with everything that is happening, what the Nazis are doing. I am fed up of feeling helpless and frustrated.'

Eva nods. Then, 'Your opa's shop is being watched. And your house too, no doubt. You are all on their radar, which is why it is taking Karl so long to arrange the requisite papers for you...'

'You know about that?' Ruth asks.

'Yes,' Eva says. 'We were neighbours back in the day. I have known your opa and oma for as long as I have been alive.' She smiles and her furrowed brow relaxes, her eyes sparkling. Then, becoming serious again, 'Your father...'

Ruth's breath catches. 'Yes, I know...' She swallows. 'I know Papa was executed in prison to prevent him from leaving and continuing with his activities.'

Eva nods, her eyes stark. 'I'm sorry.' Then taking a breath, 'If you join me, you might be...'

Ruth tastes bile as she says, 'I know. But I am prepared to take that risk.'

'You will be on the radar of the Gestapo even more so than you are already.'

'I will be careful,' Ruth says. 'I... I hate that they have all the power. I cannot... I refuse to let them win. Especially when Papa has given his life for the cause.'

And now Eva steps forward and wraps her arms around Ruth. She smells sweet, of buds dancing in the spring breeze.

'Good,' she whispers in Ruth's ear. 'Come and find me after worship and we will talk some more.'

They have just settled down for worship, when...

A whisper travels through the synagogue, taut with fear, thrumming with anxiety. 'Ernst vom Rath is dead.'

Over Elijah's tousled head, Opa, Oma and Ruth share expressions of horror and worry as the ripple swells, becoming a storm, rife and seething with tension that can be cut with a knife.

For everyone understands that when the repercussions of the shooting were so bad, then those of vom Rath dying are going to be worse...

32

RUTH

When the first window shatters, they are praying. For Herschel Grynszpan and his family. For vom Rath and his.

It begins with a hum.

The reverent hush of the synagogue disturbed by a droning from outside, persistent. Growing in volume. Distinctly ominous.

Then the windows shatter in a multitudinous explosion of crystal, one after the other.

One shard of twinkling glass strikes Mama even as she ducks, pulling Ruth and Elijah down with her, her face stark with horror and shock. The spear of broken pane pierces the pale skin of her arm, drawing blood, crimson on white.

But they have no time to do anything but cower, for the humming buzz is now a roar. Suddenly very loud and very near.

The violence of kicking boots, ruthless fists and furious swearing; hateful Jewish slurs defiling this holy place.

And then they are inside. Pulling scrolls. Slashing screens. Tearing holy books. Cutting down anyone daring to stand in their way.

A sudden flash. Bright, flaming orange. The strike of a match. A scream. More.

Pain. Anger. Incomprehension. Terror.

The acrid tang of smoke stealing breath.

The evil tangerine dance of flames, hungry, grasping, destroying all that is precious, beloved, revered, sacred.

The charred, yellow scent of agony, choked dreams, burning hopes.

And suddenly, a stampede. Opa lost in the ominous swirls of fiery ash, capped by crimson, dark as hell. Oma falling. Mama trying to help her up and falling too. Elijah sobbing beside Ruth, clinging to her.

'Go,' her mother whispers to Ruth. 'Take your brother and leave.'

'You come too.'

'I can't leave Oma.'

Oma's eyes shut, tears squeezing from behind closed lids.

'She's twisted her ankle,' Mama cries.

And now Ruth sees through the navy haze stinging her eyes, Oma's leg swelling.

'Please. Just go. Get yourself and your brother to safety.'

'But, Mama...'

'Ruth.' Her mother gasps for the breath the fire-tipped smoke has stolen from her.

Around them, mayhem. Screams, pleas, hatred, chaos, defilement, devastation, death.

'Papa... he reached out to the family who had disowned him, for us. He wanted us to escape...' Mama gives another shuddering gasp as she points around her, '...this. He loved you and Elijah more than life itself. You *were* his life. Go, please. We will be happier knowing you've escaped this madness. We'll see you soon, *meine lieblinge.*'

33

RUTH

Ruth swallows, unable to speak for the sorrow flooding her mouth, tasting of the sea.

'Oh, Ruth, my *bubbale*, I'm so sorry,' Esther says.

My *bubbale*. Beloved. Her opa and oma's terms of endearment for her and Elijah.

My *bubbale*. She tastes love and grief, sorrow and regret for what might have been.

It is Isaac who breaks the silence, for Esther appears as overcome as Ruth is. 'We didn't know the extent of it. We put together what happened from the carefully curated news reports of the Kristallnacht, the Night of Broken Glass.'

'Yes.' Ruth nods, gratefully taking the handkerchief Esther offers and blowing her nose.

'Eva, her letters... There weren't many. And she couldn't tell us much, if anything. Of course, even if she had, the censors would have got at them...' Esther says, sniffing. 'I cannot begin to imagine how... The horror of it. And you... you experienced it.'

'Yes,' Ruth says simply, her mind's eye bombarded by images of the mayhem, the agonised cries, Oma's foot swelling rapidly, Mama gesturing at her children to run, her beloved face obscured by the burning haze...

Opa lost somewhere in the chaos. Eva and her children too.

Ruth keeping hold of her sobbing, coughing brother and pushing blindly through the swirling clouds of smoke that choked them, fiery breath scorching their skin. Walking away from Oma and Mama...

'I'm so sorry,' Isaac says.

'Yes.' What else can she say? What can anyone? She takes a breath, says, 'Afterwards, we heard that several synagogues and Jewish houses of worship had been destroyed, mostly by arson. The fire departments did nothing; they let the buildings burn. They only took action if the fire was in danger of spreading to non-Jewish dwellings. Jewish businesses and houses were looted and destroyed, Opa's shop and our house among them.' Ruth sniffs, blowing her nose once again, grateful for the hand-kerchief. She takes a deep breath. 'In the event, Oma's caution was right. Our paperwork to leave Germany and gain entry elsewhere did not arrive in time. Perhaps we would have left after Kristallnacht. If nothing else, if our paperwork was still delayed, we might have considered sending Elijah on the Kindertransport, to Britain, perhaps. But it was a moot point, for after Kristallnacht...'

She cannot continue for again, the images come. They ambush and assault with bloody relentlessness.

Esther lays a gentle hand on Ruth's. It blurs before Ruth's eyes as she thinks of her brother's small palm, tucked trustingly in hers.

Oh, Elijah, what wouldn't I give to hold your hand in mine just once more...

She opens her mouth but nothing comes.

'You don't have to,' Esther says.

This is the first time she has narrated it all. Eva, having also lived through it, had held Ruth, offering comfort in this way, knowing without words what Ruth had gone through.

In any case, then, with it all too raw, the horrific nightmare branded into her mind, Ruth could not speak about any of it. Now she can and it helps.

It helps.

'I need to,' she says and taking a deep breath, she prepares herself for the hardest part. The saddest chapter in this litany of sadness.

34

RUTH

November 1938
Munich, Germany

She takes Elijah and runs, blindly, billowing smoke at their heels, squeezing the breath from them in ash-tipped gasps, past the hysteria, the sobbing people, the agitating rioters setting fire, crashing furniture, slashing Torah scrolls and holy books, feeding sacred texts into the devouring blaze.

Even as terror takes her captive and she clutches her brother close, his small, sweaty palm tucked in hers, she worries whether her mother and grandparents will be okay, a small, brutal voice whispering, *They most likely will not. This is why Mama asked you to take Elijah and escape.*

Her brother, usually so compliant, hangs back. He is shaking, shuddering with dread. His teeth are chattering. His eyes are bloodshot. It is too much for him.

'I want to go back, to Mama, to Oma and Opa,' he sobs.

'Please come with me, Elijah,' she cries. 'It's dangerous here. You heard Mama. She said to go to safety.'

'But I'm worried that I will never see Mama and Oma and Opa again. Just like I never saw Papa again,' Elijah wails.

She stops as, around them, looters savage and destroy. She's terrified and yet, her brother's words wound more than all that's going on around them.

He is crying so hard that it's difficult to get the words out and yet he chokes them through in stuttering gulps. 'Papa... He just went away and never came back.'

Her brother might only be eight years old, but he is smart, and intuitive, having picked up, just the same as her, that now they are leaving Oma and Opa and Mama behind, there is a possibility, given that the synagogue is ablaze and Oma trapped because of her ankle, they might not see them again. Mama and Ruth thought they were protecting Elijah, but they have under-estimated him. He is an easy-going, trusting, loving child but nevertheless, her brother has grasped the gravity of the situa-tion they find themselves in. And he doesn't want to abandon his family for the very real fear that he might never see them again.

Her heart breaks even more so than it has already.

Her brother is bawling now and yet, through juddering sobs, he manages, 'I want to be with Mama, Opa and Oma and you. I want us all to be together.'

She is tempted to go back, do as her brother says.

But she thinks of Mama's words, her plea for them to escape the violence.

And in any case, she cannot see even right in front of her as they are enveloped in a thick miasma of smoke topped by flames. Even if they turned back, they would be walking blindly into a screen of fire.

She bites back her tears as she tries to think up some way of reassuring her brother, convincing him to come with her. They need to get out of here *now*. Urgency and fear tap tapping upon her chest, even as the scorch of fire is more intense, the smoke stinging, assaulting, stealing breath.

Her mother has tasked Ruth with getting herself and her brother, for their father's sake and for her own, to safety. She will do just that.

Amid the chaos, the screams of fear and upset, the expletives of the rioters, the lapping flames, branding, fiery heat, she kneels so that she is at eye level with her brother.

She puts her hands on her brother's shoulders. His nose and eyes are leaking, his breaths stuttering out of his small, achingly vulnerable chest. She wants to gather him in her arms, spirit him away from here. But first she needs to convince him.

'You are right,' she says.

Her brother blinks.

She takes a burning, ash-flavoured breath. 'But you heard Mama, Elijah. She asked me to take you to safety.'

'But, Ruth!' he cries. 'I want to go back to Mama, Opa and Oma. I want for us to be together.'

'And we will be,' she says, 'once this has settled.' She waves a hand around them. 'We will find them, I promise. But we can't do so now. We will be lost in the smoke and fire. We can't see them or hear them. Come on, Elijah...'

Someone careens into her and she falls backwards, losing her balance and her grasp on her brother. People rush past, kicking her, stepping on her. Stabbing throbs of pain punching into her chest, her stomach, her arms, her legs.

'Elijah,' she opens her mouth to call but smoke rushes in, charred black, robbing her of breath and voice.

When she manages to right herself, her brother is gone.

'Elijah!' she screams, but her throat is hoarse and scalded and a quavering, terrified whisper is all she can manage. 'Elijah!'

Smoke spears her eyes and all she can see are hazy figures wreaking destruction, wielding death.

Defaming holy texts. Desecrating this sanctuary.

Screams of fiery pain.

Echoing.

Building.

A keen that goes on and on, coming from her own besieged heart, flying out of her desperate, burning mouth. A reeling, terrified lament.

Elijah.

Elijah.

Elijah!

35

RUTH

1941
England

'I'm so very sorry,' Esther says, jolting Ruth back into the present.

Tears shine like jewels in Esther's eyes.

Isaac is digging a handkerchief out of his pocket and roughly swiping at his eyes.

Why did Ruth stop to talk to her brother, convince him? She has returned to that moment over and over again. She should have followed her instincts, grabbed him and run. Reasoned with him later, once they were safe...

But he was so upset and she couldn't bear to see him distraught. And so she had taken a moment to explain, like she had always done. It was their way, and it changed everything...

36

RUTH

November 1938
Munich, Germany

She had run through the synagogue, among the marauding mob, trying to find her brother.

In vain.

She had tried running back to where her mother and grand-parents were.

But the synagogue was burning and strange arms had pulled her back to relative safety.

She had been held in a fortress of unfamiliar bodies, breathing sweat and smoke and dread as around them Jewish houses, synagogues and shops were burnt and destroyed, looted and ransacked.

Cheers rang in Ruth's horrified, disbelieving, devastated mind as the city was given over to thugs. Well-dressed women held their children up to watch the mindless destruction. In front of her eyes, civilised people became savages united in attacking Jews with whom they'd previously been friends, had custom, shared meals, drinks, gossip and laughter. She watched, stunned, as able-bodied Jews were led away.

Afterwards, when night settled on a shattered city, when the insurgents finally returned to their – intact, unviolated – homes, she along with the other survivors who had seen too much had walked through the smoking rubble. Every one of them pausing at each dead body, praying desperately through clenched teeth and fearful gazes that it wasn't their loved one. That they had been spared.

She found Elijah just a few paces from where she had lost him, lying still, as he never was in life, his small body trampled and broken, one hand stretched out as if trying to grasp at something. Those small fingers arching. Desperately seeking help that did not come.

If only I'd searched harder. If only I'd looked instead of turning away from the smoke and dread haranguing my eyes.

Elijah's last words. 'I want for us to be together...'

She cradled his little broken body and wept. *I'm sorry, little brother. I'm so very sorry. I let down everyone I love.*

She found Oma and Mama where she had left them, Opa a short distance away.

'Papa loved you and Elijah more than life itself. You *were* his life. Go, please. We will be happier knowing you've escaped this madness. We'll see you soon, *meine lieblinge.*' Mama's last words.

I failed him, Mama. I failed Elijah. I failed you.

She was lying there, broken, wishing she was with them, wondering why she was spared, when she felt arms around her. Familiar arms. A voice in her ear, hot breath flavoured with grief. 'Come now, come with me, Ruth, *mein liebling.*'

Mein liebling. Mama's endearment. For a brief moment, although she was holding Mama's lifeless hand in hers, she allowed herself to imagine it was her mother's arms wrapped around her, whispering succour into her ear.

Then, *I don't deserve comfort. I don't deserve compassion. I failed Elijah. My sweet, innocent, beloved brother. Oh, Elijah.*

And finally, the events of the day caught up with her and she gave in to the darkness crowding her eyes, hoping, praying, entreating with all her might that it meant she was joining her family...

37

RUTH

1941
England

When she has managed to compose herself, Ruth says, softly, 'After I had lost everything and everyone I loved, I was only able to go on thanks to your sister.'

'Eva,' Esther says. Her sister's name on her lips is a hymn of longing and pain.

'Eva saved me. It was her arms wrapped around me, when I fainted that horrific day after I found out that I had lost everyone dear to me. She and her children had managed to escape to safety and once she made sure her children were with friends she trusted, she came back to look for us.' Ruth takes a minute. Then, 'After she found me, catatonic with grief, she took me to the safe place she and her fellow resistance crew had arranged. As if setting fire to our places of worship, looting and destroying our homes and businesses was not enough, the Nazis then asked Jews to pay recompense! Many were marched off to concentration camps. And while the anti-Semitic violence and discrimination was condemned by other countries, they didn't welcome Jews either. If you were a Jew, you were a pariah.' Burning anger and sorrow fight within her. With difficulty, Ruth swallows both down. 'In any case, during those first weeks after Kristallnacht, I was in no state to do anything except wade through a life I didn't want to live. I was lost to grief.'

Esther once again places her palm upon Ruth's, gives Ruth's hand a gentle squeeze. *I'm here for you,* she is conveying with her gesture, just as her sister had in those terrible days after...

'It took a while for me to come to terms with what had happened. Eva and her children helped. Those children, they brought Elijah back to me in their way. I grew to love them and Eva, even though I was afraid to love anyone for fear of losing them too...' Ruth tastes salt and sorrow in her mouth, her heart ravaged with grief.

Oh, Eva, I hope you and the children are all right, even as I fear that you are not.

'The only way I was able to endure the guilt of surviving when all my loved ones were dead was by being active in the resistance. It helped that I was fighting the Nazis who had killed my family in some small way.' Ruth takes a breath. Blows her nose. 'Then, even though we had been very careful in covering our tracks, moving from safe house to safe house every few months, they found us. And when they came for us, Eva saved me once again, pushing me out of the back door, asking me to deliver her letter to you, knowing that otherwise, I would not go. Thanks to Karl, I had the relevant paperwork to escape. My passport with my name, Ruth Ravinder. Ravinder was clearly not Jewish but even if they had queried my first name, there was no J on my passport, thanks to Opa's connections, the strings he and Karl pulled. Nobody stopped me. My Indian identity, I couldn't hide. It was stamped upon my dusky skin. But my

Jewish one... That I could and did, even though it felt like a betrayal and went against all the principles I'd so passionately defended.' Ruth sighs. 'Eva... She gave me the gift of a life I don't deserve.'

'Don't ever say that,' Esther says fiercely and in that moment, she sounds so very like her sister. Feisty, loyal, wonderful Eva.

Ruth smiles through her tears.

'That's exactly what Eva used to say when I lamented about why I had been the one to live. Why not Elijah, who had his whole life ahead of him?' Her voice breaks.

Esther's hand on hers steadies her.

She smiles at this woman, Eva's sister. 'And she gave me the letter for you. Asked me to please deliver it to you in person. It was her way of ensuring I didn't do anything stupid. That I would escape like she wanted me to.'

Esther manages a wet smile. 'That is Eva through and through. In her letter, she says only that she loves me and that she and the children will see me when it's all over.'

Then they are all crying, even Isaac, who clears his throat vehemently and blows his nose.

'Yes, let's hope so,' Ruth says when she can speak again.

'That's all we can do in these times. Hold on to hope even as we despair,' Isaac says, his voice gruff with sorrow.

'In any case, just as Eva intended, here I am, while she and the children...' Ruth cannot continue.

Esther gently squeezes Ruth's hand. 'We are so glad you are here,' she says, Isaac nodding agreement.

Ruth can see that they mean it.

And this, too, is a gift she does not deserve. But a gift freely given. A gift all the same.

38

RUTH

They sit together, Ruth gathering her thoughts after telling her story.

It is quiet and yet the silence is companionable. It is... healing.

Ruth kneads her hands. She can taste the guilt in her mouth.

Why me? Why do I get to live, sit here with kind people who have listened to me, allowed me to open myself to them, while Eva, so much more worthy than me, and her children, mere innocents, are suffering?

Esther's hand on Ruth's imparting comfort. 'I understand. We feel the same. Helpless. Useless. Asking ourselves why we are spared, a childless couple, when our fellows are dying. But we go on, knowing Eva wants to hold on to the hope that we are alive. She sent you to us because, wherever she and her children are, they want the assurance that we have met, that together, we are thinking of them and waiting for them to join us when they can.'

Esther pauses to take a breath. It is the longest speech she's made since Ruth arrived so unexpectedly into her life, but her eyes glitter with a passion that makes her husband sit up straighter and his eyes shine as he looks from her to Ruth.

'Stay with us, Ruth. Eva wanted that. That is why she sent you to us. We would love to have you,' Esther says earnestly.

She turns to her husband, who nods, and looking at Ruth, clears his throat. 'We would like that very much.'

'We all carry guilt, every single one of us, for surviving while others are dying,' Esther says. 'I make up for it by doing what I can control: scrubbing the house, going prepared to the Underground when there is an air raid, knitting for the soldiers, helping with the Women's Voluntary Service. It is not enough, I know, but it is something.' Esther smiles gently at her. 'We are all doing something. Every single person here on West India Dock Road.' Then, softly, 'Will you think about staying with us at least for the time being?'

And, sitting in that narrow house, blackout curtains drawn, dark with shadows, rife with memories and missing, dotted with photographs, each faded picture telling a story of happier times in a Germany where Jews were not persecuted like they are now, beside a woman and a man who long and ache and remonstrate with themselves just as she is doing, their hearts weighted with guilt and pain just like hers, Ruth says, 'I would love to stay here with you. You are both very kind, thank you.'

Isaac smiles and nods at Ruth.

Esther throws her arms around her. She smells of wilting roses and nostalgia, sweet ache.

A sudden, high-pitched klaxon punctures the night into a million screeching shards, startling Ruth, so she jumps a little Esther's arms.

'Ah, that's the air raid siren now,' Esther says. 'Come. I have my things ready and waiting by the door.'

Ruth helps Esther and Isaac with the bags Esther has packed to take with her – *so many? How long will this air raid last?*

Together, they hurry out onto West India Dock Road to join the surging mob swelling into the street, a busily moving mass who hail the Rosenbaums and Ruth with brisk nods.

'Ah there you are!' They smile at Ruth as if she is a long-lost friend and finally, after sharing her story with Esther and Isaac and now being welcomed so openly and easily, assimilated into this motley crowd making their way down the steps of the Tube station, Ruth feels the burden, the pain she is carrying, ease just a little.

PART III

39

CHARITY

Charity takes a bolstering breath as she stands at the gate of the sugar factory. She has walked by these gates countless times, but today will be the first time she will actually be going inside!

The cloyingly sweet scent of sugar clashes with the almighty reek wafting from the pile of disintegrating animal carcasses at the soapworks next door.

Just beyond, the shimmering ripple and swell of the Thames, barrage balloons dotting it, which at night flames orange from the deadly cargo dropped from German killer machines.

The noise is deafening. The whirring of the dock cranes competing with the hawkers yelling about their wares, and the workmen repairing the tramway down the street.

Over by the river, tons of dehydrated veggies are being packed into boxes to be sent to the troops.

'I always include a note in mine,' one of the packing girls had confided to Charity as she walked past on her way to the sugar factory, a wistful smile gracing her face. 'My 'arry is out there.' The girl clutched at the heart-shaped locket on the necklace twinkling silver-bright upon her chest, which she opened to show Charity.

It contained the miniature of an earnest-looking young man in uniform. 'I wish them luck in the note, and I send kisses too, hoping they somehow reach my 'arry,' she said, dropping a kiss upon the young man's likeness, closing the locket and resting it gently upon her heart.

Now the impressive gate is opened by an older man who nods at Charity. 'Ah, you're the new girl.'

'Yes,' she says.

'Come on then, follow me,' he says, leading her inside.

The gate shuts behind her but Charity doesn't notice. She is bowled over by the sheer size of the operation being run: the huge number of warehouses, the whirring and clanking of giant machines, bags of sugar being loaded onto lorries. Each task conducted with the utmost efficiency; everyone – a few men but mostly women in overalls – operating the machinery so very confidently and flawlessly, it appears to Charity's untrained eye. They seem to know exactly what to do and when, not a minute lost.

Will I be able to manage this? It all seems so hopelessly compli-cated and yet these amazing women, in their dungarees, their hair tied back in blue checked scarves, make it look effortless...

Charity is guided into one of the huts where a man in a boil-ersuit holding a clipboard asks for her name and references, which Mrs Porter, who operates the Mobile Canteen Service and Mr Stone, foreman at his factory back in the day, have kindly given.

He glances over them and announces, 'Ah, good, good, you will be in the syrup shed.'

The syrup shed! Charity tastes the sweetness of the words in her mouth, hugs them to her, although she is feeling over-whelmed.

'Now then, you 'ave to 'ave a medical first.'

Nerves flutter in her stomach, not least because she was too excited and a wee bit apprehensive to eat much breakfast, despite Divya's best efforts. *Hope I pass.*

Divya had given her a hug and said, beaming fondly, 'They are so lucky to have you, Miss Charity O'Kelly. Don't you forget that.'

'I second that,' Veer had said. He had paid an unexpected visit to the curry house, a detour on his way to his duties at the Home Guard, to wish her luck, his eyes glowing as he smiled at her.

'We all do,' the patrons of the curry house, which meant the entire street and then some, had asserted.

'You're so lucky, Charity, to be working with all that sugar. Try and see if you can smuggle some for us,' Paddy had said for the umpteenth time, awe and desire battling in his voice, Connor nodding along, Fergus chuckling fondly and riffling his littlest brother's hair.

'The surgery's thataway,' the man in the boilersuit nods, pointing.

There's a surgery here, *and* a bar and a recreation room! Wait till Charity tells the boys; she can picture Paddy's face falling open in wonder.

In the surgery, which Charity finds after only a couple of wrong turns (this place is *huge*), sugar girls cheerily pointing her in the right direction when she appeared a little lost, a nurse checks her heart, her blood pressure, her hair for nits and declares her good to go.

And then she is given a set of dungarees and a scarf for her hair, similar to the dungarees and checked scarves that she had seen the other women wear, which gives her another thrill, and led to the syrup shed, where the gooey, honey-coloured nectar is packaged into Lyle's Golden Syrup tins.

She stands at the entrance to the shed, watching the other women chat among themselves as they work, briskly, in tandem, not missing a beat. Some of them look up, and upon seeing her, smile and nod in welcome. And she feels her heart swell with joy.

I've arrived. My dream has finally come true. I am a sugar girl now.

40

CHARITY

The sugar girls are a motley bunch, ranging from just fourteen years old to middle-aged, and yet they are all kind and jolly, chatting above the sound of the machines, singing merrily together, Charity, after a moment or two of shyness, joining in.

'You get two ten-minute toilet breaks; make the most of them,' they advise. 'We do not go back until the very last second.'

At lunchtime, they eat their sandwiches perched on the wall outside, trying to ignore the stench of burnt timber and the reek of leather wafting on the smoggy breeze, and grumbling about the rationing and the shortages.

'Oh, what I wouldn't give for beef pie rich with dripping and lard, followed by spotted dick with plenty of currants.' Edna, who is next to Charity in the assembly line and had shown her the ropes, sighs.

'What I miss are lobster patties,' Ethel remarks wistfully.

'Liver and bacon followed by apple fritters,' Alice says, a dreamy smile on her face.

'Fruit jellies and lemon ices,' Joan, barely out of school, whispers.

'Get away with you,' Marge groans, jogging Joan's arm playfully. 'Ain't you sick of sugar given we're working with it all day?'

'Not that they let us try it, do they?' Joan frowns.

'It ain't 'arf bad 'ere, whether they let us 'ave sugar or not,' Alice pipes up. 'My siblings and me sleep four to a bed. There's eleven of us, ain't there. Bread tickets've saved us from starvation more than once. But always an 'and to mouth existence, ain't it. Ma and us lot made cigarettes from home 'til I got this job. Pa, before 'e signed up, travelled to markets looking for things to sell. 'E worked in the rag shop too, 'e and me brothers, trying to keep ahead of the relief man. Awful shame, ain't it, taking alms from the council? Me ma and pa are proud folk, but there were times when we'd no choice but to make use of the soup kitchen, much to Ma and Pa's shame. But we 'aven't 'ad to since I got this job.' She grins happily.

Charity sends a silent prayer of thanks heavenward, realising afresh how lucky she is. It had been far from easy, managing the lodging house on her own from the time she was fourteen, bringing up her siblings and looking after her parents. But they had always had enough to eat, a roof over their heads and kind neighbours and friends who looked out for them, not to mention the Ursuline nuns.

'I worked as a chambermaid.' Martha shudders, her gaze faraway. 'I'm so glad to be 'ere now, let me tell you.'

'I've 'ad a few jobs, me,' Annie, the tall, lanky girl sitting next to Alice, says, 'but this one's by far the best.'

'Where 'ave you worked, then?' Marge asks.

'When I left school, I was earning eight shillings a week sweeping up in the timber factory,' Annie says. 'Da was a timber merchant and got me the job. It was either that or working for the lady butcher next door.' Annie shivers.

'A lady butcher, you say?' Marge asks, nose scrunching.

Annie nods. 'She's a creepy old bird, is our Enid, with 'er men's cap, the shawl around 'er shoulders with bits of gristle, blood on 'er apron and toothy grin, wielding 'er cleaver like nobody's business, threatening any man who walks in that she'll cut off 'is you-know-what if they give 'er chat.'

Charity smiles, wondering what Paddy would make of Enid, given how scared he is of Mrs Neville, who he is convinced is a witch.

'After working at the timber factory, I was a machinist for a Jewish firm. Then I was in the old weavers' 'ome a spell. Then the 'at-making factory before I came 'ere.'

'You've been around,' the others exclaim.

'I 'ave an' all,' Annie says proudly.

'I would collect orders from wholesalers. I was always running up and down, this way and that,' Joan says.

'Give over!' Marge cries. 'You're only fourteen and this ain't your first job?'

'I've been earning since I was thirteen,' Joan says proudly. 'There's nine of us, so every shilling 'elps.'

'I bet it does,' Marge says.

'My younger brothers 'awk the afternoon and city editions of the evening papers after school, they do,' Joan says. 'My da's laid up, you see.'

'Tell me 'bout it. My da's chest wheezes something terrible. The landlord does nothing about the damp in our slum no matter 'ow much we complain,' Ethel grumbles.

'I'm sorry, gel,' Marge says. 'Thank goodness for the sugar factory, eh? It's not like the other factories where women suffer in sweaty labour and bear the brunt of suffering at home too. Here, at least they pay us well enough and look out for us too. Do you know, Mary from the Hesser floor...'

Marge pauses, seeing Charity's puzzled expression and reading the question she is hesitant to ask.

'That's where they pack the sugar,' she explains kindly. 'You'll learn soon enough. Anyway, Mary had a breakdown and they sent her to the coast to recover, all expenses paid!' Her voice is bright with wonder. 'And look it, I was only ever a heartbeat from destitution until I started working here. I'd not a ha'penny to rub together. It was plenty hard going at times, mind you. Me ma thanked the Lord when I got this job. "Landed on yer feet," she told me, and that's true, that is. She's not to be crossed, me ma, but she speaks sense, she does.'

'That she does,' Peggy, who lives in the same tenement block as Marge and her ma, agrees.

Although she's only been here for half a day, given how talkative the sugar girls are, Charity has learned that Peggy's home had been bombed in the Great War. She was the only survivor, pulled out of the wreckage, barely alive, an orphan at ten. Afterwards, as she had nobody to take her in, she went to the home for waifs and strays in Shoreditch.

'I'd peer in through the Nottingham lace curtains, at families sitting down to dinner in the light of lamps, and wish myself inside,' Peggy tells Charity matter-of-factly. Then, smiling, 'But it all worked out and 'ere I am, with all of you sugar girls for family.'

'We are family an' all,' Ethel says, throwing her arm around Peggy.

Marge smiles fondly at Peggy. 'Not one to moan and always looking for the silver lining, is our Peggy.'

'That's all of us women. We are the beating heart of the East End,' Peggy declares.

'You can say that again,' Helen says, nodding at Peggy. 'My ma and her ilk, in their crossover aprons and button-down boots, rule the cobbles, helping birth babies and lay out the dead. Our narrow East End streets might be brutal but they are also full of community and camaraderie.'

'Hear, hear,' the others cheer.

'My ma lived her life by these rules, which she passed on to me,' Peggy says. 'Never wear slacks if you can help it. No risqué red lips either, she warned. Also, she advised me to put away a little every day, even a shilling would do, for a rainy-day fund. You never know when it will come in useful, she said.'

'I don't agree with not wearing slacks,' says Lizzie, a tomboy, who likes to play footie at breaktime with the few men who work at the factory.

'And I don't agree with the no-red-lips rule.' Joan pouts, showing off her bright-red lips.

'My sister doesn't either,' Ethel says. 'She's getting married soon. We've all been paying into a wedding club every month.'

'Ah, good to 'ear!' They all cheer.

'You don't need a club an' all,' says Big Mary (called thus to distinguish from the other Mary, Charity is told by a helpful Marge). 'All you need to give as gifts at a wedding are salt, so the 'appy couple always 'ave good, well-seasoned food, soap, so they're always clean, and coal, so they're always warm.'

'Did you know it's good luck at a wedding to have a chimneysweep turn up at the church?' Edna says. 'And make sure to tell your sister to have horse hair stitched into her wedding gown, will you?'

'Why?' Ethel scrunches her nose.

'It's supposed to give a marriage strength,' Edna says wisely. 'And I'm sure your ma knows this but in case she doesn't, it is tradition for the mother of the bride to sew the last hem on the wedding dress, thus leaving their mark on the most important dress in their daughter's life. East End mothers are held in high esteem.'

'You know a lot about weddings, our Edna, given you're not married,' Marge says archly.

'My ma used to work for a wedding seamstress, didn't she?' Edna says.

'When are you getting married then?' Marge asks, winking at Ethel.

'Not for a while. I'll 'ave to give up working here, don't I, when I marry? In any case, my 'arry is at war, ain't 'e?'

'Make sure to sleep with a slice of wedding cake under your pillow, won't you?' Edna says.

'And why would I do that instead of eating it?'

'So you dream of your future 'usband, silly bint.'

'That's dangerous, that is,' Marge muses.

'Why's that then?' Edna queries.

'What if Ethel dreams of someone other than her 'arry?'

And everyone giggles as they stand and pat themselves down to go back to work as their lunch break has come to an end.

It is wonderful, the shared laughter and gossip as the women link arms with Charity, so readily and heartily welcomed into their fold, as they tell her stories about their experiences and introduce her to the girls from other floors.

From the time she was a little girl, Charity had wanted to join this sodality of sugar girls. And now, she finally is one. The work is hard and she is tired by the end of the day, ready for home. But it is a good tiredness; it does not weigh her down. She does not have to worry about the accounts adding up and whether they can make it through another month without folding as she had when she was running the boarding and lodging house. Being a sugar girl is just as rewarding as she had hoped it would be.

Once she has completed her first ever shift at the sugar factory, Charity goes to Mrs Kerridge's basement to check on Mammy.

'I'm fine,' Mammy says, smiling lovingly at Charity. And she continues, pausing between each word to collect her breath, 'I've had a very good day. All the ladies of the street popped in to see me, one after the other. Divya brought me my meals and in between, I've been inundated with all manner of snacks. I have heard more gossip than I know what to do with.'

Charity is reassured. Mammy is looking better than she has in ages. The ladies are good for her.

'They are worried for Jack Devine. It seems he has not written in a while,' Mammy says.

'Yes, we're all concerned for him,' Charity says.

'I am praying for him,' Mammy says. Then, 'You don't have to worry about me, my love.' And, gently cupping her face, 'You look like you have had a good day too.'

'I did, Mammy,' Charity says, beaming, thinking of how the girls had welcomed her, showing her how to fill the tins, promising her, when she faltered, that she would get the hang of it soon enough.

And she had.

After checking with her own eyes that Mammy is all right, Charity comes straight to the curry house.

'How was it?' Mrs Kerridge, spokesperson for the street, asks, even before the door to the curry house has fully shut behind Charity.

The whole street is here, looking brightly at Charity, waiting to hear about her day, except for Veer and Fergus, who are yet to arrive.

Connor and Paddy come running to Charity, flinging themselves at her, even Connor, who thinks he's too old for hugs now.

'You smell like taffy, so delicious, I could eat you,' Paddy says and Charity laughs. 'You didn't manage to steal some sugar for me, did you?' Paddy asks, looking up at her, eyes wide and hopeful.

'No, my love, sadly, we're not allowed to,' Charity says.

Paddy's face falls briefly before he once again breathes deeply of her.

She has changed out of her uniform of dungarees and scarf before coming to the curry house – the dungarees are a little loose and she will bring out her sewing kit tonight when waiting out the air raid with Mammy in Mrs Kerridge's basement and work on them – but the honey-gold aroma must still be clinging to her person.

Divya comes up and ruffles Paddy's hair. 'How about trying some of my oat biscuits, Paddy? Or carrot cake, perhaps?'

'It's very good, Paddy,' Mrs Boon says through a mouthful of cake. 'You can't hardly tell there's no sugar.' And to Divya, 'I don't know how you do it.'

Once her brothers release her from their embrace and go back to watching Mr Stone and Mr Brown's chess game, Charity looks about the curry house.

Miss Ravinder, who had arrived so dramatically at the curry house yesterday with a letter for Mrs Rosenbaum from her sister, is here, sitting beside Mrs Rosenbaum. The painful shadows under the girl's eyes are still as stark as ever, but both she and Mrs Rosenbaum look lighter somehow. In fact, Charity thinks that Mrs Rosenbaum, for one, is looking younger, the worry lines crowding her face and dragging her lips and eyes down not so evident.

When, periodically, the IRA bombed parts of London and relations between the Irish immigrants and the English became strained, Charity had felt worried and upset, especially when there were repercussions – name-calling and the odd bit of bullying and fisticuffs – for the boys at school. But in a day or two, it had largely blown over and the East Enders for the most part were a kind and warm bunch and neither Charity nor her brothers had ever felt targeted or in danger.

Recently, when out and about with Veer, Charity has experienced hatred, venomous slurs flung at them, but even so, she cannot begin to imagine how it must feel to have your people persecuted, your loved ones *killed*, just for being of a particular race.

Even Mr Rosenbaum, quiet and nearly always impassive in expression (except when he thinks Mr Brown or Mr Stone makes a silly chess move), is looking lighter. He appears more animated, smiling often at his wife and Miss Ravinder.

'Miss Ravinder, what a difference you have made in just one day!' Charity heard Mr Stone exclaim as she was entering the curry house, before all attention turned to her. 'Thanks to you, Mr Rosenbaum is not interrupting our game and is refraining from his tuts and sighs about how much better he could play, without actually playing, of course.'

Miss Ravinder had smiled and Charity noticed that when she did, her entire face lit up from within so she looked luminous, even more beautiful than she was.

'I hope you are planning to stay,' Mr Brown said. 'You have changed our friends.'

It was Mrs Rosenbaum, usually so quiet, happy to fade into

the background, who said, squeezing Miss Ravinder's hand, 'Yes, she is staying with us and we are grateful.'

'Hooray!' the curry house cheered and Miss Ravinder blushed and that was when Charity entered and the focus shifted to her (Miss Ravinder appearing relieved), with Charity's brothers running up to her and throwing their arms around her and Mrs Kerridge asking the question that was on everyone's lips:

'How was work then, our Charity?'

'I love it,' she says and the curry house cheers again. 'Thank you for looking after Mammy for me. She said she was spoilt by all of you,' Charity says, making eye contact with each of them.

'Ach, it was our pleasure, gel, to have a chinwag with Moira. It was just like old times,' Mrs Neville says and the others enthusiastically agree.

'I'm lucky to have you all,' Charity says and they beam as one, even as they protest that it was nothing.

Divya arrives bearing a plate of oat biscuits, carrot cake and spiced apple drops. 'I'll be back with the tea. Sit down, Charity, tuck in,' she beams.

Charity takes her friend's hand. 'Thank you for taking Mammy's meals to her today, in between your busy schedule here.'

Like the others, Divya waves her thanks away. 'I enjoyed sitting with her. She is lovely, your mammy.'

Today, Divya appears even more worn out, Charity thinks, feeling the niggle of worry about her friend balloon into full-blown anxiety. Something is definitely not right with Divya and Charity is determined to find out what it is. She has ignored the warning voice in her head long enough; there have always been more pressing demands on her time. No more. Divya has been such a good friend to her and to her family, and Charity will do right by her.

'Divya, do you have a minute?' Charity asks, deciding that now is a very good time to find out what is bothering her friend, for Veer is not here yet. Once he arrives, Charity will eat supper with him and they will walk to the end of the road together before parting ways. 'I'd like a chat,' Charity says as Divya places a steaming cup of tea in front of her.

'Eat first,' Divya says. 'You must be starving. Then we'll talk.'

41

CHARITY

Charity finishes her tea at record speed, even as she answers everyone's questions.

Once she is done, she tells Divya, 'I will give you a hand with supper.'

'Charity.' Divya smiles. 'I have supper prepared already. I only have to make the rice, which I can do while you are giving me company.'

In the curry house's kitchen, once the rice is bubbling away, Charity places her hands on her friend's shoulders, and turns her round to face her.

'Now then. What is it that you are not telling me?'

Divya takes a breath and her eyes sparkle with tears.

They cause Charity's heart to flip with anxiety on behalf of her friend, somehow knowing that they are not wholly to do with Raghu's death. Charity understands that Divya will always miss him, grieve for him, but she knows instinctively that this is something else, something more.

'What's wrong?' she asks, her heart pounding with concern.

'I don't want to worry you, Charity; you have just started a new job. And you have your brothers and your mammy and—'

'Listen,' Charity interrupts, her hands on Divya's shoulders, looking into her eyes. 'You are my best friend. I care for you. I've noticed for a while now that something is not right. I should have done this earlier. I am sorry.'

'No, you had enough on your plate. I didn't want to bother you.'

Charity sucks her teeth. 'Now you're making me angry. You're my friend. Nothing you tell me is a bother. I *want* to know what's worrying you.'

In response, Divya takes Charity's hand and places it upon her stomach.

It is hard, rounded and is that...?

Does she feel...?

Could it be...?

Charity looks up, meets Divya's gaze, awe and amazement coursing through her.

This is why Divya appears exhausted and yet jubilant, haggard and wasting away and yet rounded at the same time.

'Divya...?'

'Yes.' Divya smiles through her tears. 'I'm pregnant.'

42

CHARITY

'Oh, Divya, a miracle!' Charity is ecstatic on behalf of her friend.

'Yes,' Divya breathes. 'A miracle. Something of Raghu's.'

Under Charity's hand, which is still on Divya's stomach – which is harbouring a child! – Divya's babby obligingly flutters.

'I felt it move just now! Your babe!'

Tears of wonder fill her eyes, mirroring those shining in Divya's.

'It never gets old, no matter how many times I experience it,' Divya says, smiling wetly.

'Hello there, little one,' Charity coos. 'Your Auntie Charity says hello.' Then, looking up at Divya, 'Why didn't you tell me?'

'I... You had so much going on with the lodging house being bombed, your da's death and your mammy weaker than ever...'

'But you are my friend,' Charity says softly, taking Divya's hands in both of hers.

'Yes. I... I'm still coming to terms with it...' Divya takes a breath, her voice soft. Tears bejewelling her eyes, adorning her lashes with sparkly diamonds.

Charity holds her, still in awe from the magic of Divya's

babby – Divya's babby! – dancing beneath her touch. Responding to it.

'I love this child and I will protect it with my life,' Divya says. 'But, Charity...' And now Divya's eyes are huge and worried as they gaze at her friend. 'What am I to do?'

Charity sits Divya down in the chair in the kitchen.

'Mrs Smith is judged harshly for having a baby that is not her husband's.' Divya takes a shuddering breath. 'And me... I...'

Charity squeezes Divya's hands as she considers what to say, how to console her friend.

The truth is, she is angry with herself. She has been too absorbed in her life, her grief and upset and now, after having made up with Veer and started work as a sugar girl, with her happiness, to see what her friend was going through.

A part of her knew something was going on with Divya and she meant to ask, but there was always something else pressing...

And now too, when her friend is looking to her for advice, she is busy berating herself.

Get a grip, Charity.

But what can she say to make her friend feel better? After what Charity herself has experienced when being out with Veer, she knows that Divya is right to worry, that having a babby out of wedlock is not going to be easy.

She takes a breath, composing herself. Then, 'I'm so sorry,' she says, tasting remorse, bitter blue, in her mouth, 'that you've been agonising about this all on your own when you should be celebrating your joyous miracle of a child. I feel terrible about it.'

'Charity, you've nothing to—' Divya begins.

But Charity cuts her short, pulling her into a hug.

'You will be alone no longer. From now on, I'm with you every step of the way.'

Divya smiles and it is a gift. Her face is splashed with tears, which she wipes with her apron.

'Thank you. I feel better for telling you.'

'You should have told me earlier. You shouldn't have had to worry on your own.'

Divya nods, acknowledging it. 'Now you know.'

'We will put our heads together to think of what to tell everyone,' Charity says.

'We have to do it soon,' Divya says, twisting her apron. 'You know how the matrons are; they will ferret it out sooner rather than later. If you noticed, they will too.'

'Don't worry, we will come up with something,' Charity assures her, although as to what that something might be, she is at a loss to say.

But she must sound confident enough for Divya throws her arms around Charity. 'Thank you so much.' She smells of spices and relief. Her beloved friend. 'From the first time I set foot on West India Dock Road, you have helped me, been there for me. It is a blessing,' Divya says.

'I should have—'

'You are here now. That's enough.' Divya sniffs, then, wiping her face with her apron, says, 'We'd better get out there before they miss us.' And, smiling at Charity, she continues, 'Your Veer will be here soon, wanting to hear about your day. Charity, it was your first day at work and I have—'

'No,' Charity interrupts Divya. 'Don't. I wanted to know what's going on with you and I am glad that now I do.'

There's a knock at the kitchen door.

Both Charity and Divya turn towards it, Divya whispering,

'See, they've missed us and are wondering where we got to,' to Charity before saying out loud, 'Come in.'

It is Miss Ravinder.

'Sorry for interrupting.' She is hesitant. 'Mrs Kerridge sent me to find you both.' She looks embarrassed.

'Ah, she's hard to resist at the best of times. Everyone else is wise to her ways and quick to come up with an excuse, so she picked you, I imagine,' Charity says.

'You can help take some of the food out for me.' Divya smiles.

'Thanks,' Miss Ravinder says, smiling.

She really is so beautiful when she smiles, Charity muses again.

'All of you on this street have a knack of making everyone feel instantly at home,' Miss Ravinder says.

Divya beams. 'Charity was the one who first made me welcome here.' Her gaze so fond as she looks at her friend that it sparks tears in Charity's eyes.

'Well, you and everyone in your wonderful curry house have made me feel very welcome,' Miss Ravinder says.

Divya touches her hand. 'I'm so sorry for everything you've been through,' she says simply.

'I am too,' Charity says.

They all know, for Mrs Rosenbaum had told them, with Miss Ravinder's permission, that she lost her family the night of Kristallnacht.

Miss Ravinder sniffs. 'Thank you. It means a lot.' Then, smiling at Divya, 'When is the baby due?'

Charity and Divya exchange a shocked glance. Divya's hand, which had travelled instinctively to her belly, trembles as she strokes it, the colour leaving her face.

'Oh, I'm sorry. I...' Miss Ravinder loses steam as Charity

holds her friend and sits her down on the chair. 'I'm sorry,' Miss Ravinder says again, wringing her hands, her cheeks inflamed.

'Miss Ravinder,' Charity begins.

'Please call me Ruth. Miss Ravinder sounds so formal, I keep looking around to see who is being addressed.' Then, taking a breath, she says, 'I'm so sorry. I seem to have spoken out of turn.'

'Miss Rav... I mean Ruth...' Charity begins again.

But even as she tries to formulate her next words, Divya speaks from where she is sitting on the chair, her voice soft. 'I'm sorry we've upset you just when you said we made you feel so welcome.'

'No, it is I who am sorry. It was not my place to comment,' Ruth says.

Divya waves her apology away. 'You took me by surprise, that's all. I haven't told anyone yet. I only just shared my news with Charity before you came in.'

'Ah,' Ruth says.

'How did you know?' Divya asks.

'Well, you see, for the last couple of years, since before the war started, in fact, we have been in hiding. In the rare instances when we came into contact with new people, we had to rely on body language to determine if they were really on our side or if they would give us away. I became very good at it.'

'Ah,' Charity says and Divya nods.

'I realised from the way you were holding yourself,' Ruth says to Divya, 'your hand going to your belly every so often, that you were pregnant. But I should have also read that it is a secret you're keeping, that you haven't shared it with everyone. This mistake when in hiding could easily have got me killed.'

'Yes,' Divya says.

Ruth smiles. 'I like that you are honest.'

'Ruth, could I ask that you please not tell anyone until I'm ready?' Divya says.

'It's not my news to share,' Ruth says.

'Thank you.' Divya smiles.

Ruth hesitates, then, 'I... I'm sorry to speak out of turn again but... if I guessed, someone else will too. So if you want to share the news on your terms, it must be soon.'

'Yes, that's what we were discussing just before you came in,' Divya says, looking at Charity. Then, taking a breath, caressing her stomach where her baby grows, Divya says, eyes sparkling, 'Ruth, this child is a gift. The love of my life, he died on the battlefield at the beginning of this year. I went to see him at Christmas and this babe is the miraculous result. His legacy. Something of him living on even though he is gone. But...'

She takes a breath. Another. Charity gently places a hand on her friend's shoulder, squeezing it, offering comfort.

'You weren't married,' Ruth says softly.

'Yes,' Divya says.

'It shouldn't matter. Love is what matters,' Ruth says fiercely, and Divya beams at her, her face speckled with tears.

'Thank you for saying that,' Divya says, when she can speak. 'It shouldn't matter, but it does.' She takes a breath. Then, 'You see, I love that I am part of the community here on West India Dock Road. And I will need them more than ever if I am to bring this child up on my own, in a world being torn apart by war. But... if they knew that this child was created out of wedlock, they might turn against me and boycott the curry house.'

Ruth nods, her forehead scrunched in thought. Then she says, 'Can't you say you married in secret?'

Divya and Charity share a glance.

'Now there's an idea,' Charity says.

'It's wartime,' Ruth says. 'Like you said, this child is a gift. This is why I commented on your pregnancy just now without thinking. I consider it worth celebrating: a budding life in the midst of all this death and doom. By rights, nobody should care whether you're married or not.'

'But they will,' Divya sighs. 'Most of them are staunch Catholics. Good people who follow the Bible to the letter.'

While Ruth and Divya have been speaking, Charity has been thinking hard.

'Tell them that you married Raghu when you went away at Christmas, Divya,' she says now.

'But they think I went to see an *ayah* I befriended on the ship on my way to England,' Divya cries, bunching her apron.

'Tell them you lied about that. That you went to see Raghu and he proposed and you got married, immediately, for he was going back to the battlefield and you didn't know when you might next see him.'

'Yes,' Divya says. And then, wringing her apron again, 'But I think they will see right through my lie when I tell them I am pregnant.'

'They might. But we will stand by you,' Charity says, looking at Ruth, who nods firmly.

'Yes,' Ruth says. 'I know I've only just met you but I will too, for what it's worth. It is wartime. People are dying. A child is a wondrous gift.'

Her words are bright but when she says the last sentence, a shadow crosses her face, her gaze becoming haunted.

Charity instinctively throws her arms around Ruth.

Ruth freezes in her arms for a minute before she hugs back.

Charity opens her arms and invites Divya into the embrace.

'Divya,' Charity says, when her friend is enclosed in her

arms, 'we are with you, all right? Whatever happens, we will stand by you.'

'We will,' Ruth says. 'And although I've only just met them, I think Esther and Isaac will too.'

'Thank you,' Divya says, her tears spread across her face, lending it a salty sheen.

'The street will come round, Divya, even if they do not believe you at first,' Charity says. 'They are good people, one and all.'

Divya nods, sniffs and wipes her face with her apron.

'Now, we've dallied long enough. They'll be sending in a search party any minute. Let's go,' Divya says. Then, cocking her ear, 'Ah, that's the front door.' And managing a smile for Charity, she adds, 'I think your Veer is here.'

43

DIVYA

Dear Jack,

How are you doing?

I must admit that myself and all here at West India Dock Road are more than a little worried about you.

Since you wrote to say that you were taken prisoner of war, your letters had been arriving regularly. We look forward to them as you know.

I read them out to everyone on the street.

But lately, I have sent you several letters with news from everyone and haven't heard back.

Here's hoping that you are all right and that it is just the wartime post taking its time.

We heard on Mr Stone's wireless that some mail ships have been bombed. So it might be that.

In any case, I am continuing to write to you in the hope that even if we are not receiving your letters, you are getting ours. For I know how much they mean to you – you tell us so in every letter.

Now, before I fill you in on news from the street, I wanted to assure you that we are all praying for you. The entire street, and Father O'Donnell every day at mass, and the Ursuline nuns too. So rest assured, God is looking out for you. We are all reassuring ourselves with this too.

So, I have two big items of news for you from here.

First, Charity started her new job as a sugar girl over at Tate & Lyle's today!

And she loved it. She said it was every bit as wonderful as she'd dreamed it would be.

You should have seen her – her face glowing with joy and fulfilment. She appears transformed. It is wonderful to witness. I wish you were here and fiercely believe that you will be, soon.

And now to the second piece of news.

We have a new arrival on the street. Her name is Ruth Ravinder. She is about our age and is half-Indian, half-Jewish.

She turned up at the curry house yesterday, a beautiful, golden-complexioned, caramel-haired young woman saying, hesitantly, 'I have a letter for Mrs Rosenbaum.'

Needless to say, the curry house was abuzz. All last evening and all day today, the matrons were coming over with new nuggets of information gleaned about Miss Ravinder.

'It seems she is an orphan,' Mrs Kerridge reported.

'Her mother was Esther Rosenbaum's childhood friend.' This from Mrs Neville.

'She's going to be stopping at Esther and Isaac's for now.' Mrs Boon.

Ruth joined us at the Underground station last night during the raid and Mrs Smith's girls were all over her.

She teared up when she saw Mrs Smith's little bubba. He was born in the Tube station during a raid a few weeks ago and we all helped – I wrote to you about it after, do you recall?

'He reminds me of my brother,' Ruth (she's asked us to address her by her given name) said softly and a haunted look came over her.

She lost her little brother, only eight years old, along with the rest of her family, the night of Kristallnacht.

I remember Mr Brown reading out loud from the newspaper after it happened, over at Charity's boarding and lodging house.

The curry house was not around then, although I cannot imagine a time without it. I was cooking for the lodgers in Charity's kitchen in those days. And now the lodging house is no more...

I remember Mr Brown's voice was a whisper of shock, beset by tremors, as he read out loud to all of us about the Nazis' senseless anti-Semitic violence over the course of one night, the night of the broken glass, as it came to be known. All of our faces slack with the horror of it.

What a tragedy, we'd thought.

What we didn't realise was that that was just the beginning...

Anyway, now onto other, more cheerful news from the street.

Mrs Boon came into the curry house yesterday, beaming. She had been to the pictures with her niece, who is a nurse. Joan works so very hard, she says. 'Like you girls,' she added, nodding at me and Charity. Mrs Boon thought her niece deserved a treat and took her to see Under Your Hat. *She said that it was a load of laughs and that it was wonderful to hear Joan chuckling. 'Being at the hospital like she is, there's not much in the way of joy.' Mrs Boon's eyes were sparkling. 'Afterwards, Joan hugged and thanked me, telling me how much she had needed the outing. She recounted some of what she had seen the past week and it was enough to make my eyes water and my skin tingle.'*

'What had she seen then?' Mrs Kerridge asked.

Mrs Boon sighed deeply. 'A teenage boy who had lost all his hair because he saw a woman's head blown off after she pushed him out of the way of a bomb. A woman with one eye destroyed and, if that wasn't enough, the veins and arteries of her hand exposed. A man with shards of glass sticking out of his face from a shattered window. An East End boy who grew up without shoes, joined the army and climbed up the ranks to become staff sergeant, only to be invalided out due to severe lung damage from inhaling gas. A man with club foot, polio damage to both legs and who lost part of his chest in an operation to save him when he contracted anthrax, fighting very hard but succumbing, finally, to an air raid. It seems all the doctors and nurses gathered to bid him farewell. There was not a dry eye in the place, Joan said.' Mrs Boon paused. 'And all this and more, she encountered in just one week, mind you.'

'Puts things in perspective rather,' Mrs Kerridge said, her face grim, no doubt thinking of her own boys.

In other news, we have all become a dab hand at hoarding food. Tins of pilchards, pease pudding, Carnation milk, boxes of fig rolls, arrowroot biscuits, packets of tea, tins of custard, Ovaltine, tins of National milk hermetically sealed to protect against gas attack... you name it, we've stored it.

Now, I've told you in previous letters that Mrs Murphy is becoming very confused and that we are taking turns looking in on her, making sure she remembers to eat and takes shelter during the raids. One thing she hasn't forgotten to do, and takes great joy from, is her singing. In the Tube station, Mrs Murphy's is always the loudest voice, although valiantly out of tune, so it comes across a screech, causing children to cry and those nearest her to flinch and move away a little (although this is generally not possible in the station as it is always packed and so they just have to grin and bear it).

I've just read this back and I am sorry to put a dampener on things. I didn't mean for the letter to turn quite so dark. I am going to cross out the bit about Mrs Boon's niece's encounters in the hospital.

Ah, now there's the siren. I must be off.

I will write again soon.

Meanwhile, we await your letters and hope they reach us soon.

Keep safe and well.

We are praying for you.

Love from Divya and all at West India Dock Road

44

DIVYA

2 May 1941

My dearest Raghu,

As you know, through my letters which are piling up beside my pillow, I have agonised about sharing my news about this amazing child we have created together with the world. But finally, I did it. I told everyone on the street. You must have been looking out for me, for it gave me strength. Also, having Charity and Ruth by my side helped enormously.

I told you about Ruth Ravinder turning up at the curry house in my last letter, didn't I? Well, now we are on a first-name basis – yes, that was quick. Bear with me and I'll tell you how it happened.

So, Ruth coming to the curry house asking for Mrs Rosenbaum was a turn-up for the books. I love this phrase and I use it whenever I can: turn-up for the books. The English have such wonderful phrases, don't you think? I do love the language.

As soon as she heard from the beautiful stranger that she

had a letter from her sister, Mrs Rosenbaum fainted – I don't think I told you this.

You should have seen Mr Rosenbaum's face. He was by her side in an instant. And the way he spoke her name, so tender and worried, a lifetime of love in his voice! I have never seen him so vulnerable.

You know, I always thought Mr Rosenbaum was the strong one in their relationship.

Mrs Rosenbaum is so demure, content to fade into the background, allow her husband to take the limelight.

But I had it wrong.

He needs her more than she needs him.

I think if, God forbid, something happened to him, Mrs Rosenbaum would be able to go on. But if it was the other way round, Mr Rosenbaum would not last more than a few days.

And here I am living on without you. But then I now have something of you to get me through the days.

Mr and Mrs Rosenbaum have not been blessed with children.

'The poor dears, it is their lasting sorrow,' Mrs Kerridge has said. 'Esther dotes on her nephew and niece but of course she hasn't heard from them since Hitler started his pogrom against the Jews in Germany.'

And then this girl turns up with a letter from Mrs Rosenbaum's sister. Ruth Ravinder. Half-Indian, half-Jewish. Golden skin and hair like honey. But oh, her face, the sorrow dragging her features down, mapping it with lines too old for her years. Her soulful eyes, that have seen too much, lending a solemn gravity to her beauty.

Well, since she arrived, although it's only been two days, what a transformation in Mr and Mrs Rosenbaum! Their gazes are bright with a sense of purpose.

I cannot begin to imagine how it must feel to have your people discriminated against, hurt, killed. Actually, given the racism you and I have endured, the ostracism I can under-stand. But for an entire race to be targeted – that, I cannot. Which is of course why we are at war.

And to be part of that race and having to wake up each day to more horrible news of fresh terrors Hitler is employing on your people, your loved ones among them...

I can see now how much it must have been affecting Mr and Mrs Rosenbaum.

But since Ruth arrived, they are different people and it is a joy to behold.

But... I have digressed. Another word I have learned from the dictionary little Paddy passed on to me: digress. A mouthful but beautiful.

By the way, I need to find a place to store these letters to you (there's no space on my bed any more). Corresponding with you is a habit formed after you went to war without leaving me a forwarding address and which I continue even now you're gone forever.

One day, my love, when our child is old enough, I will share these with him or her. For in these letters, I have recorded my feelings not only about you but about this wonderful miracle growing within me. A testimony of our love for each other and for our beloved babe.

Yesterday, when Charity came to the curry house after her first day at work, she walked into the kitchen and asked me right out what I was keeping from her.

I should have told her before but somehow, I couldn't find the words.

She has asked me often, 'Are you all right, Divya?'
Knowing something was the matter but unable to guess
what.

She is such a good friend, so kind and loyal. She cares
deeply for the people she loves.

But even so, I hesitated to tell her. I worried that she
would be shocked. That even though she is my best friend,
this, having a child out of wedlock, would be one step too far
for her.

In any case, yesterday, her first day as a sugar girl
notwithstanding, when she came to find me in the kitchen
and asked me what was the matter, I took her hand and put it
on my belly where our baby danced, responding to her
touch.

You should have seen her face! The joy there. The awe.

Oh, but I have never loved my friend more than I did
then.

And once again, I wished with all my heart that you had
been there to experience it too, that wonderful miracle of our
babe making their presence felt.

In any case, Charity was so supportive that it eased my
anxiety somewhat.

Perhaps I had been worrying for nothing, I thought.
Perhaps the residents of West India Dock Road, whom I have
come to think of as extended family, would also be as
accepting.

Charity and I were discussing how to break the news to
the others when Ruth knocked at the door of the kitchen.

Right away, she asked after my pregnancy. She had
guessed!

I would have thought the matrons would – you know how
eagle-eyed they are. But it was this girl our age, who has

endured so much death and destruction, her whole family killed by the Nazis, who noticed.

And you know what she said? 'There's death everywhere. A new life is a joy. A legacy to be celebrated and cherished.'

So beautiful and profound. I told her so and she smiled and it was the saddest thing I had ever seen.

Anyway, sharing my news with Charity and Ruth gave me the courage to finally come clean to everyone.

I took a deep breath and went out to face the residents of West India Dock Road, all of whom were gathered in the curry house.

The women were nattering away while waiting for their food.

Mr Rosenbaum and Mr Lee were watching the game of chess between Mr Brown and Mr Stone, while Charity's brothers were keeping score of who had won which game.

Usually, Mr Rosenbaum would be tutting and shaking his head and offering a running commentary about the many mistakes made by the chess players. 'I say, you should have taken his queen. There was an opening right there.'

To which, Mr Stone would retort, brusquely, 'I have a plan.'

'Yes, to lose,' Mr Rosenbaum would huff.

At which point, there would be the start of a war which Mr Lee would gently defuse.

But yesterday, there was none of that.

Mr Rosenbaum was quiet, keeping his counsel. Every so often, he looked across at his wife and seeing her face relaxed in a way it hadn't been before, he turned back to the game with a gentle smile upon his face.

My mouth was dry and heart somersaulting with fear as we left the kitchen, even though I was flanked by Ruth on one *side, carrying a tureen of cabbage soup, and Charity on the other, hoisting bowls of carrot and potato hotpot and lentil curry. My hands were shaking so much that I was glad I was hefting the spiced rice to go with the curry and the ginger-bread for afters – no danger of spills.*

'Here they come.' Mrs Kerridge beamed. 'Our youngsters, bearing supper.'

Everyone cheered while Veer and Fergus, who had arrived while we were in the kitchen, rushed to lend us a hand (Veer asked me to address him thus, rather than the more formal Mr Singh, when he and Charity got back together).

'Me and Connor are the youngsters,' Paddy said, hands on hips, and everyone laughed. 'I wasn't joking,' he said, face scrunched, but he glowed, his protest forgotten, when I handed him some gingerbread.

Once everyone was tucking in, I sat with the ladies, Charity beside me, squeezing my hand, Ruth next to Mrs Rosenbaum, offering support with her gaze.

I recognised the loss pulling Ruth's lips down and shad-owing her eyes, for it is what I saw in the mirror too.

Her expression was that of a much older person, weighed down and worn out by life, the burden of going on when her loved ones were snatched from her. It hurt to look at her face full-on, there was so much sorrow there.

And yet, right then, that was what gave me the courage to launch into my revelation. For Ruth had suffered so very much. And yet she had survived. And here she was, looking at me, offering encouragement.

So I took a deep breath and said, 'I have something to tell you all.'

They looked up, mid-chew, stopping eating to focus on

me. Knowing from my tone that what I was going to say was important.

'What is it, child?' Mrs Kerridge speaking for everyone.

'I…' I fiddled with my apron.

Charity put her hand on my knee and squeezed it.

Over by the men's table, Veer looked at us.

Usually, Charity sat with him and they chatted away. Today, however, she'd briefly told him about her day but then said that she needed to be with me.

'Miss Ram, you were saying?' Mrs Kerridge prompted.

'I… I haven't been honest with you all,' I said.

There was silence among the women. They were so quiet that the men craned over to look, Mr Brown and Mr Stone stopping their game.

'You haven't been honest about what?' Mrs Kerridge asked, her voice sharp.

'I… Do you remember when I shut the curry house at Christmas?'

'Oh yes.' Mrs Boon sighed with feeling. 'We missed your food, I can tell you that much.'

'I hope you're not planning to do it again, Miss Ram!' Mr Stone cried.

'You said you were going to visit a fellow ayah whom you had met on the ship to England,' Mrs Kerridge said severely.

'I always smelled a rat there,' Mrs Neville said, tapping her nose. 'Was it a man, then?'

The curry house was silent, waiting on my reply.

I felt pinned by their gazes. These people, my friends, regarding me sternly, suspiciously. My knees, my whole body was shaking. I was reminded of when I stood up for you when everyone thought you had started the fire at the pub.

I could not meet their eyes, these people whom I regarded as family.

Charity squeezed my knee again, but even her steadying hand could not stop the tremors rocking my body.

Ruth steadily met my gaze, offering strength. I thought of all she must have gone through, her family killed while she narrowly escaped, and living with guilt because of it. Hated for being a Jew, reviled for being brown.

And I thought, I can do this.

In my stomach, your babe, your legacy, jumped. Had the little one picked up on the panic that its mother was experiencing?

I opened my mouth, tasted fear, bilious yellow, even as I said, 'It was Raghu I went to see.'

'The lascar,' Mrs Kerridge said.

Was that a censorious note I heard in her voice? Almost definitely. Even so, 'Yes,' I said.

Mrs Kerridge's lips disappeared. The other ladies looked just as grim.

Mrs Neville sighed. 'I thought as much.'

My eyes shied away from the women's narrowed gazes. Instead, I looked at Ruth, who imparted courage.

'He was recuperating at the Chalmer Grange convalescent centre in Guildford. He had been wounded in the battlefield. He was about to go back and we...'

The curry house was so quiet that I could hear Paddy's breathing from across the room.

Everyone was waiting for me to continue.

I took a breath. Another.

Charity patted my knee. My friend, there for me.

I took yet another breath. Thought of those few hours I spent with you. Perfect. Not nearly enough. But they had to be. They had to last a lifetime. And they had created our child.

I thought of you, of your face as you loved me, and I lied, looking right at them, these people who had become my family, their unsmiling faces. 'He proposed to me when I went to see him. He was returning to the battlefield after Christmas. We didn't want to wait until he returned. There was a chaplain on the premises. And so…' I took another breath. Charity squeezed my knee again. There was no sound at all in the curry house. Everyone was poised, waiting for my words. My lies. '…We got married,' I said. 'There was no time for a ring or anything of the sort.'

It was Paddy who broke the silence which had stretched to breaking point. He came up to me and threw his arms around me. 'That's wonderful news, Miss Ram. Oh wait, you are Mrs now?' he asked, scrunching up his nose in that endearing way he has.

I managed to smile at him, although I could feel it waver, and said, 'Yes, I am Mrs Kumar.'

And do you know, even as I was speared by the assessing gazes of the people I loved and cared for, it was a gift. A precious, beautiful gift to take your name, own it, say it out loud.

'That is why you received the telegram when he died,' Mr Stone said.

'Yes,' I said. Did this mean they had accepted my lie?

'Why didn't you say, Miss… I mean, Mrs Kumar?' Mr Brown tutted. 'We would have been happy for you.'

'We…' The lies tumbling out of my dry mouth, bitter blue. 'We wanted to get a blessing from a Hindu priest, when he returned, before telling everyone.'

Mr Brown nodded, looking sad. 'A shame that you

couldn't get to do so. A tragedy, Mrs Kumar, to be widowed so very soon.'

'Yes,' I said.

But all the while, I was waiting for the ladies of the street to voice their opinion. And as always, they were looking to their leader, waiting to follow her lead.

Mrs Kerridge fixed me in her unflinching gaze. 'There's more, isn't there?' Her gaze sliding to my stomach.

'Yes,' I said. Knowing that she wasn't fooled. Knowing that she knew, as did the other ladies, that the only reason I was telling them about my so-called marriage was because of what I was about to reveal.

'I am with child,' I said, holding Mrs Kerridge's gaze.

I cared for the opinion of these people gathered in my curry house just as much as Charity had, because of which, she had briefly broken up with Veer. They had warned her against him because she would be condemned and looked down upon for loving a coloured man. But, despite their disapproval, when she insisted on continuing the relationship, they had accepted it, because they love her. If they hear anyone saying a word against her, they stand up to them, for Charity.

I hoped that they would do the same for me: take my words on trust, even if they had a suspicion that I might be lying about being married.

They are quick to judge, and even quicker to gossip. They are brash. But they are also fiercely loyal. They care deeply and love wholeheartedly.

I wanted them onside. But I would not be made to feel ashamed.

Again, it was Paddy, sweet, innocent Paddy who broke the silence.

'Miss... Mrs Kumar...'

Oh how wonderful it felt to be addressed by your name.

'You are going to have a babby?'

'Yes, Paddy.'

Paddy beamed from ear to ear. Then, earnestly, assured me, 'Mrs Kumar, I will look after him. And Connor will too, won't you?' Addressing his brother, who nodded, shyly. 'Fergus is too big though, I think, to be interested in babbies.'

He looked at his oldest brother, who smiled and ruffled Paddy's hair. 'You bet I am, squirt. You're not much bigger than a babby yourself.'

'Fergus!' Paddy was shocked. 'I'm ten!' And turning to me again, 'Connor and I will look after him, Mrs Kumar,' he promised gravely.

'It might be a little girl, Paddy,' I said.

'I have a feeling it is a boy,' he said, beaming. 'And I will be a good role model to him. I will teach him only good things.'

'I have no doubt at all that you will,' I said.

Paddy preened visibly at that.

In other circumstances, I would have smiled. But I was too nervous for it, my heart cramping as I looked at the ladies.

They looked back at me severely. They were waiting for Mrs Kerridge to respond and would take the lead from her.

Mrs Kerridge's mouth moved.

Please, I thought.

Then, 'You are lying, Miss Ram,' she declared, her lips set in a thin line of disapproval.

'Mrs Kerridge, it is not nice to accuse your friend of lying! And she's not Miss Ram, she's Mrs Kumar,' Paddy cried, hands on hips, indignant.

But the rest of the curry house was silent. I was speared by the women's judgemental gazes.

Well, most of them. Ruth's gaze was gentle and kind, imparting love, as indeed was Mrs Rosenbaum's. And of course, beside me, Charity was squeezing my knee.

The men all looked worried, and appeared to be holding their breath, Veer, Fergus and Connor glancing anxiously from Charity to me.

I knew Charity was worried too. I could feel it in the rigid set of her shoulders, the anxious frown furrowing her forehead.

In my stomach, our babe moved.

That gave me the courage to swallow down the bile that threatened and lie again, while looking right at Mrs Kerridge. '*I am not lying.*'

'You lied to us when you said you were going to visit your friend, an ayah from the ship, when you were really meeting the lascar. Why should we believe you now?'

I took a deep breath. My voice, when it came, wavered, even as I tried to hold Mrs Kerridge's unsmiling gaze. 'That time, I lied because I did not know if Raghu had left for the battlefield already. I did not know if he would see me. But not only was he happy to see me, he proposed to me, and we decided not to waste any time and got married then and there.'

Charity's hand was on my knee. Ruth's steady gaze was urging me on.

'Why not tell us when you got back?'

'Because I had lied already. I didn't know how to backtrack.'

Mrs Kerridge was undeterred. I agreed with Mr Barney

then: the interrogation skills of the ladies of West India Dock Road were second to none.

'Why didn't you tell us when you received the telegram?'

And now it was Charity who spoke up. 'She was grieving.'

Mrs Kerridge did not look at her, only at me. Her gaze unflinching. 'I tell you what, Miss Ram. You found out you were pregnant, the father of the child dead and you stuck, in an impossible situation. And so, you've come up with this ruse.' She sniffed and stood up, her knees creaking. 'I've lived long enough to know when someone is taking me for a ride. Do not make fools of us, Miss Ram. We cared for you, welcomed you into our fold. But you have lied and are still lying to us.'

And with that, she walked out and the rest of the matrons got up and followed, their suppers half-eaten, a waft of gritty, smog-laden air drifting inside as the door shut behind them, leaving only the men, Ruth, Mrs Rosenbaum, Charity and her brothers in the curry house.

Silent shock in their wake.

Until the boys, Charity's brothers, bless them, all three, even Fergus, came up to me and congratulated me.

'This is great news, Mrs Kumar,' Fergus said.

'Why did Mrs Kerridge say all that? Why was she mean to you?' Paddy asked.

'Doesn't matter, squirt,' Fergus said. 'We know Mrs Kumar, don't we?'

I could have hugged the boy but he is so much taller than me. In any case, he read my mind and hugged me instead, and I was so grateful for it.

I might have been judged and found guilty, ostracised by the ladies of the street, just like that time after the fire at the pub when they thought I was in cahoots with you, a felon, but now I had more people on my side.

'Is the babby in there?' Paddy asked, pointing at my stomach, his face rapt with awe.

I took his hand and placed it on my belly.

After a bit, 'Oh, oh, oh,' he glowed. 'I felt him move.'

'The baby is saying hello to you,' I said.

'That means he likes me!' Paddy beamed.

Then Connor was doing it too. Both boys alight with joy.

And although it didn't take away from the fact of the women, their gazes shrewd and disapproving, walking away, shaking their heads, it eased my upset a tad.

Charity hugged me. 'They will come round,' she whispered, her breath fiercely hot and sweet in my ear.

Veer shook my hand. 'Congratulations, Mrs Kumar.' And, his eyes shining, 'Raghu would have been over the moon. Shame that he's not here to celebrate with you.'

'Yes,' I said, blinking away the hot tears that stabbed at my eyes.

Veer pulled a handkerchief out of his pocket and blew his nose. Then, 'I believe he is watching over you and his little one,' he said.

I smiled, overcome. 'That is exactly what I believe too,' I said.

For I know you are, my love. I know you are.

Ruth and Mrs Rosenbaum hugged me too.

'A child is a blessing,' Mrs Rosenbaum said. 'And they will see it sooner or later.'

'If nothing else, they will miss your food,' Mr Stone said.

I think that all the adults remaining in the curry house, while they perhaps did not quite believe that I had married

Raghu, loved me enough to accept my lie, go with it. And I was grateful to them for it.

And I have decided that that is enough for now.

'Thank you,' I said, tears in my eyes.

'In this time of war, a child, a new life on this street, is a gift.' Mr Brown smiled.

'I make toy for bubba,' Mr Lee promised.

As she was leaving, Charity embraced me again, repeating, firmly, 'They will come round. They care for you. They do.'

I hope so. But even if not, I will soldier on.

In any case, pariah or not, it is a load off my mind. I did not realise just how worried I was, how much the approval of the street mattered to me. I was pleased beyond my wildest dreams to be carrying your child and yet I was anxious about sharing it with the world.

But it's done now.

I will get through this, we will, our babe and I. We have people who care for us, and that is a blessing. A gift, like this child, that I do not take lightly.

All our love my dearest,

Yours always,

Divya and babe

45

CHARITY

Charity's brothers linger on in the curry house, peppering Divya with questions about the babby, while Charity walks with Veer to the end of the street where they will part ways.

But even her love's gentle presence cannot calm Charity.

He smiles softly at her. 'I know you are angry.'

'Incensed,' she says.

He holds her and whispers in her ear, 'I'm glad it's not at me.'

'Are you afraid of me now then?' she asks archly.

He pretends to consider it. 'Well, perhaps a little. Although I must say, you are very beautiful when you are angry.'

Despite herself, she smiles. 'Only then?'

'Always, but even more so when you are angry.'

She smiles again.

'And your beauty is multiplied ten times when you smile when you are angry.'

She laughs. 'Only you can make me laugh when I am boiling inside,' she says.

He looks at her, warmth and love and admiration and adoration in his molten-caramel gaze and says, simply, 'I'm glad.'

She relaxes in his arms, breathing him in, her love.

After a bit, he says, 'I'm so happy for Divya.'

'So am I,' Charity says.

'It's one good thing to come from all this devastation, the loss of life.'

'Yes, and why can't those narrow-minded women see that?' Her mouth is bitter with fury.

'They will,' Veer says, 'for you will make sure of it.' The radiance of his tender gaze envelops her. 'I am so proud, so lucky, so incredibly blessed that somehow, by some miracle, you, amazing, formidable, loyal, wonderful woman, are mine.'

When she goes back into the curry house, her brothers are seated by Divya, Paddy promising earnestly, 'And Connor and I will make sure that he is fine in the Tube station. If he cries, we will console him.'

'Come on, boys, time to go home,' Charity says. 'Divya needs her rest.'

'Of course.' Paddy nods solemnly, standing up with his brothers.

Then, bending down, he speaks directly to Divya's stomach. 'Bye, Babby Kumar. We will see you tomorrow. Sleep well.'

Divya gathers Paddy in her arms, dropping a kiss upon his hair. Above his head, her gaze meets Charity's, her eyes bright. She looks different already, lighter somehow, as if the very act of sharing her secret has released her.

'Goodnight, Charity,' she whispers. 'Thank you for today. I couldn't have done it without you. And your brothers, they do me a world of good.'

Charity is so proud of her brothers for being so wholeheartedly accepting of and wonderful to Divya.

She is impressed with Fergus for what he did, hugging Divya, telling his brothers, confused by the matrons' reaction, 'We know Mrs Kumar, don't we?' The fondness and conviction in his voice, even though, unlike his brothers, he understands exactly what has happened.

As they leave the curry house, Connor and Paddy skipping on ahead, she says to Fergus, 'You and your brothers were great in there with Divya.'

He looks her in the eye. 'She loved him; that's what matters.'

'Yes,' Charity replies, touched, tears stabbing her eyes. 'When did you get so wise?'

He grins. 'I've always been wise. Wiser than you, in any case. You let Veer slip away, didn't you? We had to talk you into getting him back.'

'Ah, that...'

'When are you getting married?'

She blushes. Fergus chuckles.

Paddy is chattering away excitedly about his plans for the babby as they walk back to Mrs Kerridge's in the gathering twilight and how he will be a good role model and what he will teach him while Connor flits between them, trying to listen to both conversations.

'Mrs Kerridge and the others weren't kind to Mrs Kumar,' Connor says suddenly.

Connor rarely speaks if he can help it; he only does so when there is something that needs to be said. Charity's heart, once again, balloons with pride.

'No, they weren't,' she says, patting Connor's head.

'You're going to give them what's what, I hope, Charity,' Fergus says.

'I definitely am.' Charity bunches her palms into fists.

'That's our girl.' Fergus beams appreciatively and Charity smiles.

Her brothers have turned out all right, and she is grateful for it and also happy that they know right from wrong, that they see people and not propriety, that they are, above all, kind.

Dusk is falling and the street is dark, with blackout imposed. Very soon, the sirens will sound as they have done without fail these past few months and a rush to the Underground station will ensue. Broken nights are what they are all used to.

Charity will bed with her mammy in Mrs Kerridge's basement, the two of them praying together.

In the morning, Charity will head to work, which she already loves, despite the long hours she's worked today. The camaraderie, the easy banter of the sugar girls, the joy of being part of the factory workforce. Of doing something useful, keeping Britain in sugar during the war.

The factory has been battered by the bombing, but it is still going, like all of them.

As Charity and her brothers approach Mrs Kerridge's house, they see the clique of women gathered on the stoop. Mrs Kerridge chatting with Mrs Neville, Mrs Boon and the posse of matrons who walked out of the curry house after Divya shared her news.

They hear Mrs Kerridge declare, loudly, 'If she is married, I will eat my hat.'

'But you are not wearing one.' Paddy is perplexed.

'Go on, boys, indoors with you. Try and get some sleep before you've to go to the shelter,' Charity says.

'But...' Paddy protests.

Fergus takes charge, herding his brothers inside.

As he brushes past Charity, he whispers in her ear, 'Give the ladies a piece of your mind.'

Once she hears the clatter of the boys' footsteps receding, Charity turns to the huddle of women.

In the darkness, their eyes gleam bright as beacons, their faces set in identical glowers.

'What does it matter if Divya was married or not? She loved Raghu. He died giving his life for the war effort. She has a child to remember him by. Isn't that lovely?' Charity says, trying to keep her voice even, although she is fuming.

'So I was right. They did not marry,' Mrs Kerridge says. 'That's shocking, that is. I did not expect it of Miss Ram. "Mrs Kumar" indeed.'

'This is how she has always been where that lascar is concerned. Didn't she stand up for him, turning against all of us when the public house was on fire?' Mrs Neville says, tutting.

'She was right in doing so. Raghu wasn't responsible,' Charity says. 'And you are all missing the point. Like I said, what does it matter? This is something wonderful for Divya, whom we love and who has fed us all through the war. We should be happy for her, celebrating with her.'

Mrs Kerridge tuts too now. 'Listen here, Charity, love, I warned you about these people, didn't I?' she says. 'They are different. They don't follow rules and they—'

'You don't mean that. Divya is human, just like the rest of us. Every one of us would do what she did in the same circumstances. Her love was nearby, he was going off to war again, she went to see him. Wouldn't you? I don't see how colour comes into it.' Charity takes a breath, tasting ire, bright red, in her mouth. 'This is Divya, who has fed all of us the past few years,' she says again. 'She has told us she was married to Mr Kumar, that she is having a child by him and it is our duty as her friends to believe her, to trust her, to be with her now that she is bringing a child into the world without the man she loves, who died giving his life for this country. She has cared for every one of us, looked out for us when we were down. She brought care packages to Mrs Porter when she was in hospital. She is on the rota to help with Mrs Murphy and with my own mammy. She is loyal, she would do anything for us and if one of us were in her situation, she would be there for us without judgement. I know this for a fact and you know it too. And now, just when she needs us the most, you all abandon her because of some silly principles. Who cares about them, especially when we are at war?'

'Just because we are at war, that does not mean we abandon propriety and do what we like. It is a slippery slope to lawlessness.' Mrs Kerridge sniffs.

'What law has Divya broken? She has loved. She is having a child...'

'Out of wedlock, whatever she might say.' Mrs Kerridge huffs. 'She lied to us.'

'She has cared for us, fed us, looked after us,' Charity reiterates firmly. 'All she is asking is for support as she brings a child into this war-sundered world.' She looks at each woman in turn. 'I thought you were better than this. In any case, I am tired. I am going to the basement to be with Mammy. Goodnight.'

She turns on her heel and walks indoors, but not before she hears Mrs Kerridge tut again and say, 'That coloured man she's seeing has turned her head.'

Charity is fuming as she heads to the basement, and so she does not realise that Paddy and Connor are waiting for her until she bumps into them.

'What are you both doing here?' She tries to keep her voice light.

'We heard what they said. And what you said. They are saying Miss Ram, I mean Mrs Kumar lied, aren't they?' Paddy says. Both boys' bright eyes, innocent and wide-gazed, look to her for answers.

From the top of the stairs, Fergus peers down, his hair, always just that little bit too long, falling over the banister. He smirks at her while raising an eyebrow as if to say, *How are you going to answer that?*

'Look, boys, Mrs Kumar has always been good to you, hasn't she?'

'Yes. But... she did not marry Mr Kumar?' Paddy asks. 'That's what Mrs Kerridge and the others say she lied about, isn't it?' His voice soft with the worry that furrows both his and Connor's faces.

'If Divya says she married Mr Kumar, I believe her. And in any case, it is none of our business. Mr Kumar is dead. She was and will always be upset about it. She misses him immensely but now she is having his babby. That is something to celebrate, is it not?'

'Yes,' Paddy says solemnly, Connor nodding along.

'And I hope you will, like you promised Mrs Kumar, be good role models for the babby.'

'The best,' Paddy says gravely. 'And we will help her with him too.'

'I would expect nothing less. Now, will you come to see Mammy with me?'

Paddy and Connor nod, while Fergus clatters down the stairs, winking at Charity and giving her a discreet thumbs up.

46

DIVYA

My dearest Raghu,

I went to church today.

I often visit, for I find peace there. And somehow, I also feel closer to you over there.

I visit early on those mornings when I am not on the rota for the Women's Voluntary Service, after the all-clear at the Tube station, and before I have to go back to the curry house and make a start on breakfast, before the church rouses in prayer and devotional hymns are sung at morning mass.

The church is always open.

'It has already been bombed, what else is there to take? People can come and find solace anytime they need it,' Father O'Donnell says.

I come to church just as dawn tints the horizon creamy grey. The air is rife with smoke and fiery debris, urgent with the keening of fire engines tending to the newly homeless and dispossessed. The sanctuary of the church, the peace I find there, has been even more of a godsend since I shared the news about our baby and the women of the street stopped coming to the curry house.

For I worry, Raghu, about what I am doing, bringing a child into this tearing-apart world of violence and fury and enemy fire and disapproving friends. Are they still my friends if they don't believe me, turn away when they have no choice but to encounter me, edge as far away as possible from me in the cramped confines of the Tube station, where we are all sheltering from the bombs above?

Yes, I consider them so, even if they want nothing to do with me.

I agonise over whether I can keep this child safe when people are dying every minute, when nothing is certain or assured, not the roof over your head, which can be blown off any second, nor the ground under your feet, which can erupt, a crater opening up and swallowing you whole, like it did the trolley bus full of people over in Balham. I am sometimes so terrified of the responsibility I bear that I struggle to breathe. I have to keep myself safe until I give birth to this child and then keep both of us safe. Can I?

The world might be at war, but that doesn't stop the hatred, the prejudice. Many people will only see the child's colour and judge him or her for it.

What am I doing? I think, panic clasping my heart in a vice.

And that is why I come to church. Here, I can breathe, even when my worries tend to overwhelm me. I snatch a few moments of communion with you. I think of you, imagine you watching over us, myself and our babe. I stroke the bump and our babe responds to my touch. I wonder if this child will have your features. Your nature. And I find the courage that has briefly gone into hiding. I sit on a pew in the bombed-out church, the smoggy, grey awning of sky patching the holes in the ceiling, scribbles of birds here and there, my feet resting upon the graves of the long dead.

I look up at Jesus on his cross, his face wrought with pain, obscured by the blood dripping from the crown of thorns piercing his head and yet, his eyes, while haunted, also loving. Accepting. Kind.

Despite everything that's going on outside, here, with the gentle light of dawn straining through the stained glass windows, those still intact, that is, and dancing patterns on the tiles beneath which are buried the older patrons of this church, ones from previous centuries, casualties of ancient wars, there is a gravity, a sombre peace. The faint scent of incense lingers alongside the smoke and the dust. I can almost see the prayers of the devout who have been here making their way to the heavens, like the winged birds whose shadows cast aspersions on the dust-harangued, muddy blue of the morning sky.

The other day, the Ursuline nuns found me in church. They were visiting before dropping in on Charity and her mammy and brothers, to wish Charity all the very best for her new job.

'It's you,' they said, beaming at me and in their kind faces, I saw the angels who had rescued me when I fainted in front of their convent after having been let go by the Ellises who had brought me to England as a nanny. The nuns had given me succour and hope. They had led me to Charity and in this way, changed the course of my life, for I had found my home, my community and my livelihood on West India Dock Road.

They knelt down beside me and we prayed together.

Afterwards, they asked, 'How are you, child?'

And perhaps it was the fact that they were nuns, or perhaps it was because they had taken me in when I was at my lowest and saved me, that I told them the truth. I just couldn't lie to them about being married to Raghu.

They should have by rights been shocked. In their faith, it is considered a sin, I know, to be pregnant outside of wedlock.

But they smiled, beaming benediction and joy.

'A gift from God. What a wonder,' they said.

And it brought tears to my eyes.

'I... I am scared,' I whispered.

'You have nothing to be afraid of,' they reassured. 'God will show you the way. He will not fail you. He will be with you at every step. We will pray for you.'

Their assurance gave me hope that everything would work out. That I would be able to bring this baby into this world being rent apart by war and keep him or her safe.

Ah, there's the siren now. I have to go, my love,

More soon,

Yours always,

Divya and babe

47

RUTH

Ruth is in the Underground station, staying close to Esther and Isaac. She knows it's easy to become separated in the panic, the collective fear of the crush of people, the threat of violence, death: a hand slipping from a loving grasp, a brother lost forever.

She is swept along in the flow of people, this mass of humanity all sheltering from the bombs above. These people who have accepted her into their fold.

She is slowly getting used to life on West India Dock Road, her life for now. She cannot think of it as anything but temporary given her experience, knowing how life can change direction in an instant, stop in a heartbeat, more so during these uncertain times.

But for now, she is here and she is settling into the rhythm of it.

'Thank you, Eva,' she whispers when she is in the Tube station, sitting snug between Divya and Esther, playing with Mrs Smith's girls and looking after her baby while she tries to catch up on sleep.

'I don't get a minute to myself at home, thank you kindly,' Mrs Smith says, smiling with gratitude as she hands her bubba over to Ruth and Divya.

Shadows crowd her eyes: tiredness and sadness. She's recently been widowed, her husband one of the many casualties of war.

Her little boy, with his golden skin and huge, brown eyes, reminds Ruth of Elijah.

Elijah, who was born when she was twelve. Her parents had told her that they were worried that she might not take to this usurper. After all, she had been a much cosseted only child until then.

'But from the first moment you saw your little brother, you were besotted. You wanted to do everything for him,' Mama would say, smiling.

Oh how she misses them: Mama, Papa, Elijah, Opa and Oma.

But here, at West India Dock Road, with Esther and Isaac and Divya and Charity and Mrs Smith's girls and her infant boy and all the others, she feels the ache of missing ease a little.

'Thank you, Eva,' she whispers when she is in the curry house too, sitting between Charity on one side and Esther on the other, Divya plying her with delicacies she has never tasted before, and others which remind her of Mama, Elijah and her sojourn in India, each of which is a gift.

And she thinks, *I must find a way of giving back, serving this community who have made me feel so very welcome.*

Once she, Mama and Elijah had returned to Germany from India, they had felt hounded. But here, among people of all colours, each with their own trials, Divya growing a child while the father, the love of her life, lies dead in a foreign battlefield, Charity, who endures abuse from outside the community for loving a man of a different skin colour, Ruth is beginning to feel at home.

Ruth was coming out of the curry house the other evening, running across to the Rosenbaums' house – hers too, now – for a shawl as Esther was feeling the cold when she came across Charity, leaning against the wall outside, trying to regain her composure.

She looked devastated. It was obvious that she was biting back tears.

'What's the matter?' Ruth asked.

'Ah, nothing,' Charity swallowed, trying for lightness, but the angst in her eyes gave her away.

Ruth contemplated whether to take Charity at her word and pretend as if nothing was amiss.

But it did not sit well with her.

Charity was clearly upset, sniffing and trying to gather herself together before facing the others.

Ruth decided that she could not in all conscience leave Charity to deal with whatever was causing her agony on her own, not when she had *seen* her, clocked her pain.

'It doesn't appear to be nothing,' Ruth persisted. 'Look, I am very discreet. I promise this won't go any further.'

Charity nodded and managed a wet smile, but her eyes were pools of distress. 'My... We... Veer and I, we walk to the end of the street together, and then I come back to collect my brothers while he goes on to his lodgings.'

Ruth nodded encouragingly, knowing more was to come.

Charity took a shuddering breath. 'There were these men, they made fun of us, called me names, said I should be ashamed of myself for liaising with Veer.' Charity swallowed.

Ruth laid a hand on hers and squeezed gently. It was obvious she had more to say.

'It happens more often than not. I should be used to it by now. And sadly, I am, although it makes me angry every time. Today too, I was so angry that I was speechless for a minute. When I opened my mouth to retort, Veer said, "It's all right, Charity, leave it. Please don't engage." And then, he said, once again, what he's said several times before, that perhaps I should reconsider being with him. I said I would never, that I wanted only him.' Charity took another deep breath, which caught on a sob. 'He smiled, but his gaze was haunted. "I hate that you have to endure this, become used to this if we are together," he said and his voice was so very sad. "I wish it was different," he said.' Again, Charity stumbled on a sob. 'He says this every time someone heckles us, but somehow, today, it got the better of me.' She smiled at Ruth and it was bright with pain. 'He fought for our country, lost his arm and injured his leg in service of it, and this is the thanks he gets.'

'My mama and papa,' Ruth said gently when Charity had finished, 'they went through the same thing.'

Charity looked at her, silver pearls of tears ornamenting her eyelashes.

'But they loved each other very much. They created me and my brother.'

In the dark, Charity's eyes sparkled as they fixed upon Ruth's face, following her every word.

'They were so right together. That was what mattered. That is *all* that matters,' Ruth said firmly.

'Thank you,' Charity said and this time, her smile reached her eyes.

Ruth gave in to instinct and hugged Charity.

And when Charity hugged her back, it filled a small part of the aching void in her heart.

48

DIVYA

4 May 1941

Dearest Raghu,

You know I told you that the women of the street have been cool to me, no longer frequenting the curry house, turning away from me in the Tube station, since I lied about being married to you and revealed my pregnancy to them?

I had expected it. I knew they would see right through my flimsy lie.

It is like the time I was shunned from my childhood village after my parents died because everyone decided that I was the harbinger of bad luck – that I had brought about my parents' death.

But not quite like that...

For then I had no choice but to leave the village.

But here, I clung to the hope that the ladies would come round...

I'm pretty sure Charity gave them a piece of her mind, for many of them have since approached me, offering help and advice.

Mrs Boon cornered me when I was coming back from the church, looking furtively up and down the street for any sign of Mrs Kerridge, before advising me to rest often and listen to my body, and that she was there if I needed anything. I was touched beyond measure, tears prickling my eyes.

Mrs Ross gave me a potion which she said helped with her morning sickness.

When I went to visit Charity's mammy with meals and snacks for her while Charity was at work, she smiled at me and said in her gentle voice, even though each word required effort (and was appreciated all the more for it), 'How are you today? How is your babby?'

And when I told her that I was all right and the baby was doing well, she smiled and said, 'A gift from God, my dear. My children have brought me great joy. Your bubba will for you too.'

I was moved to confide in her then. 'Mrs Kerridge and some of the others are not happy. They—'

'Ah, they will come round. They are not happy with Charity's beau either but he makes her happy. If God has given you this blessing, who are we to judge?'

I came away from seeing her feeling better, calmer, more optimistic.

Charity's mammy may not be a nun but she has that same aura about her: the gift of peace and gentleness that she can impart with just a look and a kind word.

And like she assured me, the ladies of the street are coming round, slowly but surely.

Mrs Kerridge and Mrs Neville are the only ones who still turn the other way when they encounter me.

But... they are good, kind people at heart and fiercely loyal to those they care about. So I am holding out hope that, like Charity's mammy said, they too will come round. And I am feeling even more hopeful after what happened at the Underground station last night.

I sat as usual with Mrs Rosenbaum and Ruth – Charity was waiting out the air raid in Mrs Kerridge's basement with her mammy – keeping Mrs Smith's girls and her baby boy occupied so their mother could have some well-deserved rest, such as it was, in the cramped confines of the platform, with enemy aircraft raining havoc overhead.

The women of West India Dock Road pretend, when they are with Mrs Kerridge, to ignore me, although, as I said, many of them had approached me privately with offers of help.

Mrs Edwards from East India Dock Road shot me an assessing glance, her gaze travelling to and resting upon my stomach, and then she nudged Mrs Kerridge none too gently. ''Ere, is it true what I 'eard, that your Miss Ram from the curry 'ouse is pregnant out of wedlock?' All this said while she sniffed with disdain, not knowing, perhaps, that her loud whisper would carry very well indeed, especially given the other ladies had fallen silent in anticipation of the fresh gossip. Or perhaps she didn't care if I heard.

She continued to huff, in that same loud whisper, 'What else'd ye expect from these coloureds, eh? They're all the same: no morals, any of them.' No doubt she felt smug in the knowledge that Mrs Kerridge would concur.

I pretended I hadn't heard her snide remarks, jogging Mrs Smith's bubba on my lap.

It hurt what she said, though, I cannot lie. Especially that reference to my colouring.

However much I think I belong here, when someone says

something like this, thoughtlessly, I feel defeated, upset. Realising that I would always be different, my colour setting me apart. That it would always be used against me.

Would it be the same for my child?

I would protect him or her with all my might, I promised myself. If such comments were directed at my child, I would not be keeping quiet and pretending not to have heard Mrs Edwards.

I looked at Mrs Smith's sweet, innocent infant in my lap. A brown child born to a white woman, causing great scandal. Some openly insulting him. Others hesitating to touch him, inching away from him as if his beautiful, golden hue might be catching. He is a happy little babe, and for now at least, completely unaware of the difference shown to him because of his colouring.

Mrs Smith had recently received the dreaded telegram.

'It's a shame an' all but at least 'e died unaware of 'is wife's playing away, spared 'aving to accept a child that wasn't 'is,' the ladies had pronounced.

Beside me, Ruth heard Mrs Edwards' words and flinched. She was just about to say something – I saw her open her mouth to – when Mrs Kerridge said, in a tone that could freeze water, 'I don't know who told you this nonsense, Penny. Mrs Kumar is married and is expecting her first child, although sadly, her husband died fighting for this country. Whoever is spreading this malicious rumour, please tell them to stop.'

And with that, she turned away.

I was so touched, I felt tears start. I am quite emotional nowadays, perhaps because of the pregnancy. But I could have hugged Mrs Kerridge right then.

What did I tell you?

The women of West India Dock Road, whatever they might think in private, protect their own in public.

And I am one of their own. Even if they are shunning me and not coming to the curry house right now.

'Give them time,' Charity has said.

I will give them as long as they want.

For Mrs Kerridge's stout defence of me warmed my heart.

Isn't that something?

Much love, my beloved.

I miss you but you are always with me,

Divya and babe

49

RUTH

Ruth is visiting Mrs O'Kelly with Esther while Charity is at work, when the Ursuline nuns pop in.

They are good for Charity's mammy, Ruth can see, for she perks up in their presence, her entire being glowing.

The nuns pray with Charity's mammy and afterwards, they walk out into the mellow May morning together with Ruth and Esther.

The sun is shining, bringing the debris and piles of bricks where houses should be into sharp focus, making the dust haze glimmer and wink like golden treasure.

'You said, when we were in the basement, that God has a plan.' Ruth can't help challenging the nuns. 'But how does that square with all that is happening? The mayhem, bloodshed, so many lives lost...' She cannot continue, her voice breaking as she thinks of Opa, Oma, Mama, Elijah, dead in a place of worship...

The nuns do not take offence. Instead, they smile at her, saying gently, 'God has His ways. Everything He does has a purpose.'

'Forgive me, but I cannot see the purpose of man turning on man. And, please tell me this: why are some people spared while others, just as innocent and blameless, are not?'

Why was I spared while my sweet, happy brother's life was cut short so ruthlessly?

Even though she doesn't voice the last question out loud, the nuns intuit it. 'God saved you for a reason,' they say softly. 'You will understand when you find it.'

Ruth discovers a kindred soul in Mrs Devlin, who lost everyone beloved to her to the Great War. And, to make matters worse, all mementoes of her loved ones were destroyed when her home was bombed in this one.

Ruth too is in a similar situation, having lost everything: their house gone, seized by the Nazis, alongside Opa's shops, no photographs or keepsakes of her family except in her mind.

Mrs Devlin tells her, 'You find a way to go on even after everything is lost. You take one day at a time and if that is too much, then one hour at a time.'

Ruth has followed Mrs Devlin's advice to the letter.

And she has found her place on West India Dock Road with Esther and Isaac, Divya, Charity and the others.

'I'm so glad you came,' Esther says often.

'It's thanks to your sister,' Ruth replies.

'Yes, Eva was always perceptive and kind,' Esther says, her wistful gaze traipsing the annals of her and Eva's shared childhood. Then, focusing on Ruth, 'I'm so pleased you have made friends with Charity and Divya.'

'I am too,' Ruth says, smiling.

It is becoming easier to smile, her cheeks no longer hurting from the effort. The Rosenbaums and West India Dock Road have given her so much: a sense of belonging, of acceptance.

She wants to give something back.

The women of the street do their bit for the Women's Voluntary Service.

Divya serves the street by running her curry house as well as volunteering with the WVS as and when she can. Charity works at the sugar factory.

Ruth wants to do something too. But what?

The answer comes to her one morning as, alongside Esther, Isaac and the others, she heads out of the Underground station and blinks in the light, rife with plaster dust, the scent of smoke and fire.

A thick cloud of ash and dust coats everything, stinging their eyes. The Thames glimmers with an oily sheen, topped by the residual spitting of orange embers. Silver-grey barrage balloons dot the smoggy sky.

An ambulance races past, keening, driven by a woman, Ruth sees.

And she recalls her father teaching her to drive Opa's car. 'You're a natural. Like me,' Papa had declared, smiling proudly at her.

Ruth had loved the freedom of being behind the wheel.

She had driven her father and Opa to the shop every day, collecting them in the evening. 'Our own chauffeur,' Opa had beamed, 'and what an impressive one too.'

She knows then what her contribution will be for the war effort.

Later that morning, she runs her plan by Esther and Isaac.

'I have decided that while I'm here, I'd like to be an ambulance driver, and help in this way.'

Isaac nods his approval. 'That's a noble thing to do.'

Esther hugs her. 'It will be dangerous,' she says, looking worried.

'I will keep safe, as far as I can,' Ruth reassures her.

Isaac adds, 'Nowhere is safe, my dear,' smiling tenderly at his wife.

Esther nods. 'You do what you have to. We are proud of you.' She smiles even as she knots her hands anxiously.

That afternoon, Ruth goes to the St John's Ambulance office.

'Um... I'd like to sign up to drive ambulances, please,' she says to the woman at the desk, her hair pulled back into a severe bun, who peruses her from over the top of her thick glasses.

Ruth stands up very straight as she is given the onceover by this woman.

She must pass muster, for finally, the woman asks, 'You can drive?'

'Yes,' Ruth replies.

'Driving an ambulance is very different to driving a car,' the woman says.

'I will manage,' Ruth says, keeping her voice firm and confident.

'It will not be easy. Much of the driving will take place in the blackouts during the German bombing campaigns. The roads will be dark and covered in debris.'

'I understand, but I want to do it nonetheless,' Ruth says.

The woman nods and permits a minuscule lifting of her lips.

'In addition to driving the ambulance, you will also be responsible for looking after it: servicing it and the like.'

Ruth nods. 'I'm up for it.' Recalling Sunday afternoons spent with Opa and Papa and Elijah, tinkering with the car, Mama and Oma supplying them with *Krokerle*, the spiced, hazelnut cookies melt-in-the-mouth delicious, and *Knieküchlein*, the doughnuts which were her brother's favourite. He would fall upon the plate even before Mama had set it down, his face dotted with sugar and grease. The scent of engine oil and contentment.

260 of 324 RENITA D'SILVA

The woman's voice cuts through Ruth's reverie and she packs away the heartwarming yet painful memory to take out and cherish later.

'Turn up tomorrow at 8 a.m. sharp for training.' And now the woman's severe expression relaxes a tad.

'Yes, ma'am,' Ruth says.

'It's Agnes,' the woman says. 'I'll see you tomorrow...'

A pause, which Ruth fills: 'I'm Ruth.'

'I will see you here in the morning, Ruth,' Agnes says.

Ruth goes back to West India Dock Road with a spring in her step.

She is going to be an ambulance driver, working for the war effort.

Opa, Oma, Papa, Mama, Elijah, Eva, I am giving back. I am doing something useful.

Eva, thank you from the bottom of my heart.

PART IV

Charity is in the curry house; she is on a later shift at the sugar factory so she has time to have breakfast before she starts work.

The curry house is quiet in the way it has been since Divya shared her news and the ladies of the street chose to boycott her. Only Mr Stone, Mr Brown, Mr Lee and Mr Rosenbaum are here. Veer is off doing his duties for the Home Guard. Fergus is at his shipbuilding apprenticeship at the docks. Ruth is out and about in her ambulance, attending to the wounded.

Ruth's face had been glowing when she told them about signing up for the St John's ambulance service.

'That's a brave thing to do, our Ruth,' Mrs Neville had declared.

And Ruth had beamed, and blushed both at the same time, Charity guessed as much because of Mrs Neville addressing her as 'our Ruth' as from the woman's praise.

Mrs Rosenbaum is mopping her stoop and cleaning the house, after which she will make her way here.

Paddy and Connor are at school, such as it is. They are not being taught much since nearly all the teachers have left to join up and most children have been evacuated. Much of the school operates as a rest centre with a couple of small rooms reserved for the children who are still here. Classes are clubbed, which means Paddy and Connor and Mrs Smith's girls, although of different ages, are all together, much to Paddy's lasting joy, for not only is he in the same class as his older brother but he also gets to boss over Mrs Smith's girls, who are younger than him. The older children teach the younger ones, it appears.

'Such are the sacrifices in these times of war.' Paddy sighs like a little old man, having heard the phrase somewhere and decided to use it himself. 'I can't tell you what a chore it is to teach those girls.' He emits another deep sigh, heavy with suffering. 'They giggle, fidget and are *so* distracted all the time.'

The women of the street are conspicuous in their absence at the curry house.

But Charity thinks it is only a matter of time before they start frequenting it again. For one, Charity is sure they all miss Divya's food; she does not know how Divya manages to concoct delicacies despite the scarcity of ingredients.

Divya has told her that the ladies of the street have approached her individually with advice and offers of help, with the exception of Mrs Kerridge and Mrs Neville.

'I very much believe that the ladies being nice to me has something to do with you, Charity,' Divya had said, smiling at her.

'She gave them a talking to, she did,' Paddy had told Divya earnestly.

Divya had enveloped Charity in a hug, whispering in her ear, with warmth and love, 'Thank you, my friend.'

Her bump snug between them, the babe cavorting happily within, blessedly unaware of the tensions its innocent presence had caused.

Divya, face glowing and eyes shining, had told Charity about how Mrs Kerridge had defended her to Mrs Edwards from East India Dock Road.

Even so, Charity thinks it is not enough. She herself has been cool with Mrs Kerridge. She likes the woman very much; she has been there for Charity through thick and thin, a mother figure to her with her own mammy indisposed. But she is too quick to judge.

And yes, perhaps she defended Divya to a woman from another street but that does not excuse how she behaved when Divya shared her news and how she still will not talk to her.

Charity watches Divya as she flits about, making sure everyone is fed. She is glad to see her friend looking lighter, the worry lines that had dragged her face down no longer in evidence now that she's shared her news with everyone.

The constant nagging voice in Charity's head, that she was letting her friend down, has finally been silenced.

'If you need anything at all, promise me you'll ask,' Charity says, every time she sees Divya.

'I will, Charity. Thank you.' Divya smiles. 'Nearly every single person on the street has offered help, remedies and advice. Me and this bubba,' she beams, rubbing her bump, which is showing now she is no longer bothering to conceal it, 'are truly blessed.'

And Charity marvels at her friend, who always looks for the light even on the darkest of days, for the good even when the going is tough.

When Divya brings Charity her porridge and tea, Charity hugs her, saying, impulsively, 'I'm so lucky to have you, as is the entire street.'

'What's brought this on, eh?' Divya laughs.

And, unbidden, Charity thinks of Ruth comforting her when

she was in tears outside the curry house and trying to compose herself after she and Veer had encountered those racist men. It was so short and precious, Charity and Veer's time together and it had been ruined by their slurs.

Although most of the time, Charity managed to keep it together, that evening, it had all suddenly got on top of her.

She spends every night worrying about people's reactions if she and Veer were to marry, even as she prays alongside her mammy in Mrs Kerridge's basement.

Charity would very much like to marry Veer. That evening, before the men shouted their racist abuse, Charity had brought up the subject of marriage with Veer.

But he had been hesitant. 'I would love nothing more. But... Charity, I want the best for you. And when you are with me, you will not get it.'

That look in Veer's eyes, the pain there! It had lanced her heart, making it bleed.

She had countered with, 'I want you, Veer. Only you. Look at Raghu and Divya. He thought he wasn't good enough for her and they lost so much time. And now they will never have it.'

Veer had looked so very sad.

Charity had stood on tiptoes to kiss him and that was when the men had directed their horrid, racist curses and insults at them.

Ruth had been so very kind to her that evening outside the curry house when Charity had struggled to keep it together. And hearing Ruth share that her parents too had suffered similar trials and yet, that they had soldiered through, creating Ruth, a wonderful, amazing woman, a testament to their love for each other, and her brother, gave Charity hope.

Now Charity thinks, *I will count my blessings. Like Divya, I will look for the silver lining. I have a roof over my head. The people of the street who are family. A gentle mother, who even though she is in pain and frailer than ever, does not complain. Three wonderful brothers who are sheer joy. A man I love and who loves me. A job I adore. Good friends who will do anything for me, both here on the street and at work too.*

For she is now part and parcel of the tight knit community of sugar girls.

Tate & Lyle are good employers, who look after their workers.

When Charity started at the syrup shed, Marge had eagerly asked, 'Are you any good at running? The girls on the Hesser floor win all the prizes on Sports Day, although we beat them at the beauty pageant. Hmmm... you're pretty enough. You'll do nicely.' And, linking arms with hers, Marge had declared decisively, 'You will enjoy our social outings to the seaside. They are a heap of fun. The management put on a bus to ferry us there and back an' all.'

The girls are a jolly lot, singing as they work at full volume, whether they can carry a tune or not. They laugh and natter good-naturedly and when Charity dons her dungarees and her scarf and gets to work, she feels part of the sisterhood that she'd once looked up to and she loves every minute of it.

Sometimes, especially on payday when they're feeling flush, they eat lunch at the pie and mash shop opposite the factory; it's not as good as Divya's food of course but with the other girls chatting away, it's wonderful all the same.

The work is hard but Charity was prepared for it. She doesn't have the responsibility of running the lodging house, the constant worry of whether it is bringing in enough to keep going for another month at least. She is just part of the workforce. Does her job, collects her wages and that's that.

Most days, when she goes into work, there is some sort of drama.

'Charity, there you are, did you hear about the fight between Penny and Janice?' Marge said the moment she entered the syrup shed yesterday.

'No, what—?'

She did not get to finish her sentence, Marge interrupting her with, 'They were at it, pulling clumps of each other's hair, kicking, biting, the works, all this over a boy. Both of them have been suspended.'

The other morning, the syrup shed was buzzing, the girls wide-eyed as they gossiped in thrilled whispers.

'A priest came to bless the sugar and made away with some in his cassock!' Aggie, who relayed this titbit, was known to bend the truth, so Charity wasn't quite sure whether to believe her.

When Skinny Tom (called thus to distinguish him from the other Tom, who had joined before him and so didn't have a qualifier) didn't turn up to work two days in a row, the rumour doing the rounds was that he had been sacked for smuggling sugar in his rolled-up dungarees.

When Skinny Tom turned up a fortnight later, a new rumour circulated.

'The foreman took pity on 'im as 'e has several mouths to feed. Although, mind you, 'e's not allowed to roll up 'is dungarees no more.'

Charity has learned that her colleagues like assigning nicknames.

Joan, who 'puts on airs and graces although she's from Bethnal Green', is 'er Ladyship.

Then there's Little Betty and Big Betty, Tiny Maggie and Smart Maureen and Pretty Polly.

All in all, they are an affectionate lot, looking out for each other.

When Big Betty left her wage packet on the bus, everyone pooled in a coin each so she had something to take home.

Each of the girls is dealing with her own challenges, and the others try to help the best they can.

Ange is unmarried and pregnant but refuses to accept it, hoping that if she buries her head in the sand, the problem will resolve itself. The others try to talk to her, the nurse as well as the manager, the fore lady, the charge hands pitching in, but she refuses to accept either their help or advice, intent on denying that there's anything the matter.

Charity's heart, like those of the other girls, goes out to her. She thinks of Divya then, how she carried her pregnancy alone for so long, while grieving for her beloved Raghu.

'Unless Ange accepts our help, there's nothing we can do.' Marge sighs.

Tiny Maggie has got herself engaged just because all her friends are engaged, even though her heart is not in it.

'But he cares for me. He's given a ring he bought with three weeks' wages,' she cries. 'I can't say no now.'

'You can always say no,' they advise.

Stepney Annie (so called to distinguish her from the other Annie) desperately wants to be a charge hand and works twice as hard as everyone else to get the promotion so as to please her mother. 'Even though it's always been me brother who's 'er favourite, John this and John that. 'E works in the railways, reserved occupation, see, which suits Ma fine. Whatever I do isn't good enough,' she says, eyes shining. 'I know this and yet I bend over backwards to please her. Just once, I want 'er to tell me I matter. That she cares for me too. Just once.' All this while working extra hard, her hands never stopping, her words, bright with hope. 'If I get the promotion then she'll see me, won't she? She will be proud of *me*.' Her eyes glowing.

She gets the promotion.

'Well?' everyone asks when she comes in the next day.

She shrugs, defeated, shoulders slumped. 'Ma didn't even listen to me when I told her. She was too busy ironing John's shirts.'

Charity is jolted back into the curry house by the sound of the door opening, a waft of grit-laden morning breeze stroking her face.

It is Mrs Jennings, the postmistress.

All eyes in the curry house fixed upon her, tentative, apprehensive, hopeful all at once.

'Let us hope there's a letter from young Mr Devine,' Mr Brown says in his deep voice.

They are all worried about Jack, who still has not written.

'The longest he's gone without communicating with us,' Divya has agonised, voicing all of their fears, her brows knitted in concern.

Mrs Jennings looks as sombre as ever; her job must be so hard, Charity thinks. Delivering mostly sad news during this time of war to anxious loved ones, their faces crumpling as she hands them the telegram that tells them their beloved is not coming home, thus changing the course of their lives, remorselessly trampling all hope.

Now, she hands a letter to Divya.

'Ah, what's this? Looks official.' Divya sounds worried.

'Don't know, gel. Haven't seen one like that before,' Mrs Jennings says.

'Thank you, Mrs Jennings. Would you like a cup of tea and some porridge, perhaps?' Divya, ever polite, even though

Charity notices that her brow is furrowed, her gaze settling on the letter in her hand.

'I'm all right, gel.'

'Here are some apple drops for the road.'

'Thank you kindly.' Mrs Jennings smiles.

Once the postmistress has left, Charity pulls out a chair for Divya, who sits down, giving her a grateful look.

She takes a deep breath and tears the letter open.

Charity squeezes her knee like she had done when Divya told everyone about her pregnancy.

Divya's eyes fly down the letter, even as her hand creeps up to rest upon her heart.

Tears bud in her eyes and fall down her face, unchecked.

Charity kneels next to Divya, asks gently, 'What is it? Everything all right?'

Thinking the worst, even as she wonders what could be worse than Raghu being dead? It can't be about Jack; for one, it's not a telegram and secondly, news about Jack would go to his father, surely?

Everyone is looking their way, the men having stopped their game.

Mr Lee is chanting something which sounds like a prayer.

Divya takes a breath, another. She opens her mouth but nothing comes. It appears that whatever was in the letter has robbed her of speech.

'Divya, love.' Charity thanks the heavens that she has the later shift today and is here now for her friend. 'What is it?'

Divya swallows, then gasps, as she turns to Charity.

'It is Raghu,' she manages.

'Oh?' Again, Charity thinks, what can be worse than Raghu dying?

Divya is trying to squeeze out the words through her tears.

And now Charity sees that the emotion she is holding back appears to be joy.

Joy...

The concern squeezing Charity's heart in a stranglehold relaxes its grip.

'Yes?' Charity prompts.

'He has been awarded the Victoria Cross for bravery,' Divya says. 'His superior officer has written to me. The citation went up in the *London Gazette*, he says.'

And even though there are only the six of them in the curry house, they cheer so loud that the news is up and down the street and all the way to the docks within a few minutes.

Charity hugs Divya, feels her heart beating against hers, her baby jumping in her belly.

'Mr Kumar is a hero,' Mr Stone declares.

'You can say that again!' the others cry.

And Divya glows.

All through her shift, Charity thinks of Divya's face, the pride there, mingled with longing for a man who was never coming back, the way her friend's face had shone, brighter than the syrup Charity is canning.

And she resolves to hold her loved ones a little closer, appreciate them and celebrate them more. Her heroes, who are still alive and with her. And once again, she tells herself, *I am so lucky. So very, very lucky and blessed.*

51

DIVYA

8 May 1941

My dearest Raghu,

My hero! Recipient of the Victoria Cross!

Oh, what a glorious gift that letter was!

What a wonderful legacy for your child! Our bubba may never meet you but they will know of you, through my stories and also through your brave actions and will be so very proud.

You are being hailed a hero by everyone in the street – yes, even the ones who were quick to judge and blame and point fingers at you for the fire at the pub. But, as I said, they are good people at heart and they are all very proud of you.

Now, it doesn't much matter if they have their suspicions that I may not have married you.

I am carrying the child of a brave man who gave his life for his country, saving several of his comrades while doing so, and they declare this to all and sundry.

You were worried that you were not good enough for me.

You tried your hardest to stay away even though you loved me.

Look at you now! Although I must admit, I cried in private at your suffering. I could picture you hurt, your body riddled with wounds, and yet still bravely facing the enemy, putting yourself in danger while rescuing your colleagues.

I bled for you, Raghu.

I always knew you were amazing and now the world knows too.

And, of course, the women are back in the curry house.

Mrs Kerridge apologised to me.

This is the second time she's done it. And again because of you.

The first time was after they all denounced you as the one who started the fire and ostracised me because I stood up for you, maintaining that you would never knowingly hurt someone.

Today, Mrs Kerridge came into the curry house, followed by the other ladies of West India Dock Road, and she looked me in the eye.

'I am sorry, Mrs Kumar,' she said.

Oh, I am Mrs Kumar to you now, am I? I thought but didn't say out loud.

Mrs Kerridge famously never apologises.

But she has, to me, twice now.

I nodded. Then, after a beat, I said, 'Would you like some tea and oat biscuits?'

'Yes please.' She beamed.

And within minutes, it was as if the ladies of the street had never boycotted the curry house.

Raghu, what I have learned from all this is that whatever comes my way, I can and will take it.

I am strong. I survived your death. And the matrons of West India Dock Road shunning me did not affect me as much as I thought it would.

For I know my worth now. And it doesn't depend on them. Or anyone, for that matter.

I am Divya. Proprietress of the curry house on West India Dock Road. Beloved of a hero awarded the Victoria Cross for bravery. Soon to be a mother.

Yes, sometimes, I am so scared that I cannot breathe. I worry about how I will protect our child with death and devastation all around us, when life is so precarious.

But I will do so, I know that now.

I will protect our babe and all those I love with my last breath, endure anything that comes my way, take it in my stride. Just like you did.

Me and our babe are so proud of you.

Love, always,

Divya and babe

52

RUTH

When Ruth's ambulance is called out to East India Dock Road, just after midnight, her heart thrums in urgency, panic drumming a tattoo in her chest.

Careening into the street, she sees that it is brightly lit as fire rages, orange sparks leaping into the sky, devilishly gleeful, firefighters at work, trying to contain the flames, while others emerge from the smoking buildings bearing casualties.

Ruth parks the ambulance, opens the doors for the firefighters nearest her to bring in the wounded.

'Worst bombing we've seen so far.' The firefighters shake their heads as they gently carry a charred, soot- and blood-covered body into the ambulance. 'And that's saying something.'

At first, Ruth doesn't recognise the bloodied woman until she addresses her in a soft, barely there whisper. 'M... miss R... Ravinder.'

Ruth's heart stills before beating again faster, desperately fearful.

Oh no.

Mrs Smith, her battered, bleeding hands clutching...

No.

It can't be. It cannot.

And then the bundle in her arms moves, lets out a weak wail.

'The girls?' Ruth asks, heart in her mouth.

'T... the T... Tube s... station. I... w... went back... to get his b... blankie... A m... mistake,' Mrs Smith manages between agonised gasps. In her arms, her little boy wails again. Is it Ruth's imagination or are his wails getting weaker?

Her mind is inadvertently transported to the carnage at the synagogue, Elijah with her one moment and the next, missing, nowhere to be found.

She opens her mouth, and despite the fear swirling inky blue, her voice is thankfully steady when she says, 'I'll get you to the hospital and you'll both be right as rain in no time at all.'

But Mrs Smith grasps her hand, her other clasping her babe to her bruised chest. 'T... too late for me,' she pants. It is an effort for her to speak, and Ruth sees that her face is devoid of colour, that her eyes are straining shut. And yet, she manages to keep them open, fix Ruth in her gaze. 'P... please. M... my girls. M... my b... bubba...'

As if on cue, the infant lets out another wail.

Ruth feels tears sting her eyes. No, she cannot cry. 'Not too late, we'll be there in—'

She is interrupted by Mrs Smith's hacking coughs. Blood gushing out of her mouth.

Mrs Smith's eyes are shut but with great effort, she opens them again. 'T... they...' Mrs Smith is finding it hard to form the words. 'M... my ch... children... L... look after t... them. P... please. P... promise m... me.' Her clasp on Ruth's hand is weak but urgent. 'T... they... h... have n... nobody e... else. P... p... please.' She coughs up blood again.

'I promise,' Ruth says.

Mrs Smith nods. Smiles wanly. Her face pale as dew on the underside of a leaf.

The baby emits another weak mewl.

Mrs Smith strokes him, still smiling. 'I l... love y... you,' she whispers. Then, to Ruth, 'P... please... t... tell my g... girls... I l... love t... them.'

She closes her eyes.

53

RUTH

Once Mrs Smith's little boy, Jimmy, is checked out at the hospital and pronounced to be as well as can be in the circumstances, Ruth promising to keep an eye on him in case he shows signs of concussion or shock, Ruth goes in search of his sisters.

They are with Esther. She had taken them home from the Underground station when Mrs Smith had not turned up, plying them with the *matzo* crackers they loved.

Esther takes one look at Ruth's expression and the baby in her arms and guesses at what has happened.

The girls, Betty and Joan, turn as one, their eyes wide and questioning.

Betty's face contorts in fear, her mouth opening but no words coming out, unable to frame the question she wants to ask, as Ruth gently lowers herself beside her and her sister, Esther squatting on their other side.

Betty appears to have understood what is going on, while her sister, younger by a year, is clueless.

'Ah, you have Jimmy,' Joan says innocently, cooing at her

brother, who is asleep in Ruth's embrace. And then, she asks the question Betty is unable to. 'Where's Ma?'

Betty flinches and shuts her eyes, tears squeezing from behind them and dusting her downy cheeks.

Seeing her sister's upset, Joan's face crumples too.

Ruth gathers the girls to her, the baby balanced in her arms. Esther puts her arms around them all, and they stay like that, holding the girls as they wail, their cries waking the baby, who joins in.

54

DIVYA

Dear Jack,

    We still haven't heard from you.

    I cannot lie, we are all very worried.

    We are praying for you and trying to convince ourselves that your silence is because of the post being unreliable due to war.

    In any case, we are all fiercely hopeful that you are all right. That we will see you again very soon. Put us out of our misery, please, will you?

    As to the goings on here, I am sorry, but I have some sad news. East India Dock Road was bombed and Mrs Smith was one of the casualties. But, thankfully, her children were spared and are safe and well.

    Also, I have some personal news that I'd like to share with you. I have had several conversations with myself and with Charity about whether to tell you this, and have decided that I must. You are my best friend and you need to hear it from me. And I hope that you'll understand, Jack. I went to see Raghu Kumar last Christmas. He was injured in the battlefield and was convalescing in Surrey. He has since died in action and has been awarded the Victoria Cross for bravery as he saved several of his regiment whilst gravely injured. I am mourning him and miss him dearly but... I have something of his to cherish. I am pregnant! Raghu died not knowing of his child. I must admit that I am nervous about bringing a new life into this war torn world, but... I am also happy and excited too. I hope that you will be happy for me.

Now, for other news.

You will never guess – the air raids have stopped!

I didn't want to write too soon but it's been more than a week now, nearly ten days to be exact, and there have been no raids! We are, all of us, cautiously optimistic.

Although we can't quite believe it – it's been non-stop since last September, could this really be the end? Or are they just lulling us into a false sense of security before starting the battering again?

London experienced one of the most incessant and devastating raids on the night of 10th May. The House of Commons was bombed. Even though the bombings are commonplace now, hearing about it on Mr Brown's wireless nevertheless shook us all.

In any case, fingers crossed that the Jerries have finally given up and the raids are behind us.

And fingers crossed too that your letters will arrive all at once in the coming days and we will have worried for nothing.

We are all well, Jack, and waiting for news from you.

More soon,
Much love,
Divya and all of us here at West India Dock Road

55

CHARITY

When Charity goes down to the basement after work, her mother is gasping for breath, her face bloodless, papery skin translucent.

'Mammy!' Charity kneels beside her mother, fighting down panic.

She takes her mother's hand in hers. It is so very fragile.

Mammy turns to her. She is gagging for breath and yet still her face appears peaceful. Her eyes full of love.

'I will get the doctor,' Charity manages through a mouthful of salt and terror.

Mammy shakes her head. No.

'Please, Mammy.'

But Mammy shakes her head again.

The hand Charity is not holding is clutching at rosary beads.

Mammy's Bible is beside her.

Tears bud in Charity's eyes.

'Shall I get the boys?' Charity asks, tasting sorrow, navy blue.

Mammy shakes her head again.

She does not want the boys to see her, to remember her like

this, struggling for breath during her last few minutes on earth. For Charity understands that this is it. Mammy is dying.

During their times together in the basement, Mammy had prepared Charity. 'I don't have long,' she'd said, each word an ordeal for her. 'I have spent the better part of my life in bed. I am ready to move on, my heart, to meet the Lord, join your da. I have had the privilege of watching the four of you, my treasures, grow into wonderful people. I know you will look after and look out for your brothers like you have been doing all your life. Paddy and I have been so blessed to have such a wonderful daughter,' Mammy's eyes were soft with love and pride, 'and sons who are a credit to their sister, for you brought them up, Charity love.'

Charity understood and yet a selfish part of her wanted to hold on to Mammy.

She had spent much of her life resenting her mother for her illness, for it meant Charity had to take on the responsibility for her brothers and the lodging house too. And yet, when Charity was at her lowest, when she had let Veer go, it was Mammy who comforted her, told her that the best relationships were hard won, that you had to work at them, that people would always talk but that you had to follow your heart.

Since then, Mammy and Charity had been more like friends. Charity loved her time together with Mammy in Mrs Kerridge's basement during the air raids. She would climb into bed beside Mammy and they would pray together. She even managed to catch some sleep at times despite the threat of the enemy overhead.

Mammy radiated peace. Calm.

Charity had never appreciated this before when Da was beside Mammy, alternately raging and crying. Da would draw all the energy with his demands and his tantrums. And when not tending to Da, the boys required Charity's attention.

But when the boys started going to the Tube station with the other residents of West India Dock Road and after Da passed, it was just Mammy and Charity waiting out the air raid in Mrs Kerridge's basement and they had become very close.

Mammy, when preparing Charity for her passing, had said, 'You have chosen to love a man who, while perfect for you, is different to everyone else. Not all will understand. They will not be kind.'

Charity had nodded. She knew that already, had experienced their cruelty.

'But you are strong,' Mammy had said, eyes shining, her gnarled hand cupping Charity's cheek. 'And loving him has made you stronger.'

Yes, Charity had thought. It had.

'You cared for people's opinions before. You no longer do so. I heard that you gave Mrs Kerridge and the other ladies a piece of your mind when they refused to accept Divya and her baby.'

'Yes,' Charity had said, overwhelmed by the pride shining in her mother's eyes.

'That's my girl. Now, despite people telling you otherwise, abusing you, hurling insults at you, you stand by your choices, which is as it should be.'

Charity had nodded, blown away by her mother's perception. Her mother, who was bedridden, confined to the basement and yet saw everything, somehow understanding what Charity had been going through.

'It will stand you in good stead, my love. Believe in yourself always. Whatever life throws at you, you will weather it.' Her mother's voice, although fragile, was bright with conviction.

'I will,' Charity had said, tasting the fiery truth of it in her mouth.

Her mammy had smiled. Her gaze shining with pride and love. 'And through it all,' she had whispered, 'your da and I will, alongside Jesus, Mary, Joseph and all the saints, be watching over you.'

'I will miss you,' Charity says now.

And again, with her eyes, Mammy conveys what she has said since she began to prepare Charity for her death. *I will be there with you, looking out for you, like Da is, like God is.*

Even though she is struggling for breath, Mammy smiles gently, tenderly, at Charity and holds out her arms.

And, as Charity has been doing since Da passed on, she climbs into bed beside her mother, holds her. And, picking up Mammy's much-thumbed Bible, Charity reads from it, the passage that her mother has marked: 'Even though I walk through the valley of the shadow of death, I will fear no evil, for you are with me; your rod and your staff, they comfort me.'

She reads, salt-soaked prayers, until Ma's gasps for breath become fewer and far between, until, gradually, they stop altogether, her body going still in Charity's arms, her frail hands clutching the rosary beads, a smile upon her face.

56

DIVYA

Dear Jack,

How are you?

We hope and pray that although we still haven't heard from you, you are receiving our letters.

I am sorry to, once again, be the bearer of bad news.

Charity's mammy, Moira, has passed away.

Always frail, she went rapidly downhill after being trapped in the basement when the lodging house collapsed.

I have just come back from the funeral and am sitting down now to write to you.

The service was so very moving.

The boys carried their mother's coffin, like they had their da's. Trying so hard to be brave. Mr Barney holding up Paddy's side.

The church was full to bursting.

The nuns were there, celebrating their beloved Moira's life. The choir was rousing, a host of angels, the prayers rising *straight to the sky through the bombed-out roof. The pigeons nesting in the rafters joining in the chorus with their cooing.*

There was not a dry eye in the house.

She was much loved, was Moira.

And she and Paddy have left behind a wonderful legacy in their amazing children, beloved of everyone on West India Dock Road.

Take care and we hope to hear from you soon,

Much love, Divya and all of us here on West India Dock Road

57

RUTH

When Ruth returns from work, Betty and Joan throw themselves at her.

'How many people did you help today?' they ask.

The girls' welcome and enthusiasm touches her, allowing her to set the darker, more heartbreaking aspects of her day aside, even as it summons Elijah: how he would wrap his arms around her, his whole body aglow upon seeing her, the memory of her brother, joy and pain.

She recounts only the cheery bits, and Betty and Joan listen avidly, while Esther, jogging the baby in her arms, smiles at her.

Isaac is in the kitchen, warming up milk for little Jimmy.

'He just woke from his nap. Once Isaac is ready with his milk, we can go to the curry house,' Esther says.

There is a sprightliness to Esther that wasn't there when Ruth first arrived. She looks worn out but no longer drawn. Her tiredness is purposeful. They are all adjusting to caring for two young children and an infant, all three waking up several times in the night, the girls with nightmares, the baby because he is hungry. But at least the air raids have stopped so they no longer have to traipse to the Underground station every night.

They haven't heard from Eva, don't know her fate or that of her children, and they pray for her and all their people every day.

Now that the air raids are over – although they are all wary, one ear cocked each night for the sirens – Ruth, already trained in first aid, is training as a nurse. For every life saved from the jaws of death, she is getting back at Hitler: 'See, you might try to destroy us, but you will not win.'

It was easy enough to foster Betty, Joan and Jimmy, the officials grateful that the orphaned Smith children had a family to go to, given the countless displaced because of the bombings.

The first few days were hard going. The girls missed their mother terribly and were often in tears, which would in turn set off the baby.

But gradually, they are turning a corner. With the resilience of children, they are adjusting to their new life. They still have nightmares, but not as often.

There will be difficult times ahead of course, but they will weather them. Together.

Like they have weathered everything that has come so far.

That is the nature of this war, after all.

It has not been easy encountering the racism (more so since they fostered little Jimmy), which still exists even though this is Britain and they are fighting a war against Hitler.

When Ruth is out and about with Jimmy, people curl their lips at them, some swearing and crossing the road, as if their colour is a sin.

'Our blood is the same red as yours. And this is a child, an innocent!' Ruth cries.

'That doesn't take away the fact that he's half-caste.' They snort and turn away.

If the residents of West India Dock Road are within earshot, they come to their defence. It is the fact that they need to at all that upsets Ruth.

This maligning of a race, undermining a whole group of people, has caused a war that is involving the world and yet people don't understand; they still perpetuate the difference.

Ruth despairs.

But... the people of the street are lovely.

Divya and Charity tell her that the residents of West India Dock Road were prejudiced before for they didn't know any different, but that they've come round now: to Divya and her baby, to Charity and her relationship with Veer.

And this gives Ruth hope, that in time, street by street, country by country, the world too might change, become more accepting of difference and all colours and races will perhaps one day, sooner rather than later, live together in harmony.

Now, she tells the girls carefully curated stories about her day and afterwards, with Betty holding her right hand and Joan her left, their small palms clasped trustingly in hers (like Elijah's used to once, not too long ago, the memory of his touch more vivid when the girls hold her hands, heartwarming and heartbreaking both at once), with Esther carrying the baby and Isaac following with the baby's milk and sundries, they make their way across the road.

As they enter the curry house, and are hailed cheerily by everyone, as Divya brings platters of potato fingers and carrot cookies and steaming bowls of potato and lentil soup, as everyone makes a fuss of the children, as Esther smiles like she never has before, showing off the baby, Isaac looking on fondly, his eyes sparkling, as Ruth feels the girls' small palms in hers, so trusting, so beloved, she thinks, *I came here orphaned and hurting, having lost everyone I loved in the world, Eva and her children taken to the concentration camps. I felt guilty, I wondered, why have I been saved?*

She recalls the Ursuline nuns telling her, 'God saved you for a reason. You will understand when you find it.'

And holding the warm weight of the baby when Mrs Smith begged her, with her last breath, to look after her children, when she helps people while doing her job and they thank her with their eyes, as they are too overwhelmed to speak, when the girls run to greet her when she returns after a long shift, and throw themselves at her, when they hook their arms through hers, their small palms in hers, she knows why she was spared.

For this.

Ruth will always mourn her family, worry about Eva and her children's fate, but now, she has a purpose.

She lost her family, but here, in West India Dock Road, she has found her community and with Esther, Isaac, Betty, Joan and Jimmy, she has found family.

And she is living. With sorrow. With loss. But she is living. She is making a difference.

She hurts. She cries in secret.

When she lost her family, she thought she would never be happy again.

But there are times, like now, with these trusting girls' hands in hers, with Esther beside her, the baby snuffling in her arms, Isaac looking on, his kind face aglow, with Divya smiling warmly at her, with Charity arriving after her shift, her face scored with new lines since losing her mother, and yet smiling at each of them in turn, the whole street gathered in the curry house, all talking at once, wanting to know how she is, how her day was, with Mr Stone and Mr Brown arguing over who is winning, Ruth realises that right at that moment, against all odds, she is happy.

58

CHARITY

Charity and Veer are walking to the end of the road where Charity will say goodbye to him before fetching her brothers from the curry house and returning to Mrs Kerridge's house with them.

Dusk stains the horizon. It is dark, the roads deserted, scents of dinner, roasting potatoes, vinegary cabbage and sizzling onions wafting from houses, hoots of jollity and merriment from the public house alongside the sweetly pungent aroma of hops, men standing outside, smoke from their roll-ups curling into the dark sky, shaking their heads in disgust when they see them, a mismatched couple.

Smirks and leers, insults hurled at them. 'Get someone your own kind.'

Charity and Veer ignore them and walk on.

Blackout curtains dance at windows, faint impressions of the lives being lived inside, chatter, cries, voices raised in argument and laughter puncturing the darkness. The smog-ravaged sky is pierced here and there by the first daring, silver prickles of stars.

The air raids have stopped but everyone is on tenterhooks,

wondering if tonight will be the night the sirens will scream warning once more, the sky lighting up firebrand orange as enemy machines discharge their deathly cargo.

As they move away from the pub, it feels like Veer and Charity are the only two people left in the world.

Veer has been on edge all evening, which is unlike him.

'What is it?' Charity asks.

She is still undone by Mammy's death. It hit her harder than Da's.

Perhaps because she and the boys are orphans now.

But more so, she thinks, because she had become so close to Mammy after Da died.

She misses Mammy and spending time with her in the basement with a physical ache, just the two of them in the dead of night while war raged overhead, praying together.

She knows Mammy is watching over her, over all of them; she feels her presence just like she feels Da's, hears her parents' voices all the time.

And right now, Mammy is urging her to stop, to listen to Veer, to ask him why he is restless, what is going on.

For Veer is hesitating. He is nervous.

She takes his hand. 'Whatever it is,' she says, gently, 'you can tell me.'

'I... Charity.' He looks at her and in the starlit darkness, his eyes are raw, his gaze shimmering with emotion. 'I know I don't deserve you.'

'Ah, stop,' she says.

'You are so good. So amazing.'

She smiles. 'Actually, don't stop. Do go on.'

He smiles too but his gaze is still intense. 'Charity, I have saved up enough money now and I wanted to say, I wanted to ask...'

And suddenly, she knows.

She can feel her parents' smiles, even as her heart swells.

'Will you marry me, even though you're far too good for me? I know I'm not a catch. I limp, and I have only one arm. I am the wrong colour.'

'Do not say that,' she says fiercely. 'You are just right for me.'

He smiles but it is so heartbreakingly sad. 'People will judge you, make fun of you, hate you because you chose me and I can't bear it. But I will love you to the ends of the world and back. I will make sure you never want for anything. I can rent a house and we can move in, with your brothers of course and after—'

She does not let him finish.

She stands on tiptoes and whispers in his ear, 'Yes. Yes, I will.'

She gently kisses his cheek.

'How dare you?' Someone spits vehemently behind her. 'Disgusting.'

She ignores them. She knows their future will not be easy. That there will always be ignorant people like these shouting abuse at them. That their children – and she wants children with this man – will have a hard time of it.

But then again, perhaps they will not.

For there are others like them now. Baby Jimmy, whom everyone on West India Dock Road dotes on. And Divya's child, soon to be welcomed into the world.

In any case, they will prevail. She has come through worse and so has Veer.

And like when she took over the running of the lodging house at fourteen years old, the residents of West India Dock Road will come to her aid. With the help of everyone on West India Dock Road, she, Veer and their family will be all right.

They will be just fine.

She cannot keep the smile from her face as Veer hugs her, ignoring the men heckling and flinging insults at them.

Above them, the stars shine, her parents smiling, showering them with blessings, she imagines.

But Veer's face is the brightest of all, rivalling the stars, the glow on it bedazzling.

EPILOGUE

West India Dock Road is battered. It is ravaged. And yet still, it is standing. Still it keeps on keeping on.

Divya, proprietress of the curry house, which is the social hub of West India Dock Road, cries into her pillow each night with missing, the letters beside it, testament to her lost love growing, like his baby is in her stomach.

Her love is a hero, recipient of the Victoria Cross for bravery, and she hurts for him, for what he endured, even as she is proud of him.

Ruth Ravinder works as an ambulance driver and is training to be a nurse. She encounters trauma and horror on a daily basis, but she deals with it calmly and efficiently, impressing her superiors.

For Ruth's courage has come at great cost: her loved ones killed and others dragged away to concentration camps.

Survivor's guilt is in every line prematurely etched upon her face, but with each person she helps and saves in the course of her work, some of that guilt is assuaged.

When she came to this street a few weeks ago clutching a

letter for Esther from her sister Eva, Ruth had no inkling that her life was about to change.

Again.

But it has, this time, for the better. She has family now in Esther, Isaac, Betty, Joan and Jimmy and a place to call home on West India Dock Road.

Esther Rosenbaum is not lonely any more. She and Isaac could not have children but now they are blessed with four.

Ruth, a gift from her sister, who sent her a message and with it a promise that one day, when this madness of war is past, they will meet again.

And Joan and Betty, whom she was drawn to from the first time she met them in the Underground shelter, and Jimmy, who she helped welcome into the world, wrapped in her towel, his mother lying on her blankets.

She and Isaac will make sure to keep Mrs Smith and her husband present in these children's lives by telling them stories of their parents, and they will honour the promise Ruth made to Mrs Smith by loving and caring for these innocents as if they are their own.

Isaac beams at his wife as he plays with the children and there is a sparkle to his eyes, a spring to his step.

Their house, which was heavy with loneliness and sadness, is now bright and noisy with children's laughter and chatter and cries. It is lighter. Full of life.

And now, look, dusk has fallen; the blackout curtains are drawn.

Everyone on West India Dock Road has gathered in the curry house for a chinwag alongside supper.

Veer and Charity sit side by side.

They've just rented Mrs Ross's flat, which they will be moving into, once they are wed, along with Charity's brothers.

Mrs Ross is moving in with Mrs Kerridge while she waits for news of her son, who is missing in action. She is bringing the cat who has been keeping her company. Nobody knows where it came from – another casualty of the bombings no doubt, displaced and homeless until it found shelter with Mrs Ross. Mrs Ross says, eyes moist, that the cat arrived when she was at her lowest, providing solace and a reason to go on.

'I will be glad of the company.' Mrs Kerridge smiles. 'I've got used to having Charity and the boys around and it will be very quiet once they're gone, so I am ever so pleased you and Hope are moving in, Fanny.' (Hope is Mrs Ross's name for the cat.)

Mrs Ross nods and smiles but the smile does not quite reach her eyes.

'And we can wait on news of our boys together,' Mrs Kerridge says, and now her eyes are haunted. For her younger two sons are still missing in action too, though her older boy has finally written to say he was injured but that he is now back at the frontline.

The matrons of West India Dock Road natter as they partake of Divya's cheesy potatoes and vegetable pie with carrot cake for afters.

Mr Brown and Mr Stone discuss their game and world news, with Mr Lee and Mr Rosenbaum putting in their two pennies' worth. Fergus sits with them while his younger brothers play with Betty and Joan.

Ruth and Esther beam proudly as everyone makes a fuss of little Jimmy. Divya, once she's made sure everyone is fed, sits beside them, one hand on her stomach where her own baby cavorts.

Ah look, someone has just turned into West India Dock Road.

A once jaunty young man, beloved of all the street.

Now, his shoulders sag as if burdened by the weight of the world. Weary lines are wrought onto his face. His eyes are wounds, and his face and body bear the scars, both physical and emotional of all he has endured: the suffering of a lifetime in a few endless months.

He walks down the dark street, silver gashes of stars scored across the thick, black awning of sky. He walks past the raucous pub, and when he sees the pile of rubble where the lodging house used to be, the flag that Paddy has planted upon it flapping valiantly in the nippy breeze, he shakes his head sadly.

Then he turns and looks at the curry house.

A grin splits his face and in that instant, he looks like the young man he was before he went to war.

He stops for a moment at the door, taking in the buzz of chatter from inside.

And then he pushes the door open.

There is silence within, conversations paused as all eyes turn towards this unexpected visitor.

It is Paddy who runs up to him, throwing his arms around him in joyful welcome, while the momentary silence is split open by gasps, cheers, shouts of, 'Well I never!'

Jack Devine takes a deep breath. He tousles Paddy's hair even as his gaze takes in everyone in the curry house, beloved, much longed for, clocking those who are missing and experiencing a thrum of grief, the hollow ache of loss. He notes the new faces and recognises them, for he feels he has come to know them through Divya's letters.

And now his gaze settles on Divya. From the moment she ran into his arms that fateful evening three years ago, in a sari the dazzling emerald of spring shoots and a man's coat that was too big for her, with another sari wrapped around her head like a scarf, and asked him for directions to West India Dock Road, hesitantly, in that beautiful voice redolent with the music of the tropics, her cocoa eyes fixed upon his face, he has been enamoured of her.

Her letters have got him through the war and the long, terrible months of captivity.

She is glowing, her face alight with wondrous awe.

She looks just like he remembers her. And also different. Older. Her features underscored by sorrow and pain. Her eyes carrying the imprint of all she has endured.

But it only serves to render her more beautiful.

'I have come for the curry you promised, Divya,' he says.

And the curry house erupts even as Divya beams at him, causing his heart to flip over, just as it did the first time he laid eyes on her.

* * *

MORE FROM RENITA D'SILVA

The next instalment in the West India Dock Road series from Renita D'Silva is available to order now here:

https://mybook.to/WestIndiaDockBook4

ACKNOWLEDGEMENTS

I would like to thank my wonderful editor, Francesca Best – I don't know how I got so very lucky but I am beyond grateful to have you as my editor. THANK YOU for all you do.

Thank you to all the amazing team at Boldwood for helping make this book the very best it can possibly be, and for making it travel far and wide.

Thank you, Emily Reader, for your eagle eye and wonderful suggestions during copy edits for this book.

Thank you, Shirley Khan, for proofreading this book.

Thank you, Ben Wilson, for overseeing the production of the audio version of the book.

Thank you, Rachel Odendaal, Wendy Neale, Issy Flynn, Megan Townsend and all the marketing team for the amazing marketing campaign and promotions.

Many thanks to Kathryn Smith for ensuring copies of the book arrive with me in plenty of time for the launch. Many thanks to Kate Dioufas and all the accounting team at Boldwood for all you do.

Thank you to Rachel Gilbey and all the other wonderful bloggers for giving their time to reading, reviewing and shouting out about the book. It is appreciated so very much.

Thank you to Jason Vinod D'Souza for my wonderful new website: www.renitadsilvabooks.com

Thank you to my lovely author friends, Angie Marsons,

Sharon Maas, Debbie Rix, June Considine (aka Laura Elliot), whose friendship I am grateful for and lucky to have.

A huge thank you to my mother, Perdita Hilda D'Silva, who reads every word I write; who is encouraging and supportive and fun; who answers any questions I might have on any topic – finding out the answer, if she doesn't know it, in record time – who listens patiently to my doubts and who reminds me, gently, when I cry that I will never finish the book: 'I've heard this same refrain several times before.'

I am immensely grateful to my long-suffering family for willingly sharing me with characters who live only in my head. Love always.

And last, but not least, thank you, reader, for choosing this book.

ABOUT THE AUTHOR

Renita D'Silva is an award-winning author of historical fiction novels. She grew up in the south of India and now lives in the UK.

Download your exclusive bonus content from Renita D'Silva here:

Follow Renita on social media here:

- facebook.com/RenitaDSilvaBooks
- x.com/RenitaDSilva
- instagram.com/renita_dsilva
- bookbub.com/profile/renita-d-silva

ALSO BY RENITA D'SILVA

Standalone Novels

The Secret Keeper

The West India Dock Road Series

New Arrivals on West India Dock Road

Wartime Comes to West India Dock Road

Heartache on West India Dock Road

Sixpence Stories

Introducing Sixpence Stories!

Discover page-turning historical novels from your favourite authors, meet new friends and be transported back in time.

Join our book club Facebook group

https://bit.ly/SixpenceGroup

Sign up to our newsletter

https://bit.ly/SixpenceNews

Boldwood

Boldwood Books is an award-winning fiction publishing company seeking out the best stories from around the world.

Find out more at www.boldwoodbooks.com

Join our reader community for brilliant books, competitions and offers!

Follow us
@BoldwoodBooks
@TheBoldBookClub

Sign up to our weekly deals newsletter

https://bit.ly/BoldwoodBNewsletter